LOVE

MW00627365

Cole takes my hand and doesn't even let me stop to enjoy the scenery. He leads me through a magnificent set of double doors that have horse heads carved into them, and then he continues on until we come to a room that I presume is the master suite. Cole opens both doors, and I am not at all surprised to see a saddle sitting in one corner, next to a big cushy, leather chair, and then a king-size bed that's suspended from the ceiling by thick, tan ropes.

I swallow, feeling nervous and excited all at the same time. "Does it swing?" I ask. But what I'm thinking is *Oh my God,* and I can already envision me and Cole lying atop the bed, going at it for all it's worth… until the rope breaks.

I gasp a little and put a hand to my throat.

"You all right?" Cole asks.

"Yes, I just feel… slightly overheated."

Cole grins. "It's the air-conditioning. It needs work."

Um… no. It is so not the air-conditioning, I think.

Cole reaches behind me and releases the tie that holds my red silk halter top around my neck. I'm still processing the bed when my blouse falls to the floor. Cole takes a moment to gaze at my breasts, and then he fills his hands with them. "Is this okay?" he asks. "I don't want to do anything you're not comfortable with."

I look down at his hands. "Yet, you're already holding my breasts."

"I didn't want to waste any time, in case you gave me the go-ahead."

"Go ahead," I whisper.

PRAISE FOR ALEXA DARIN

LOVE TRIP

"Want fun in the sun? Read this book. It's laugh-out-loud funny."—**Sheila Roberts**, national best-selling author of *On Strike For Christmas* and *Three Christmas Wishes*

"This book is a fun escape from reality and perfect for a beach vacation."—**Rachel Van Dyken**, *Books by the Glass*

KISS ME TWICE

"This one is a buried book treasure."—**Stephanie Queen**, *USA Today* best-selling author

"Ms. Darin has given her readers a sweet, yet tender, amusing, love story…"—**Robin Leigh Morgan**, author of *I Kissed a Ghost*

KISSES DON'T LIE

"A zippy romance that will leave you smiling."—**Susanna Carr**, author of *Pink Ice*

"*Kisses Don't Lie* is a hunka hunka burnin' fun!"
—**Geralyn Dawson**, *USA Today* best-selling author

"Thanks to Alexa Darin, Elvis lives!"—**Vicki Lewis Thompson**, *New York Times* best-selling author

"Fantastic! Full of mischief, mayhem, romance, and happily ever afters… one of my favorite books of the year… immensely engaging from the very first sentence."—**Amanda Haffery**, *Romance Junkies*

"Humorous… delightfully quirky."—*RT Book Reviews*

GOOD WITH HIS HANDS

"Sharp, witty writing."—**Meryl Sawyer**, *New York Times* bestselling author

"A promising debut."—*Seattle Post-Intelligencer*

ALSO BY ALEXA DARIN

Love Trip

Alexa Darin

Top Down Publishing, LLC
www.topdownpub.com

Top Down Publishing, LLC
PO Box 13181
Mill Creek, WA 98082
www.topdownpub.com

LOVE TRIP
Copyright © 2013, 2016 by Alexa Darin
Previously published as LIVE A LITTLE, LOVE A LOT
All rights reserved.

ISBN: 978-0-9966306-6-5

Cover design by Paper and Sage, Christa Holland

Logo designs by Lemoncraft

Edited by Blue Otter Editing, Amy Knupp

Print formatting:
By Your Side Self-Publishing
www.ByYourSideSelfPub.com

Publisher's Note: This is a work of fiction. The names, characters, places, brands, media, and incidents are products of the writer's imagination or have been used fictitiously and are not to be construed as real. Any resemblance to actual events, locales, organizations, or persons, living or dead, is entirely coincidental.

No part of this book may be used or reproduced in any manner whatsoever without written permission by the above-named publisher and copyright owner, except in the case of brief quotations embodied in critical articles and reviews.

In memory of Doug (Dougie) Price...
You were so very loved, and you are missed.

*Dedicated to every man who has ever made a
woman forget she has a broken heart.*

ACKNOWLEDGEMENTS

This book would not have been the same without the help from a guy I call SuperJeff. He and I connected many moons ago while he was a construction worker in the Caribbean, and he in no small part helped bring this story to life. So, thanks, SuperJeff, for being super helpful! Hugs to you wherever in this world you are right now!

Many thanks and hugs to my friend, Sheila Roberts, for taking the time to read this story in its early stages, and for giving me such valuable feedback.

Much gratitude goes to a great team of true professionals—Dana Delamar, Lucinda Campbell, Christa Holland, and Amy Knupp. You guys are awesome!

Thank you, Karen McCullough, for doing such a fantastic job keeping my website up and running smoothly.

Much love and thanks to Jasmine Britain. Your enthusiasm makes each new book release that much more fun.

Hugs and thanks to Pamela Mae Gunther, for providing a great friendship, and for being someone I can always count on.

Many thanks to George Castle. You make me feel like you're actually interested in this romance writing business.

Love and thanks to my old friend, Steve Marczewski, for being a constant in my life. You never fail to let me know you're there.

Much thanks to so many others, but especially Kristi Elkind, Kathy Doyle, and LaRee Lewis, for laughs along the way and so much more.

Special thanks to Irene Woodard Bennett, for your prayers and words of encouragement, when I needed them most.

More special thanks to Phil Struck, Kathleen Rossi, Sandra Fann, and Jill Czarnecki, for suggesting such great character names.

Thanks to Thomas Bryant, for providing so many smiles along the way.

Most especially, thanks to Gary R. Maynard, for being a cowboy a girl can believe in.

And, finally, thanks to Jennifer Love Hewitt, for inspiring the title of this book.

Chapter One

Men. First they love you, and then they leave you wondering what the hell just happened. And that, I imagine, is why so many of us women turn into pineapples, all hard and prickly on the outside, with our sweet centers hidden so deep inside that only an act of God can bring our sweet back out.

Even so, being that I'm all but drooling over a man in a white straw cowboy hat, I think it's entirely possible I have not yet turned all the way hard and prickly. Which makes me a gidiot. Girl idiot. It's what I call women who lose all sense God gave them when they find themselves in the vicinity of a hot man. The man in the cowboy hat is hot. I have officially become a gidiot.

Gidiot Taylor Grant.

I'm also a defense attorney with the prestigious Seattle law firm of Burns, Stockwell, and Taft, which is known for hiring the best right out of law school. So, I must not be too much of a gidiot. Just when it comes to men.

Or maybe it's that I'm bored. And lonely. Yes, lonely, and finding myself thinking about all the choices I've made in the past couple of years that haven't worked out in my best interest. As a result, I've spent far too much time gazing out my office window at the Space Needle, wondering what it would be like to free-fall from the top of its pointed little head. Not that I'm planning on taking the big dive, but life has been stressful lately. Too many lost cases, one painful breakup, and a whole lot of friends who would rather not hear one more word about how my man done me wrong. Perhaps I should wear a sign on my back that says, "Happy doesn't live here anymore."

Or not.

Maybe I should just wait and see what happens over the next couple of weeks. That's how long I'll be here in St. John. I've come to see my sister, Paula, who has become a bona fide island beach babe. She runs a bar here, and she's not one for allowing others to wallow in their pain or feel sorry for themselves. I fully expect she'll tell me to woman up and get over my ex. She never liked Peyton. Which is fine by me; I don't much like him right now, either.

But where is Paula? I check my watch and see she's late picking me up—by forty-five minutes—and then I remember her fondness for being the last to arrive at a party. That's okay. It gives me a chance to peruse my surroundings. I look to my left and see a hillside dotted with colorful houses. Then, above those, nothing but dark forest green. Trees, I think. Though the green is so thick it looks like a jungle. And now my imagination is going wild with visions of all kinds of animals swinging from vines, such as you might see in a Tarzan movie. Tarzan, I could deal with; wild animals, not so much. And I'm not big on foraging for my own food, either. Which Paula has assured me won't be an issue here.

A young couple passes in front of me, and they make their way across the sand, linked together and leaning into each other, presenting themselves as newlyweds or at least new. But that only takes me back to memories of Peyton, so I turn away and look at the man in the hat again. He reminds me of nothing from my past life, and surprisingly, for the first time in weeks, I feel a hint of sunshine and smiles. Like life is not so bad, like life goes on, no matter what… and it feels good.

And why not look at other men? I may be half-broken, but I'm not dead.

My gaze stays with the cowboy. I'm curious what his story is. He seems to be alone and hasn't once in the last five minutes pulled a cell phone from his pocket to check for messages or to take a call. Which I find refreshing and so different from the men in Seattle who become panic-stricken if they discover they've left home without their iPhones or iPads or i*Somethings*.

I squint, focusing on the cowboy's right bicep, and I make out a tattoo that looks like a set of horns. Bull horns, I think. Which is fitting if he is indeed a *real* cowboy.

My lips curve into a smile. That would be something—a *real* cowboy, here in the Caribbean.

And what might I do with a man like him if I had the opportunity?

Everything… absolutely everything.

Orgasm included.

But it isn't meant to be, because the cowboy is unaware of me and my lustings. He's found someone interesting to talk to—a woman in a flouncy yellow skirt and a lacy white blouse—who appears to be in charge of a fancy truck that's big and painted in shimmery colors of blue, green, and gold, like the scales of a fish. In fact, the parking lot is full of oversized trucks with fancy paint jobs. My guess is they're public transportation. Maybe, like me, the cowboy is looking for a ride.

I take a moment to peruse the trucks, but needing their services is not a particularly pleasing prospect as I can see I might be forced to share a seat with a pig. One of the trucks has a woman sitting near the front with a pig in her lap. And the man in the seat directly behind her looks like he might be harboring some kind of nest in his beard.

I think I'll stay put. I'm happy just to stand in the sun and wait for my sis to arrive.

I step out of my shoes and let my toes sink into the warm, white sand. It's so soothing I'm already feeling more optimistic about my future. More positive. More young. Younger. I should have done this sooner, come here to St. John. Maybe all I've really needed to be cured of my relationship blues is to spend a couple of weeks on a tropical beach.

I take another peek at the cowboy and I see he's looking in my direction. Staring right at me, actually.

I don't immediately react, though know I should turn away. But I'm hiding behind my Tom Ford sunglasses and I think I'm being cool and touristy, just taking in my surroundings.

I keep watching and waiting… for something to happen, I suppose. Then, finally, I smile, which I immediately realize is a mistake, because the cowboy has taken my smile as encouragement and he's now walking toward me.

God, what have I done? I should have known better.

My heart is pounding in my chest and my mouth has gone dry. There's no running away now.

I stand and wait for his approach, ready to tell him I don't have time. For anything. I am completely booked up my entire stay here. And maybe I'm getting ahead of myself. Could be he just wants someone to talk to while he waits for *his* ride.

"You must be Taylor Grant," Mr. Cowboy says when he steps up in front of me. He's beautiful. The kind of beautiful that makes a woman want to spend all day between the sheets. No lunch, no dinner, just sex. He doesn't wait for me to respond, just reaches for my hand and continues with, "Name's Cole McKenzie."

I'm so completely caught off-guard all I can think is that I must look like hell after spending so many hours on a plane. Like that matters. I'm not here shopping for a man. Though if I were, the cowboy would be a good start. "Attorney at law, may I help you?" I say. And God only knows why I feel it important he know I'm an attorney, but now he does, and so I guess he also knows I'm not a woman to be messed with.

"Your sister sent me." He gestures toward the jungle, into places unknown. "She's back at The Fish Shack, waiting." His drawl is unmistakable. An honest-to-goodness cowboy, here in the Caribbean. Imagine that.

"Excuse me?" I say. Our palms languish together as I gaze

into his eyes. They're the bluest blue you could ever imagine. He *and* his eyes are damn beautiful. I feel shaky, like I might fall at his feet.

"Your sister. She sent me to get you."

"I'm confused. I don't remember my sister ever mentioning you, or that someone else would be picking me up."

Cole smiles. "Maybe she forgot."

I take back my hand. If Paula really did send him, it's likely she and the cowboy are involved. Which means the cowboy and *I* will not be engaging in any X-, or even R-rated, activities. Then, again, maybe he doesn't even know Paula. He hasn't once called her by name, only referred to her as my sister.

I feel my lawyer antennae going up. Being a defense attorney has done a number on my level of trust with strangers. Men, in particular. And though *this* man has given me no reason not to trust him, his failing to mention Paula's name is a red flag I can't ignore.

"Are you sure?" I ask. I'm stalling, hoping he'll say something to reassure me.

"Sure as the sun is shining, Taylor Grant… attorney at law," Cole says. He's grinning, mocking me. But I don't care. It's not the worst thing a man has done. "Like I said, Paula is waiting." He reaches for my bag.

Ah, there it is. He's used her name. I should believe him now. But for some reason, I can't. I trusted Peyton, and he blindsided me.

"Wait," I say. "I don't mean to sound paranoid, but I think I'd feel better if you could at least confirm your identity."

Cole leaves my bag resting in the sand. "Sounds fair." He peruses the beach, like he's looking for someone. Then he waves at some old guy at one of the flower stands. "See that fella over there?" He points to the old guy. "He can vouch for me."

I look, squinting into the sun, and I see the man wave in our direction. I lift a hand and give a halfhearted wave back.

"Are we good?" Cole asks.

"No. Not really. I don't know how you could possibly know

my name, or that Paula is my sister, but riding off with you into the jungle without something more substantial than a wave from another stranger seems dumb at best. You could be anybody. You might not even know my sister. You and that old man could be in cahoots."

"Cahoots?" Cole looks amused.

I look at the old guy again. He doesn't look so bad. Still. "You know what I mean. The two of you could be plotting something."

Cole laughs, big and hearty, like I've just told him the best joke ever. "What might me and that old fella be plotting, Taylor Grant, attorney at law?"

"I don't know. Kidnapping... or rape." I feel silly even saying it.

Cole laughs again.

My ire is up now. "What, you think women don't get kidnapped while on vacation? It happens all the time." I rattle off several cases in recent history to prove my point.

Cole nudges his hat back, exposing beads of perspiration. I feel his pain. It's getting hotter by the minute, standing here in the hot sun. "I'm not sure why that old guy and me would want to kidnap you," he says. "Seems like you might be a lot of trouble. And as mean as I might look, I'm not into rape. Women tend to join me in bed of their own free will."

My forehead furrows. "I don't need details about your dating past. I need proof that you know my sister."

"Seems like we're at an impasse," he says. "You don't want to take any chances, I get it. But trust me, Taylor Grant, your sister really did send me to get you. And I'm not a rapist... or a kidnapper." He presses his lips together, thinking. "Tell you what. You wait here and think about it, while I go get some wind on my face." Then he grabs my bag and starts off across the sand.

I'm surprised at first, and then concerned. If I don't stop him, there go all my clothes, as well as my female supplies—makeup, hair product, unmentionables.

"Wait!" I shout at his back, but he doesn't even break pace.

My mind is racing. I spin around and look for anyone who

might be witness to what's just happened. But no one is paying any attention. The only thing I can think to do is shout again. So I do. "Help! I've been robbed!"

My noise gets a few looks, but it's more like I'm an annoyance, me with my loudness on this peaceful sunny day. I think I even see someone yawn. No one cares that a woman is being robbed in broad daylight.

I point at Cole, who's still walking away from me. "He took my *bag*!" I explain. Nothing. "He's a *thief*!" I say, incredulous at their indifference. Finally, I turn and look at the old man at the flower stand. He's busy with a customer.

Suddenly, I feel alone. Alone in paradise.

Where the hell is Paula?

I finally get it together and I take off at a brisk pace through the cushion of sand in shoes that are hardly proper for chasing down a thief. Not only that but the cowboy has long legs, and they have one speed—fast. Soon my bag is all the way across the beach. And by the time I catch up, Cole has made it to the parking lot and is standing at the side of a well-used Jeep, with my bag already in the backseat.

"Here we are. You can relax now," he tells me.

"Didn't you hear me calling to you?" I put a hand to my throat. "I was screaming so loud I think I might lose my voice." Not only that, but my wind is gone and I'm sucking warm air. It's the humidity and heat, I tell myself, but the sad truth is I'm out of shape, which is what sitting behind a desk seventy hours a week has done for me. Thank you, Burns, Stockwell, and Taft.

"Your voice sounds fine," Cole says. He looks unconvinced. "Paula told me you might resist, you being an attorney and all. She warned me you're a suspicious type and that I might have to take charge."

Paula! I should have known she was behind this nonsense.

Cole nods in the direction of the woman he was talking to several minutes ago. "If you'd rather, you can catch a ride on Lady Bella's Island Express. You'd better hurry, though. She looks about ready to leave."

I glance back at Lady Bella and her truck. I consider going with her, but I'm still trying to catch my breath and doubt I could make it across the parking lot. Too, I'm beginning to believe Cole really does know Paula. If he was a kidnapper, he could have easily grabbed me by now and thrown me into the back of his Jeep, along with my bag. But he hasn't. He's still standing here, arguing with me.

"What'll it be, darlin', me or Lady Bella?" Cole presses me.

Darlin'? Damn.

I catch my bottom lip in my teeth. "You. I'll go with you," I say. So, there it is. Proof positive I'm a gidiot.

Chapter Two

I just wanted to look. I told myself there was no harm. But now here I am riding in a strange car with a strange man, and I'm not at all certain this is something I'll survive.

The good news is Cole and I are going so slow, because of all the ruts and dips in the road, that if he *does* turn out to be a psycho killer, I'll be able to jump out and run for cover in the bushes. Bushes meaning jungle. All the green and thick and nothing else, it *has* to be the jungle.

My gaze goes to Cole's right thumb. It's slightly off, like it's been broken. This gives me something to focus on other than the fact that my fillings are practically being jarred out of my teeth. But the good news is I don't feel like I'm in any immediate danger. So I try to relax. I rest my head back against the seat, only half closing my eyes. I don't feel *that* safe.

My mind wanders and I go back to the moment I found Peyton's note. *Thanks for the memories, but I need more* is what it said. I must have read it a thousand times, sure that I was adding or subtracting words that held more of an explanation. But no. *Thanks... I need more*. His message was loud and clear. Life without me was not only possible, it was desired... and good-bye.

Just good-bye.

Aren't there supposed to be signs? Did Peyton want more sex... money... sleep? Truth be told, I never confronted him to find out. I was afraid I wouldn't like his answer. And, now, every time I look at another man, I feel like I shouldn't because I won't be smart enough to know when the end is near. But that shouldn't be a problem with the cowboy. We've not even begun. Nor will we. I'm too afraid, now, of taking chances.

As usual, thinking about Peyton makes warm tears form behind my eyes, and I can't help it or stop it, so I turn my head and stare out at the vegetation.

"You okay over there?" Cole asks.

I nod, smiling tightly. I'm not really okay, but I will be. Give me two or three years.

"Paula's been half-crazy waiting to see you," Cole tells me.

I choke out a laugh. "Yet she sent you to pick me up."

"I expect she wanted to make sure the place was just right for your arrival."

How could it not be? Isn't this paradise? I think as I watch the passing greenery and the occasional splash of color—red, yellow, magenta—which, I'm sure, are flowers. Their fragrance is so sweet and thick I feel like I'm eating it. And I wish I were. My stomach has begun to feel like a hollow pit. I declined the in-flight meal, saving my hunger for the delicacies I was sure I'd receive upon my arrival, but now I'm wishing I'd had at least a snack.

I hear twittering and chirping overhead, and I look up into the sky, where hundreds of birds are soaring above us, flaunting their colorful wings. I've never witnessed such a thing. They're so enchanting I don't want to take my eyes off them.

I watch the birds make their way through the trees, and then they disappear. But a few minutes more and I hear noises that aren't nearly as enchanting. It sounds more like screeching from someone being murdered. I turn in my seat to see the source, but I can't see a thing through all the green. "Do I need to duck for cover?" I ask Cole.

He laughs. "It's nothing to worry about. You'll get used to the noise."

Oh. Okay. But I lean into the middle of the Jeep, where I feel safer. Cole and his muscles are a comfort, plus he smells good. Like the sea and the wind. It's an incredibly sexy combination.

After several minutes, the "noise" of the jungle dies down, and I decide to put my overworked imagination to rest. I close my eyes, finally trusting that Cole will get us to our destination in one piece.

Barely a minute passes and I'm giving in to my fatigue. It was a long journey getting here. Plus, I haven't slept in two nights in my excitement to see my baby sis. I hadn't intended to wait so long to visit, but then life got in the way, and, well, that seems to be the excuse we all use when life becomes too complicated for fun.

As Cole and I bounce along the rough road, I become aware of how incredibly clean and fresh the air smells. It's like breathing pure oxygen. Washington has fresh air, too. But not like this. In the past few years, Seattle and surrounding cities have become so crowded with cars, people, and buildings that it feels stuffy. Too much stuff. Too many people. Sometimes, I feel like I might suffocate.

My thoughts go back to Paula. Why is she here? I promised our mother I'd come and find out, though I would have come anyway. I haven't seen her in two years, and I have plenty of questions of my own. Before she left Seattle, Paula and I had been talking about how, after her graduation, we'd open our own law firm. We were both excited for the chance to work together and be our own bosses. Just one more year of law school for her, and we were really going to do it. But then along came a man named Ramone, who caused Paula to lose her mind. She thought she was in love with him and they came here to St. John on a lover's-package cruise, where he ended up breaking her heart by hooking up with some beauty queen who'd come in on another ship. Then Ramone and the beauty queen sailed off into the sunset... and Paula decided to stay and make St. John her home.

Our poor mother has been wringing her hands ever since, and now I need to be able to tell her that Paula is happy and healthy and not being held captive by some sex-slave organization.

I glance over at Cole and wonder if he's the reason my sister is still here. It's crazy, but I'm hoping, instead, that Paula is sweet on some bronzed surfer dude. Or how about a shopkeeper who surfs on the side? Or perhaps he sells flowers at one of the roadside stands.

Yeah, that's it. My sis is hung up on a flower salesman.

So not. It *has* to be Cole. He's just Paula's type. Tall, muscles galore, gorgeous. In fact, I'd bet ten mochas, topped with whipped cream, that Cole is exactly why Paula hasn't come home. He was probably there for Paula when she needed consoling… and the rest is history. It sounds probable enough, though I may have to use my finely honed interrogation skills to find out for sure.

The tedious travel over the dirt road finally gets to me, and as bars of sunlight flicker like the flash of a camera over my eyelids, I go to that serene place between sleep and wakefulness. I begin to drift off, thinking about all the fun Paula and I are going to have, and how she and I will reconnect and get back to being sisters. But then the Jeep jumps violently, and it's like I'm on one of those wild carnival rides. I grab for the closest thing—the door handle—and wrap my fingers around it, but it comes off in my hand.

I toss the handle to the floor and come fully awake, eyes wide open, looking to see what in God's name is going on. We're about to be hit head-on by another vehicle, a small truck.

I don't want to go through the windshield, so I jam my foot into the floorboard, like that will help, but Cole's arm is already against my chest and I'm pinned to my seat. I can barely breathe, in fact. *This is it*, I think… and I haven't even seen my sister.

I'm ready, braced for impact. But then Cole somehow maneuvers the Jeep around the oncoming vehicle, and it's crisis over. Just like that. Cole and the other driver smile and toss each other a wave, like a near head-on collision never happened…and

I'm practically in cardiac arrest. My heart is pounding and my mouth is hanging open with no words coming out.

"That was a tourist," Cole explains. "Takes 'em a few days to get hold of driving on the left." He glances down at my hand on his leg, which, until now, I hadn't realized was there. "Let's save that for later, darlin'. Plenty of time to get to know each other while you're here." He smiles as he says it, but I find no humor in almost being killed.

I frown and yank my hand from his leg. "We could have died!"

"But we didn't," he assures me.

No. But now I'm beyond frustrated. I just want to get to wherever we're going. "How much farther?" I ask, my voice sharp.

"Close. St. John is only nine miles long. Just seems farther because of the road conditions."

"*Nine? Miles?*" I'm incredulous. When Paula told me St. John was small, I thought she meant small*ish*. Certainly, not head-of-a-pin needle small. I could walk end-to-end in under two hours. Okay, maybe three, but *Jesus*.

"You'll get used to it, soon enough," Cole tells me.

No. I won't.

I sit for a minute, letting it sink in. And by "it," I mean everything. I cannot fathom why my sister would leave behind all the comforts of life to live on a tiny piece of land that's so far from home and everything she knows, simply because some guy who had a nice tan and spoke with a luxuriously romantic accent sweet-talked her, then duped her. There has to be more to her heartbreak story than a Latin lover turned bad.

And now I feel like a shit. A shitty sister. I'm all but consumed with guilt for not coming to see Paula sooner. She obviously needed me. I would have advised her to come back to Seattle, maybe get some therapy, and then get back on the dating horse. Though who am I to talk? I can't even get over a rat who wrote me a good-bye note on the back of a napkin.

I'm still scolding myself when the Jeep rolls to a stop. I'm relieved at first, glad to finally have arrived at my sister's home. But when I notice my surroundings, I'm taken aback. Cole has parked the Jeep at the back of a large hut.

"What's this?" I ask. Certainly, this is not where Paula lives. My sister *certainly* does not live in an oversized hut. I won't believe it until I hear it.

"This is where Paula lives," Cole confirms. He points to the sign above the door. "Also known as The Fish Shack." He hops out of the Jeep and grabs my bag and takes it over to the wood steps that lead up to the door of the hut.

I hear a dull roar and I look and see a view most would kill for. It's a blanket of turquoise that seems to go on forever—the Caribbean Sea—just a mere seventy-five yards across perfect white sand.

"That's your sister's back yard," Cole tells me.

I admit I'm envious of my sister's view. "But she lives in a hut," I say.

He steps back over to my side of the Jeep. "Don't worry, Taylor Grant. Before you know it, this will seem like home."

Chapter Three

The back door of Paula's Place bangs open, and I immediately forget about all the foolishness of my sister living on a beach in a hut. Paula is standing before me, and all I can do is squeal in delight. I rush to her, and she and I come together in a tight hug that catches me off guard. She feels different somehow, like she's all grown up.

I ignore my emotions and whisper in her ear, "You little snot," and she knows exactly what I'm talking about, because she lets out a wicked, knowing laugh as she hugs me even tighter.

"I guess I deserve that," she whispers back.

I'm no longer angry. All transgressions up to this point are forgiven.

I need to take a good look at her, so I step back, and immediately, I see that she's not my bratty little sister anymore. She's a woman.

I smile and put on a brave front, warding off tears that are so near the surface I can already feel their presence. I silently vow not to turn into a blubbering fool, but I don't know how long I'll be able to contain myself.

"Little Paulette," I say, which earns me a stern look. Paula hates being called Paulette. Our mom wanted to name her something fancier than plain old Paula, but she couldn't bring herself to go for something like Pensee or Paseala or Pazice or Paili. Which are all fine, if you don't mind spending half your life spelling your name to others.

Personally, I'm fond of Pippa. It's Italian and it means love of horses, which is fitting, considering our father has a smidgen of Italian blood running through his veins. And, well, my sister does love horses. But that's just me, and I guess naming her Pippa would have been the pragmatic choice.

"That's sis, to you," she admonishes.

"Correction duly noted," I say.

Paula laughs and grabs my arm and she pulls me along, past a bundle of bananas that are hanging just outside the door. They're ripe and fragrant and I'm tortured by their smell. Paula sees me eyeing them. "You want one?" she asks.

Cole doesn't wait to hear my answer. He picks one and hands it to me. "It'll be the best you've ever had," he promises, grinning.

I take the banana, and the three of us enter the hut through a door that looks like it was made from a leftover piece of plywood that was pulled from a construction site. I immediately press my lips together to stop myself from reacting. Or *over*reacting. This is Paula's home. I'm not going to do the big-sister thing and point out every little flaw I see about the life she's chosen.

Not yet, anyway.

Once inside, Paula makes a quick left turn and pushes through a wall of ceiling-to-floor strings of shells and beads that separate the main room—the bar, from what I can tell—from a much smaller room, which must be her bedroom, as it contains two cot-type beds and two blocks of wood that I suspect are makeshift nightstands. Cole follows with my bag, which he sets atop one of the cots. Then he leaves us, which I appreciate. I'm eager to have some alone time with my sister, to get caught up, before she and I become too involved with her friends and having fun.

"Well, what do you think?" Paula asks. She's beaming like

she's just given birth to this place.

I do exactly what I think is expected of me. I look around as though I'm making an honest assessment. Other than the cots and nightstands, there's a wood chest and a cabinet that back in civilization might be called an *armoire*. I don't see a closet, so I'm guessing the *armoire* is it. But really, it's nothing more than a plain hunk of wood with doors. The floor is plain, too. Bare, except for two shaggy pink rugs, one by each cot. And the windows have lacy coverings, but no glass.

I guess I wasn't expecting Paula's life to be so much different than mine. But it is and now I can't think of anything to say. And maybe that's not even it. Maybe I'm reacting to Paula being here so far from home and seemingly doing fine without me. Which I hate. I don't want her to be fine without me. I want her to need me. I want her to be so glad to see me that she finally realizes she wants to come home.

Because *I* need *her*.

"Well?" Paula presses me.

I look at her, don't want to tell her what I really think. She doesn't *really* want to know. "It's… quaint," I manage, though I can practically feel my nose doing a Pinocchio impression. If I were telling the truth, I'd be tossing my hands in the air and asking her, *What the hell?* But I won't do that. Not now. It's not the time.

"Really?" Paula asks, her eyes gleaming. "I know how you love a big, soft bed, loaded with fluffy pillows."

I wrap an arm around her. "Yes. This is great." There goes another inch added to my nose. "I've been sleeping at my desk lately, so this is a step up."

"So I won't catch you trotting down the beach in the middle of the night to stay at the Westmark Resort?"

"There's a resort down the beach? How far?"

Paula gives me a squinty-eyed look. "Har-de-har."

"They're not so bad." Cole steps back into the room and nods at the cots. "I've slept on them a time or two. You'll be here just long enough to get used to them."

A big yellow dog rushes into the room after Cole, and I forget about the cots and how comfortable they may or may not be. I immediately crouch and pull the big yellow mass of fur to my chest, not considering for one minute that he might have a problem with strangers. "Hey, beautiful," I murmur into one of his big, floppy ears. "Where did you come from?"

Big Yellow responds by pushing his nose into my hair and sniffing my scent. It's an honest-to-goodness lovefest between woman and beast. His fur feels like silk and smells of honey and coconuts. He's slightly damp, too, like he's just had a bath. He's magnificent.

"Yours?" I glance up at Paula.

She shakes her head. "He belongs to Cole."

"His name's Beach Bum," Cole tells me. "Bum for short."

Bum, the Labrador retriever—most popular breed of dog in the nation for the last several years. I know this because I've been investigating breeds of dogs for some time now, so that when I'm finally able to take on the responsibility, I'll be fully prepared. And go figure, Labs are at the top of my list. Everyone else in the Pacific Northwest has one, why not me?

Cole's dog and I stay attached for another minute. Me scratching and rubbing him, and him smelling and learning me. Bum is lovely and sweet, and I could rub his glistening fur all day, but now that I know he belongs to Cole, I don't want to encourage any kind of bond. The last thing I need is a connection between myself and the cowboy, even if it is only by osmosis through his dog. Our ride in the Jeep together was nice, but now it's over and it's time for me and Cowboy Cole *and* his dog to say good-bye.

When I release Bum, I'm completely covered in dog hair. Red, tan, white, I look like a female Sasquatch. A short, blond hair floats through the air, and we all watch as it settles on the front of my blouse.

"Sorry 'bout that," Cole says. He reaches to brush the hair off and gets it with one swipe. But then he sees a few more and tries to brush them off, as well. Which is useless, because there are too many. And not only that, but being that I haven't had a man's hands in such close proximity to my breasts in a very long time, I'm practically squirming. His touch, albeit innocent, is too much. I step back, out of his reach.

"Thanks, I can manage," I say, and I step over to my bag and start digging around in it, like I'm looking for something… anything to get my mind off the cowboy and his helpful hands.

"You can unpack later," Paula says. "I want to show you around." She doesn't wait, just grabs my hand and leads me back through the beads and shells. I hurry to keep up, lest she drag me along, and she stops just a few feet into the big room we passed through when we first entered the hut. Cole makes his way to the far end of the bar and settles himself comfortably on a stool. I wouldn't be surprised if his name was carved somewhere on it.

"This is it," Paula announces. A bright smile spreads clear across her face. "This is my life. This is where it all happens on St. John. There's no other place like it. Aren't you jealous?"

More like awestruck. And not in a good way.

I give her a tight smile and, again, take in my surroundings. It's beachy. Tables made from old broken surfboards are scattered haphazardly about, coconut shells with tea candles line the bar, and all kinds of paraphernalia hang on the walls, including a shark's head that has a human leg sticking out of its mouth. An attempt at humor in the face of tragedy, perhaps?

"I feel like I'm at a seaside graveyard," I say.

Paula's face is still beaming. "It's great, huh?"

Um… yeah. *But why is one of your walls missing?* Really. One entire wall of her home slash bar has gone missing. Though to be honest, it wouldn't surprise me if there never *was* a wall.

She sees me looking.

"A hurricane hit last year. It blew my wall away. It's no big deal," she explains, shrugging. She swings around and looks out toward the big blanket of blue, the Caribbean Sea. "Now, I have a better view of the beach."

Point taken. But I'm not interested in the view right now. I'm still stuck on the gust of wind that was strong enough to rip a wall from my sister's home. The idea that she could have been hurt and alone so far from home terrifies me. If Paula were back in Seattle, where she belongs, she'd be safe. From hurricanes, at least.

"God, Paula, you weren't hurt, were you?" I ask. I'm shaking.

"I'm in one piece, aren't I?" she answers… like, enough said, I don't want to bore you with the details.

But I want the details. All of them. "What's going on with you? Why are you here? Is it Ramone? Was what happened between you and him so bad that you still can't come home?" The questions come like rapid fire from my mouth. So much for me refraining from playing the big sister card. But I can't help myself. These are questions my mother would want me to ask, and ones that *I* want answered.

Paula frowns. "I *am* home."

My heart sinks. I didn't expect such finality in her words. They hit me so deep I need to pause and catch my breath. When I can speak again, I say, "This isn't home. This is the beach. You don't make the beach your home just because life throws you a curve. Please tell me this is simply a phase you're going through, that you don't really intend to stay here."

Paula's frown deepens. "I'm not some teen going through hormone changes. I'm here because I love it. No traffic, no conference calls, no stress."

"No Ramone," I comment, frustrated. Mostly at myself. I hadn't intended to do this, pressure her into talking about him. And, anyway, he's gone, so what's the point?

Paula cuts a look over to the bar, where a man the size of a mountain is standing, wiping glasses. He appears to be ignoring our conversation, but by the way he keeps rubbing the same spot on one glass, I have a feeling he's caught every word.

"Me being here has nothing to do with Ramone," Paula tells me, lowering her voice.

I look at her, assessing. I don't know how far I can push just yet. Better if I wait until she and I are off by ourselves to get into any discussion involving past loves. "Sure. Okay," I say. I glance once more up at the shark eating the leg and I shudder. It's still not funny. "But at least tell me you're kidding about living here. I was hoping you'd have a cute little two-bedroom, two-bath bungalow somewhere on this island. This is just where you nine-to-five, right?"

The look on Paula's face tells me how wrong I am. She slaps a hand to her chest. "Nine-to-five? That's hilarious. Try seven to two."

My jaw goes slack. "That's all you work? Seven hours a day? No wonder you can't afford four walls." I'm ready to go into a full-blown rant, but I can see that Paula might be on the verge of rolling her eyes, so I stop myself. I don't want to sound like our mother.

"I work from seven in the morning 'til two in the morning," she says. "Or even later, sometimes."

I do a quick calculation and come up with nineteen plus hours. Which makes my jaw go even *more* slack. "You're up all day, and then all night, too? Jesus, Paula, when do you sleep?" I'm in total Mom mode.

Paula shrugs. "Sleep is for the dead. And don't even start with me about how that's not healthy. You work plenty of hours yourself."

"Yes, but I do it in an office, sitting in a big, cushy chair. And if I need a quick nap, I lock my door and prop my feet up on my desk."

Paula grins. "You forget who you're talking to. There are no moments for propping feet and napping when you work for a law firm like B, S, and T."

I pinch my lips tight. I have no rebuttal. "Well, I'm allowed to be concerned, aren't I?"

Paula doesn't answer. She gets sidetracked when some kind of insect passes in front of her face. She swats it away, and then it buzzes over in my direction. I lean to one side, giving it some space, and then it flies away. I dislike bugs, so much so that I won't even exert the energy it takes to squash them. Then I can't help but point out the obvious. "If you had four walls, maybe the bugs would stay *out*side."

Paula hunches her shoulders. "Maybe. Maybe not. Damn, I've missed you," she says, and she pulls me in for another sisterly hug. Plus, she plants a loud kiss on my cheek, which more than makes up for the cot she expects me to sleep on while I'm here. It's exactly how I pictured our reunion, and now I'm overcome with emotion. Life just hasn't been the same without my sis.

We're stuck in our hug, clinging to each other like it's been years, which it has. But now I see the man behind the bar watching, and I realize he hasn't taken his eyes off us since we came into the room. It seems a good time to lighten things up, so I lower my voice and give a slight nod in his direction. "Who's the geezer? He keeps staring at me. Are you sleeping with him?" And maybe that's what I'm secretly hoping, so that I can continue to fantasize guilt-free about Cole.

Paula's cheeks flush crimson, like I've struck gold. Only that can't be. No way would my twenty-six-year-old sister be interested in a man who's nearly old enough to be receiving AARP offers.

"That's my bartender," Paula answers quietly. "And he's not that much older than you."

"Ouch," I say, putting a hand to my cheek, like she's slapped me. Up until now, I thought I was doing well in the age department. "Do I look old?"

"You *are* thirty-five," Paula reminds me.

I shoot a quick glance in the mirror above the bar. "But do I look it?"

Paula laughs. "Not at all. I'm just giving you a hard time."

My eyes go back to the mirror and I see Cole watching me. His face shows nothing—amusement perhaps.

Paula catches me mirror gazing, too, and she says, "Relax. Don't get all freaked out about how you look. You're beautiful... for an old chick." She laughs again and grabs my hand. "C'mon. I'll introduce you to the geezer." She pulls me toward the old man, and I forget about my age and whether or not I look it. We belly up to the bar, and it's the same as the back door, nothing more than a plank. Granted, it's been smoothed and varnished, but still, it's nothing like the bar counters back home. One might kindly call it rustic.

I look beyond the bar and see several more planks that are mounted horizontally on the wall. They're holding a bevy of glasses and dozens of bottles of alcohol—rum, mostly. In fact, the island seemeth to runneth over with rum. Cruzan Rum, to be exact. Someone offered me a plastic cupful the moment I stepped off the plane, and I refused, but had I known what lay ahead, I might have taken an entire bottle to soften the blow.

The bottom two shelves catch my eye. Bottle after bottle, filled with colorful liquid—green, blue, yellow, red—are stacked three deep, and they give the hut's drab interior a boost, which I'm sure is their *only* purpose. No one ever really drinks all that neon-colored crap. Do they?

As though the bartender has read my mind, he grabs one of the bottles filled with blue liquid, and then he does some fancy tossing maneuver that holds my attention. Up, around, behind his back, across his front, and up once more into the air a couple of feet, only to catch it on the way back down before it crashes in a big colorful splatter to the floor. Then he uncaps the bottle and splashes some of the liquid into two glasses, after which he adds a dash of this and a dash of that, before he finishes by pushing a couple of pineapple and orange slices over the glass rims. He then slides the two drinks over in front of a man who's wearing typical tourist attire—a Hawaiian-flavored Tommy Bahama shirt and a pair of off-white, wrinkled linen slacks—who promptly takes them over to one of the surfboard tables, where a woman wearing a big straw hat awaits her tropical concoction.

"This is Tug Laguna, best bartender in St. John," Paula introduces me to the man with the magical hands. I smile. Only on a Caribbean island would you find a man with a name like Tug Laguna.

Bartender Tug glowers down at me from his hulking frame with a look on his face that could either be taken as a smile or a smirk, but I quickly decide it doesn't matter. Anyone who can handle a bottle the way he does is okay with me. I do the polite thing and offer him my hand, which he takes, squeezes, and gives back.

"Pleased," he says.

I respond in kind, but now I'm preoccupied with his looks. I know it's unlikely, but I feel like I've seen this man before. Though I cannot fathom any situation where our paths might have crossed.

It's his hair, more than anything, all sun-kissed and long and wanting to fall forward over his eyes, if it weren't for the hair band at the nape of his neck holding it in place. And now that I'm really looking, he's not at all hard on the eyes. Just old-*er*. Seeing him up close, I reassess him to be at least in his mid-forties. So, Paula was right. He isn't *that* much older than me.

I keep thinking and staring, concentrating on the warm brown stubble he has growing out the bottom of his chin. And then I've got it. He looks like Robert Redford in that movie about a man who lived off the land in the mountains. A mountain man. Yeah, that's it.

I smile to myself. Mountain man may be nice to look at, but he's so not Paula's type. No wonder she went pale when I suggested she was sleeping with him.

Tug makes a grunting sound that I take as some kind of sign that he's uncomfortable with my staring, and Paula confirms it when she grabs my arm once more and leads me off in another direction. Through a door and off to one side of the bar we go.

As we enter another room, I'm immediately blasted with hot air and the savory aroma of spices and fried food. I'm so hungry now that the smell makes my stomach hurt. I have yet to eat the banana.

We're in a kitchen. Not a residential kitchen, but more like what might be found in a small restaurant. And the grill and cooking area is definitely commercial. I look to the grill and see several pieces of fish cooking, the smoke billowing up, filling the room.

Standing in front of the grill is a man with a full head of grey hair. He looks up and flashes a smile that exposes a gold-capped front tooth, and then he wipes his hands on an apron that's tied around his neck and is stained with all manner of food source.

"You be Miss Taylor, I expect," he says, taking my hands in his. He looks at me, then to Paula, and then back to me. "You gals sho do look like sisters," he proclaims. "I cain't rightly say which one o' you is the prettier, though."

"This is Greenbeans Bowen," Paula tells me. "He's the best chef here on St. John." She cups a hand to one side of her mouth. "He's also a big flirt."

"I heard that," Greenbeans says.

"You were supposed to," Paula tells him.

So, my sis has the best bartender, as well as the best chef on St. John. I wonder if Cole has a "best something" status. I can only guess what the category might be.

"Thank you," I tell Greenbeans for his compliment. Already, I feel close to this man. He reminds me of my grandfather, who was possibly the nicest man to walk the face of this earth.

"I be fixin' you gals some lunch," Greenbeans says. "Grilled halibut, warm mango salad..." He gives me an appraising look. "Or mayhaps you be more of a mahi-mahi-in-lime-butter type o' gal, eh?"

"Halibut is fine," I tell him. "Or anything. Even this." I hold up the banana Cole gave me.

Greenbeans chuckles. "I expect that'll hold you a piece. Long enough for you gals to go take a walk. By time you get back, lunch'll be off the grill. In the meantime, that banana sho goin' be the best you ever had." He gives me a wink, and then returns to his cooking, sticking his fingers into a small bowl filled with some kind of red spice mixture, which he dashes over the fish. I'm already salivating. I don't think I can wait much longer to eat. In another minute the banana may be history.

Paula escorts me back into the other room, where I see Cole still sitting at the end of the bar. We pass by him, making our way over to the front, where the wall is missing, and Paula stops on the top step. The view is so breathtaking I feel like I'm looking at one of those fabulous island calendars. A fragrant breeze passes in front of my face, and I smell a mix of scents—flowers and sea. It's intoxicating.

"This," Paula tells me, her eyes scanning the horizon, "is why I may never leave St. John."

Chapter Four

"Wow," I say. I'm in awe as I soak in the scene splayed out before me. Now that I'm over the initial shock of Paula's living arrangements, I can fully appreciate the splendor of mile after mile of rippling Caribbean Sea. Sparkling turquoise water, so vivid and beautiful that I swear I can hear angels singing. I've seen my share of beautiful beaches—Coronado, Kaanapali, St. Andrews, and so many others—but this beach is sweet perfection, and I am thoroughly seduced.

I peel the banana as I stare, and I take a bite. Greenbeans and Cole weren't lying. It's the best I have ever tasted.

Paula allows me but a moment to savor both the view and the banana. She's impatient, though, eager to be off. I can tell because her right foot is tapping lightly, and that translates to *Hurry the hell up.*

"Go ahead," I say. "I'll catch up."

And off she goes, down the steps to the sand.

Cole approaches behind me with Bum, and Bum is as eager as Paula. He bounds down the steps, too.

I watch them, mostly Paula. It does my heart good to see her so happy and carefree. I wouldn't mind being in her shoes right now. Lately, mine have been too heavy.

I finish the banana and then toss the peel into a bin next to the door. Then I'm ready to hit the beach. But as I reach the sand, my eye catches a movement over near a wall of green foliage. When I look, I see a donkey and he's stripping a bush bare of everything but the sticks. I stop to take him in, and now I'm wondering if he'll chase me when I run past. I know donkeys aren't like bears, carnivorous, but this donkey doesn't look like he's pleased with my presence. His ears are twitching and he's giving me the stare down. A twig falls from his mouth. It's seriously unnerving.

I look over at Cole for reassurance, but he doesn't look nervous at all. Though I don't know how reliable his state of mind is, considering he's just finished off a tall beer. "Paula never told me she had a donkey," I say.

"They're wild," Cole tells me. "And they can be mean, so leave them be. Don't ever try to feed them. They might bite or kick. Then they'll be hunted down and destroyed. You wouldn't want that."

No. God, no… wouldn't want that.

I still don't know if I should move or stay put.

"C'mon," Cole says, and I guess that's my cue that it's safe for me to venture past the donkey. I move quickly, feeling a shiver as I pass the wary eye of the small beast. Cole stays beside me, and Bum comes back to join us. He doesn't bark or even seem to notice the donkey. Cole tosses Bum a stick, and he chases after it.

"What's with the donkey?" I ask when I reach Paula.

"They're wild," she tells me. "And they can be mean, so don't ever try to feed them. They might bite or kick, and then they'll be hunted down and destroyed."

"You don't say." I refrain from telling her I just heard the exact same thing from Cole.

Paula and I walk side by side at a pace that makes me feel like we're on our way to somewhere and that we need to hurry, else *somewhere* might be closed by the time we arrive. I doubt that's the case, so I slow my pace and hope that Paula will accommodate me. I'd like to enjoy the scenery. But even if I wanted to, I couldn't walk much faster in the shoes I'm still wearing— expensive strappy sandals that don't belong on a beach or anywhere near saltwater. I didn't consider that I might be walking in sand immediately upon my arrival.

I plod along, feeling pretty much out of my element. Hurricanes… mad donkeys… hot men in cowboy hats. It's almost too much to absorb.

Speaking of mad donkeys, I look back to make sure he's not following us. He's not, but I feel obligated to ask, "Are you sure you're okay here?"

Paula waves off my concern. "Don't worry about the donkey. I leave him alone. He leaves me alone. Besides"—she glances over her shoulder—"we have protection."

She means Cole. I glance back, too, and see that he's taken off his shirt. It's muscle everywhere, and I can't help but think what a fabulous male specimen he is. Solid, well-proportioned, perfect. I turn halfway around to watch him for a moment with Bum. Bum leaps high into the air, right in front of Cole's face, and Cole swings around to throw a stick far down the beach. Bum scrambles after it, and when Cole turns back, he catches me watching him, like he caught me at Cruz Bay Beach. He smiles the same as he did then, only this time it seems more personal… and it makes my heart beat faster.

"Last one in is a rotten egg," Paula says. She laughs and breaks away in a sprint toward the water. She's oblivious to the looks Cole and I have exchanged. She reaches the water's edge and stops only long enough to kick off her flip-flops. Then she plunges into a small, incoming wave and disappears. I don't know where she'll come up, but I watch and wait, and when she stands, she's waist-high in the frothy aftermath of the wave.

As I continue toward her, I approach a couple of palm trees that have a hammock swinging between them. It's occupied, with a man and a woman, senior citizens, I'm guessing, as they both have heads topped with grey hair. My look turns into a stare. They're wrapped in each other's arms and looking at each other like they're the only two people on earth, which has me realizing my mistake in coming here. This is a place for lovebirds. What was I thinking? I should be back home, staring out my window at the Space Needle.

"Are you coming?" Paula beckons to me. She's loud, to be heard over the surf, and her eyes are bright and eager. Plus, she's clapping her hands like this is her first time ever swimming. The joy on her face is a testament that one can be hurt, even broken, and then somehow recover.

I'd love to join her. I'd love for some of her joy to rub off on me. But I think maybe I need more time. My hurt is fresher than hers.

"Isn't this the best backyard you've ever seen?" she shouts. "Aren't you jealous?"

"Yes," I shout back, waving a hand at her. "It's the best. My backyard is an alley."

Paula laughs at my response, and then she splashes around in the water some more, waiting, like she really thinks I'm going to join her.

Cole and Bum take a breather from playing fetch, and they catch up. Bum's tongue is hanging out the side of his mouth. They both stand next to me. "You going in?" Cole asks.

"Maybe later," I say.

"What's wrong with now?"

I have no answer. Or maybe it's that I don't want to tell him the truth, that I've all but forgotten how to have fun and laugh and be silly.

Cole doesn't push for a response. He lets Bum rest for a minute, and then they go back to their game... while I try to ignore the warmth I felt when Cole stood next to me. He makes me aware of needs I've long ignored. Needs that I think a man like he could handle.

It crosses my mind that I might be crazy. I'm not really ready for a new relationship, sexual or otherwise. But what's the harm in daydreaming?

I'd all but forgotten about Paula, but now she's out of the

water and has a firm grip on one of my arms. I resist as she drags me into the surf, but it's all happening so fast I barely have time to slip off my shoes before I'm knee-deep in an oncoming wave. The next thing I know, Paula is dipping her arms into the water and is bringing them up toward me in a huge scooping motion. Too late, I realize her objective—to drench me.

I try to back away, but I don't move fast enough, and I'm unable to get out of reach before I'm hit with what seems like buckets of water.

I scream—loud—and then I look down at myself to see that I'm soaked through. Plus, my jungle-print bra is showing through the thin fabric of my blouse.

Paula doubles over, laughing, while I drip saltwater and give anyone who cares to look a peep show. "Wow, nice bra," she says. "I never knew you were into animal print. Big hooters, too."

My face warms. I want to swear and use all kinds of language that isn't ladylike, but how can I be mad at my sister for having fun?

I hear Cole in the background. It sounds like he's having a good laugh, too. I don't even need to look to know it's at my expense.

The only thing I can think to do is lick the briny taste of saltwater from my lips. I stand quietly for a minute and watch Paula, waiting to see if she's got more torture in store for me. Then she comes out of the water, toward me, looking so apologetic that I think we're about to have a tender sister moment where we'll hug and tell each other "I love you." But as soon as she reaches me, she says, "I'll bet you a hundred dollars you sleep with Cole while you're here." And because she knows what a huge fan I am of crude hand gestures, she adds the finger-in-the-fist thing.

My jaw goes slack. I'm dumbfounded. Did I hear her right? Did she say what I think she did? And did she really do the finger-in-the-fist thing?

Yes, yes, and oh, yes.

I'm not at all sure how to respond, but it doesn't matter,

because Paula is off again, laughing and running down the beach.

I look to see if Cole has caught any of Paula's absurdity. I don't think so, but now, because my question about whether or not he and Paula are in a relationship has been answered, I'm wondering what he might look like naked. Perfect, I bet... if the upper half of his body is any indication. I'm also wondering if he's ever had lusty thoughts about *me*.

Probably not.

I watch him for a minute. He's in his own world, just he and his dog. Then I continue down the beach, pushing my feet through the sand, half running, half walking. A minute later, Cole and Bum run by, and they keep going until they pass Paula. By the time I catch up to her, I'm huffing and puffing, and I have no more energy for thinking about having sex with Cole, or any other man.

I slow to a walk so that I can avoid beginning my vacation by having a stroke. "How do you lock up at night?" I ask Paula. It's a reasonable question, considering her place is missing a wall.

She laughs. "That's all you have to say? I've just bet you a hundred dollars you'll sleep with Cole while you're here, and you want to know how I lock up at night?"

"I didn't think you were serious." I know she was serious.

"Tell the truth. Aren't you even the slightest bit interested? Look at him. He's a god."

I don't want to tell her that I *have* been looking at him, from the very first minute I stood on Cruz Bay Beach, from the very second I laid eyes on him. That's my secret and I'm keeping it to myself. I smooth my hair out of my face and pretend to make a quick assessment. "I suppose he's a decent enough guy. But to answer your question, no, I'm not interested. And I'm certainly not going to sleep with him."

"Why not?"

Good question. "I didn't come here to get laid. I came here to see you."

Paula smiles. "That's great. But what about Cole?" She stops, hands on hips, looking all serious. "I think it would do you both good to sleep together. What could it hurt? You live so far apart you couldn't possibly develop any attachment. No attachment means no heartache."

I look over at my sis, so angelic, with her blond hair flowing and practically glowing like a halo about her head. So innocent. So seemingly carefree. So full of shit. "What happened?" I ask. "You used to be so sensible. Did your experience with Ramone scramble your brain?"

Paula's mouth twists and she gives me a stony glare. "Ramone who?"

Ah, I've touched her sore spot. Maybe my sis isn't as carefree as she pretends.

"At least admit Cole is hot," Paula continues, doing her best to pretend Ramone's name never came up.

"Fine. Cole is hot." Sizzling hot, actually.

Cole stops and turns to look back at us. Has he heard? I'm embarrassed just thinking it.

"Don't worry. He can't hear us," Paula assures me. "So, what did you think when you first saw him?"

"What do you mean?" I'm suddenly feeling like I'm back in high school, talking with a girlfriend about the new boy in math class.

Paula shoots me a *c'mon* look.

I keep my voice low. "I don't know what you want me to say. And, anyway, why don't *you* want him? What's wrong with him?"

"He has issues. Which is why he's perfect for you. You both have issues."

So, there it is. My reason for wanting to become a nun. Every man I meet who I might be interested in ends up having some kind of issue that makes him wrong for me. I don't know what issues a man could have, living here an ocean away from reality, but if they're enough to stave off my sister, then that's enough for me. The cowboy is officially off my radar.

"I'm not sure that makes us perfect for each other. I think it's a recipe for a big fat mess," I say.

"Not so." Paula shakes her head. "It would be a short-term

fling, at best. Then the two of you could go back to your own lives."

I'm not getting it and I'm not sure I *want* to get it. "Thanks, but I'll pass," I tell Paula.

"Why?"

I open my mouth and then close it. A lump has formed in my throat. How do I explain that I think I might be broken, that I think it's possible we only get so many chances, and then we're done? I think I might be done.

"I'm done with men," I say.

"Forever?" Paula asks.

"For now."

Paula stares at me for a minute and then responds, "Jesus, Taylor, I never said you had to *marry* the guy. Just have a little fun. Would it hurt you to let loose once in a while? I suspect you could use a good tumble between the sheets. And I'll bet a tumble with a man like Cole could make you forget all about Peyton."

"Ah, Peyton. That's what this is all about."

Paula presses her lips tight. She hates being caught. "Mom says you and Peyton had lunch together. She says you gave him a gift."

"We had coffee. And I didn't give him a gift. I was simply returning a shirt he left in my closet. You and Mom needn't worry. Me and Peyton are over." But are we? Right now, talking about him, what I've lost seems so big that I can't help but wonder if I'll ever be whole again. Or part of a whole couple again. The pain is still so palpable.

Peyton Harris and I were once the perfect couple. That is, until we *uncoupled.* And now the experience of it hangs over me like a grey cloud, which I'm sure has something to do with the way he said good-bye. What kind of man breaks off a relationship of five years with a few scribbled words on the back of a coffeehouse napkin? But there I go again, thinking about him and becoming all fragile and gloomy. Which I hate. I quickly wipe my eyes, but I think it's too late. Paula has seen how hurt I am. She touches my arm.

"Forget I mentioned Peyton. He's an ass."

I nod, unable to speak.

"I still think it would be good for you to hook up with Cole," she says. "Especially after the note."

My head swivels. "You know about the note?"

"Mom told me."

I say nothing.

"Have you tried talking to him?" Paula asks. "Or did you simply go straight for a vein and key his car?" She's laughing, but I think she's also half-serious.

So much for me forgetting she mentioned Peyton. But I know she can't help herself, just as I can't help wondering about the ending between her and Ramone. "Peyton made his decision and obviously didn't want to include me in the conversation," I say.

Paula sighs. "If you ask me, happily ever after is simply a fairy tale we girls are fed so that we can start our lives thinking life is sweet."

"Life is anything but sweet."

"And that's why I live on an island," Paula says.

We're both quiet, taking slow steps, making our way down the beach. A wisp of wind blows my hair about my head, and I grab it in my hands. I see Cole and Bum up ahead waiting for us. Cole is looking at me from under the brim of his hat. It makes my stomach tumble, and I imagine him naked and on top of me. Which nearly gives me a hot flash. But it also makes me wonder if I was ever really in love with Peyton. I thought so. We weren't married, but it felt like we were, and my heart felt it, but now here I am on an island in the middle of nowhere, and I'm having thoughts about hooking up with some other man.

"I suppose you know about the Yorkie," Paula says, rudely interrupting my daydream of sex with Cole.

"Yorkie?" Somehow, I don't think Paula is talking about a dog.

"Mmm, Gina. I hear she looks like a Yorkshire terrier."

Something hot and sour fizzles through me, and all at once, I feel like I'm drowning. I don't know that I can take what Paula may be about to tell me.

"Word is," Paula continues, "as soon as she heard about Peyton Harris being up for grabs, she waggled up to him and looked him in the eye all eager to please, like she was his new pet pooch. She's all blue-eyed and fresh out of law school, and even occasionally wears her hair in pigtails. *Pigtails.* Can you imagine? I mean, I wear pigtails occasionally, but I live *here.*" She spreads her arms. "I don't work for a *law* firm."

So, Peyton has himself a new girl. Another lawyer. I had no idea he was so fond of them.

"I hadn't heard," I say. It's all I can manage. Bitter words are perched at the back of my throat, and I'm afraid if I let them out, Paula will see how broken I am. I don't want to show her that part of me. I have to be strong. I have to be the big sister.

"He finally sold something," Paula goes on. "Actually, an entire series. To the Bill and Melinda Gates Foundation building in Seattle."

Great. Peyton was a starving artist when I met him. Could barely even afford to buy his morning java. I guess he's not starving anymore. At least now I don't have to worry that he might come after me for palimony. I shake my head. "I hadn't heard that, either."

The lump in my throat groweth ever bigger. I can barely breathe, let alone speak. It takes me a minute to continue. "How do you and Mom know so much about what he's doing?"

"It was in the paper. The Gates Foundation is a big deal… even here."

Yes, I'm sure nearly everyone on earth has heard about The Gates Foundation, or at least Bill Gates.

"I'm happy for Peyton," I say, but my mouth twists as I say it because it's a lie and I'm just trying to be magnanimous. The truth is, I'm not feeling magnanimous at all, and I'd rather not hear about Peyton being so successful. Or that he's happy with someone new.

"He's an ass," Paula says again. "I hope the Yorkie gives him fleas."

We both laugh, and I feel happier, lighter somehow, like this is simply a phase I'm going through and it will soon be over. Maybe by the time I leave St. John.

Paula and I are nearly caught up to Cole and Bum, but there's one more thing I have to say to my sis. "Mom's worried about you."

Paula sighs long. I think she's been expecting this talk. "She misses me."

"Yes. And she's worried." Hell, until I saw her, even *I* still considered Paula a little girl, barely old enough to tie her own shoelaces. She had no damn business being here where it was impossible for me to keep an eye on her.

She kicks her foot through the sand and looks out over the water. "Tell Mom I'm fine. Things are different here. Everyone knows me, and we all watch out for each other. And if you tell her about my wall, also tell her it isn't a problem. Most tourists aren't here to steal. They're here to relax or party. My place provides both. Neither of you need to worry about me."

But I *do* worry. I *want* to worry. If not me, who? Who is here looking out for my sister? I have to know. "Who is he? Who's keeping you here?" I ask.

Paula laughs, but it's a nervous laugh, and I know I'm closing in on the truth. "Jeez, Taylor. Maybe you *are* getting old. You sound just like Mom."

I wince at her remark. "I don't have to be your mom to be concerned."

"No, but why does my choosing to live on an island have to be about a man?"

"It doesn't. But a woman doesn't move halfway around the globe to run a beach bar by herself. Please, talk to me. Tell me what's going on in your life so that I don't have to lie awake at night, wondering." But now we've caught up to Cole, so I'm out of luck and out of time, and Paula knows it. She runs to the base of a huge tree and slaps the trunk, looking proud, like she's grown it with her own two hands.

"This is the biggest sea grape tree on the island," she shouts over to me, and she grabs a slat of wood that's attached to a rope. The rope is attached to one of the tree limbs that go way up high. "Remember when we used to have one of these in our backyard?"

"I remember. It was a Douglas fir," I tell her as I approach.

Paula shoves the slat of wood at me. "What do you say? Want to give it a try?"

I look at Cole, and then I look at the rope and the slat of wood. I think my sister has gone mad if she expects me to engage in an activity that could possibly lead to my death. Either that or she's that desperate to change the subject.

Chapter Five

"Aren't we a little old to climb trees?" I ask. "What if we fall?" I'm not joking one bit.

"You're never too old to have fun," Paula says. "And if you fall, Cole will catch you. Isn't that right, Cole?" And she proceeds to climb up, up, up, like a monkey into the tree. Like she's spent her entire life in trees.

I look and see that Cole is smiling. He smiles a lot and has yet to show concern for anything. It's unnerving how laid-back he is. I'm sure there must be something stressful about island living. Taking the ferry, for instance. I've practically torn my hair out when I've missed the ferry by just one minute in Seattle—or three. If you're not ready to load within three minutes of departure, you can expect to sit in line and wait for the next boat to arrive. It's transportation hell as far as I'm concerned. But maybe it's different here. And, too, Cole might not have any reason to island hop.

When I look back to Paula, she's reached a fork in the tree and has the wood slat between her legs. I'm holding my breath, hoping she'll re-think this madness. I can't believe what I'm seeing. There was a time not so long ago when she wouldn't even go on one of those cheesy carnival rides when they came to town. Not even a pony ride. But looking at her now, little Paulette doesn't seem to be afraid of anything. She's Wonder Woman. So unlike me.

"She'll be all right. She's done this a thousand times," Cole reassures me, his voice so soothing I almost believe him.

Paula looks down to where Cole and I are standing, and then she laughs wickedly and pushes off from the tree. My hands are balled into fists as I watch. I want to see where she lands. I'm not convinced that what she's doing is safe. Strong winds have moved in. The sea has changed, become powerful. The water is dancing. If something happens and I need to call the paramedics, I want to know exactly where to point them. Though I highly doubt there are any emergency medical services here on this minuscule parcel of land.

I feel helpless as I watch Paula swing out over the water. It's beautiful and sparkling, like millions of diamonds, but its beauty is deceiving, and I can't help but feel anxious.

She's done this before. I repeat Cole's words over and over to myself, like it's some kind of mantra, until I kinda, sorta believe them. Cole should know, after all. He's spent time with Paula that my mom and I have missed. He knows her, while we don't. I feel a moment of anger at him for that, though it's not at all his fault. Still. And why does he have to be so damn nice? I want to hate him. But how do you hate someone for being nice?

Paula lets go of the rope and drops into the water, and I continue to hold my breath as I watch and wait for her to rise to the surface. Where is she? Is she even alive? My eyes are fixed on where I think she'll surface, but the water is wild and deep, and she's taking too long.

I shoot Cole a nervous glance, but he and Bum are in a different search mode. For a stick. Neither are concerned for Paula's whereabouts or safety, though Bum doesn't count. I hear Labs will fetch a stick to the point of cardiac arrest. What's Cole's excuse?

It has to be at least five minutes since Paula dropped out of sight. Okay, maybe five *seconds*, but still, my nerves are at a breaking point. And then there she is, wet and smiling, looking at me from among the waves that are bouncing around her. *Isn't this fun? Isn't this great? Aren't we having the best time ever?*

I laugh nervously at my fearful feelings. Of course Paula is alive. People don't die swinging from trees.

She climbs out of the water. "Your turn," she tells me.

I start to shake my head—she knows I'm not much of a swimmer—but when I read her face and see that she's been thinking all along I wouldn't swing, I change my mind and look high into the tree. My breath catches. That I'm even considering swinging from a rope means I've gone just as mad as she has.

I may not be as agile as Paula, but I'm not so old I've forgotten how to use my arms and legs. I *can* do this, I tell myself, and I grab the first branch, and then the next and the next after that, taking each one tightly in one hand before moving higher. At the halfway point, I'm already out of breath... and scared shitless. But Paula made this climbing stuff look so easy, so I'm not about to back out now.

Finally, I'm at the fork, and I've nowhere to go but down. As I look around, I feel a real sense of accomplishment. It's quite the sight, looking out over the water and all the way down the white, sandy beach. I can even see the hammocks hanging between the palm trees in front of The Fish Shack. *This isn't so bad*, I think. But then I look into the water and I'm frozen. My feet and hands are glued to the branches. There's no way in hell I'm letting go of this tree.

"C'mon," Paula shouts up at me. "You can do this."

My teeth are clenched. I don't know anything at this point. "It's so far down," I shout.

Paula props her hands on her hips. "Really? You're going to chicken out, now that you've already climbed the tree?"

Okay. God. I take a big breath, and then another, trying to work up some courage. But it's no use. I *am* a chicken. I glance back down at Paula. She's still got her hands on her hips, and I can see she's getting impatient. Her jaw is set in a way that tells me I'm about to get scolded.

"What's the problem? Just let go!" she yells and claps her hands together three times, like that ought to convince me. But it only antagonizes me. I'm the big sister. She's young. And dumb.

I squeeze my eyes shut, thinking maybe if I don't look, it will be okay. It will be a soft landing. I won't drown because Paula and Cole are down there and they will save me.

"Hurry up. Let's go!" Paula shouts again.

My mind is racing for any excuse to get out of doing this crazy thing. But I'm stuck. Stuck here on this branch.

"Are you okay?" Cole calls up to me. His voice is gentle, encouraging somehow.

I look out and my eyes scan the expanse of blue before me. The water is so clear and beautiful with so many shapes and shades that it looks like a different world. A beautiful blue world. But not one I want to visit.

I see one of the shapes move and I try to focus, but then it's gone. "I think I see something out there," I say to Cole.

Cole looks, his eyes moving over the shimmery surface of the water. "What?" he shouts.

"I don't know. Something."

He grins up at me. "Are you worried about sharks? A great white, maybe?"

I frown. "I never said anything about a great white."

"Fear is nothing to be embarrassed about," he tells me. "But a great white, that'd be a rare thing to see in these waters. Most likely all you'll find around here are nurse sharks, black tip, or hammerheads. Maybe even a leopard shark. Doubt you'd see one, though. Sightings are rare. Attacks even rarer. Only been a handful around these parts in the last hundred years."

I raise my chin, want to say, *Thank you, Jacque Cousteau. Then why aren't you up here swinging from this rope?* But then Paula joins Cole in harassing me. "If you're not going in, come on down," she says. "I'd like one more turn before we head back."

Gladly.

LOVE TRIP

In an instant, I'm down, standing safely in the sand next to Cole. He and I watch as Paula does a repeat performance. It's up, up, up, and then off she goes, swinging all the way out to where the fiery yellow of the sun makes her all but disappear. Cole and I wait for her to drop, like before. But she doesn't and I'm immediately sick with fear. If Paula doesn't let go of the rope in the next couple of seconds, she'll swing back and hit the tree. I look to Cole for reassurance. "Something's wrong," he tells me.

We both squint into the sun, and I see Paula struggling. Her cutoffs are caught on the plank.

Cole sees too, and he immediately scrambles to a spot in the sand that places him just to the right of the return path of the swing. He's going to try to stop Paula. She might knock into him, but that's better than hitting solid wood.

He and I watch as Paula approaches his waiting arms. He grabs for her, but she's going too fast, and the momentum rips her from his hands. The next thing I know Paula is draped across a large log and one of her legs is folded at an awkward angle.

Chapter Six

Hospitals. I suppose they come in handy during emergencies, but they are definitely not my idea of a fun time. Cole, Tug, and I check Paula in at the front desk, with the assistance of an island native named Claire Mooney. Claire has a big smile, with wide gaps between her teeth, and I feel better just looking at her. Happier, somehow. Less frantic at what's happened to Paula.

"Yes, Paula has insurance. No, she's not married," I tell Claire. But I wonder about those details and whether or not they're accurate. Paula is busy sweating and moaning, almost like she's having a baby, so I'm not going to bother her at the moment.

After satisfying Claire's questions, I tell Paula I'll see her soon, and then I go sit with Tug in the waiting room. Cole has gone out to check on Bum in Tug's truck, and Tug is sitting on a hard orange chair looking pissed off. I go stand next to him, with my back against the wall and my eyes half-closed so that I can avoid looking at the orange chair.

I don't see the color orange as happy, and I think it might have something to do with my grandmother Grace. One day she was alive, and the next, she was gone, and I found myself looking at her while she lay in a beautiful casket wearing this orange dress

I'd never seen before. All I could think was that I hoped she wasn't stuck for all eternity wearing that awful dress.

Many long minutes pass and I can't take it anymore. I need to move away from Tug in the chair. I don't want to be filled with negative thoughts at a time like this. I step over to the other side of the hall and look at pictures that remind me of home—mountains, forests, cool blue lakes. It seems odd that a hospital on a tropical island would have such pictures hanging on its walls, but I have no energy to think about the whys of their art choice right now. I have only enough energy to worry about Paula.

Eventually, the double doors at one side of the waiting area break open, and a young man in a white lab coat and jeans greets Tug and me with a toothy smile. It briefly crosses my mind that he and Claire Mooney might be related.

"It's broken, but she'll live," the young man tells us.

Well, of course Paula will *live*. Anyone who can leave the city behind, with all its comforts and conveniences, to forge a life in the jungle will most certainly survive a broken leg. And who is this kid, anyway? He looks far too young to even be out of high school, let alone medical school. I look at his name tag. It says *Doctor* Joren Dyhr, but I still have my doubts.

"Can we see her?" I ask the infant doc.

"Through there," Dr. Dyhr says, pointing. "She'll be free to go, soon as I sign her release documents. But"—because isn't there always a but?—"the break is a bad one. She needs to take it easy. She'll be on crutches for a while. After that, she'll be fine."

Tug grunts something that sounds like "c'mon" and doesn't wait to see if I'm following before he pushes through the double doors.

Paula's room is just a few yards down a short hallway. When we get to her, she's stretched out on a narrow hospital bed that's surrounded by white antiseptic curtains, and she has a pillow stuffed beneath her injured leg. Her eyes are closed, but a frown is etched into her brow, and that concerns me. Surely they've given her something for her pain.

I touch her hand lightly, and she opens her eyes. The furrow between her brow grows deeper.

"Isn't this a pisser?" she says. "They say I need to take it easy and lounge around for a while." She shakes her head. "I can't lounge. I have things to do."

She is Wonder Woman, after all.

"I know, I know, places to go, people to see…," I agree, but it's only to appease her. I think she should be thanking the stars above that all she broke was her leg.

"Exactly," Paula says, frustrated. She pushes her head into her pillow.

"I'm sure you'll manage just fine," I tell her. "Your place doesn't seem all that busy. You have people who can pitch in and help, right?" I glance at Tug, and he doesn't nod or shake his head or even tell me where I can shove it. Which leads me to believe I'm *not* right.

Paula groans. "*Now.* It may not be busy *now.* But in another week? Tourists will be falling from the sky. The island will be overrun by everyone and their uncle, people taking advantage of the reduced rates before hurricane season hits. And sure, I've got plenty of help, but they each have their own responsibilities. Trust me, not a one of them wants my job. The Fish Shack will be a madhouse." She rolls her head from side to side and lets out an exhausted breath, like it's made her tired just talking about the days to come.

"Madhouse," Tug repeats. He looks over at me. "I bartend."

Yes, that's already been established. But evidently, he wants to make it perfectly clear that bartending is his *only* job.

Cole appears, and I feel a flutter in my chest. I'm not sure what to make of it, but this is no time to think about what's going on with me. I'm just thankful he was there when Paula fell from that rope.

"Hey, girl," he says to Paula, kissing her on the cheek.

"Hey, cowboy," she responds, their connection so palpable I'm not sure *they* haven't done the finger-in-the-fist thing.

"She be all ready to go," a nurse says from the edge of the curtain. She holds up a small white bag and a sheet of paper.

"Here be some meds and home care instructions." She makes the rounds, looking from Paula to Tug to Cole and, finally, to me.

Tug makes no move to take the bag, and Paula seems uninterested, so Cole and I both step out of the small space and listen carefully as the nurse goes over the list with us. Standing so close to Cole makes the flutter in my chest turn into more of a boom boom, and I have to really concentrate to take in what the nurse is telling us.

I can hear Paula and Tug speaking in soft tones on the other side of the curtain, not quite a whisper but private somehow. I'd been kidding before when I suggested they might be hot and heavy, but could I have been right? From what I've observed, maybe what I said isn't so far out there.

The nurse points to a row of wheelchairs along one wall and tells me to pick one. I do, and when Cole and I push back through the curtain opening, the murmuring between Tug and Paula immediately ceases.

Tug bends and, with a tenderness that belies his size, lifts Paula from the bed and lowers her into the wheelchair. It's sweet, really, like watching King Kong with his beloved beauty. He steps around to the back of the chair and pushes it out of the room and through the double doors, then it's down a short hallway, until we turn a couple of corners and go through another set of automatic double doors. Then we're back out in the bright Caribbean sun. From there, Tug has us wait while he goes to fetch his truck. Cole wanders a short distance away.

The breeze is barely a whisper, but it's enough to ratchet down the sun's heat a notch, leaving the day pleasant—that is, if Paula hadn't gone and climbed that damn tree.

"He's attentive," I say with a casual air.

"He's the best," Paula agrees. She seems to know exactly who I'm talking about.

"The best bartender, I know. You already told me."

Paula stays quiet and it's frustrating, because I'd bet my law degree that something is going on between her and the mountain man. I can hardly keep from coming right out and saying what I think, except I don't *know* what I think, because she won't give me any details. What I *do* know is that I need to choose my words carefully if I'm going to get her to talk.

"He certainly seems to have more than a passing interest in you. How well do you know him?" Well, that was certainly careful.

Paula looks at up at me from the wheelchair in all innocence. It's something new I notice she does when someone—namely me—asks her a question she doesn't want to answer.

"Who? Cole?"

"*No. Tug.* I've been talking about Tug." But before I can go on with my questioning, Tug is back with his truck, and Cole and Bum are already climbing in the back. I help Tug get Paula settled in the backseat, and then I stuff a pillow beneath her leg, and we're good to go.

The ride is silent as we bump along the dirt road. I don't know about everyone else, but I'm wondering, thinking all sorts of things. About Paula and Tug, about me and Cole, about whether or not Cole and his dog are getting cooked riding in the back. I keep glancing at them and they look happy, so I push such thoughts from my head.

We make it back to The Fish Shack with Cole and Bum no worse for the wear. I'm happy, too, because I finally get a meal. Not the one Greenbeans was preparing when Paula and I went down the beach on our little adventure, but a sufficiently delicious one—lime shrimp with mango dressing and a boatload of fries. It was well worth the wait.

When Paula and I finish eating, we spend some time catching up and getting reacquainted and it soon becomes apparent that I've missed a lot in the past couple of years. It's going to take more than a single evening to hear about her life here on St. John. One thing is certain, our lives couldn't be more different. While she's been snorkeling, wave boarding, and exploring, I've been working on building a career, helping our mother adjust to her empty nest, and living with a man I thought was my forever. To hear Paula talk, one would think her life is all about having fun.

But I know better. Life holds more than adventure. And that's the part I want to hear about.

"Don't you ever get bored here by yourself? Or lonely?" I ask. Though I know darn well she's not lonely here with all these men hanging around.

"I don't have time to get bored. It's a lot of work running a beach bar. But when I do have a little free time, sometimes I take the ferry over to St. Thomas."

"Yes, but what about companionship?"

"I get all the companionship I need from my customers."

My mouth twists. "I don't believe that for one minute. The Paula Grant I know is nothing short of boy crazy. Back home, you were never without a date on Friday and Saturday nights."

She shrugs. "Things change."

"No. Uh-uh. You're involved with someone." I'm beyond Mom mode. I've gone into lawyer mode. "And I think I know who."

Paula laughs. "You know nothing."

I press my lips tight, afraid to make an accusation before gathering enough evidence. "What are you afraid of? That I'll run home and share everything with Mom?"

"Won't you?"

"Not if you don't want me to."

"I don't." Paula's eyes fill and she quickly wipes them dry. "I know it's been hard on you—and Mom. I know she's had a struggle making the adjustment of having me gone and so far from home. But life in Seattle wasn't for me. I always felt watched over."

I feel a jab to my heart. I'm close to both my sis and my mom, and now I have the feeling Paula doesn't mind all the distance she's put between us. I struggle to find the right words to say. "We wanted you to know we were there for you if you needed us."

"I know. And I know I could come home to Seattle anytime, and you and Mom would welcome me with open arms."

I nod. "That's right."

"And then I'd become little Paulette again." She spreads her hands. "Here, I'm not Paulette. I'm Paula."

"If it bothered you to be called Paulette, all you had to do was say something."

"It wasn't that easy. And it wasn't just my name. I felt like I was never going to grow up, living in your shadow or with Mom always reminding me to get a flu shot or that I needed to do this or that. I didn't need daily reminders to live my life." She lets out a heavy breath. "It's easier here."

"I don't know what you mean by that. Easier how? You just said it's a lot of work running a beach bar."

"It is. But it's work I enjoy. I'm my own boss here. I make my own hours, and I don't have to deal with any office politics."

"You could have been your own boss in Seattle, too. It wouldn't have been long before you and I could have opened our own law firm. You could have worked as little or as much as you wanted. And as far as office politics, you'd have been the boss. With me. We would have been running the show."

Paula presses her lips together. "But I wouldn't have really been free."

Free of what? I want to ask. But I don't because I can see she's getting tired of my questions. Too, I can see her point—to a point. I don't like it, but I feel like I need to back off. Maybe after she's had some rest, she'll be open for more conversation about who or what is keeping her here.

I stand and look around the small room. "What can I do to make the rest of your day easy on you?" I ask.

"Are you offering to be my nurse?"

"I'm offering to help make sure you don't go batty with boredom." I notice her water glass on her nightstand is empty. "I'll bring you some fresh water."

"And reading material? There are some books in my closet, and also some crossword puzzle magazines."

She means her *armoire*. I find her a book first, along with a couple of crossword puzzle magazines—can't believe she's taken a liking to them—and then I bring her pitcher of water and a clean glass. After which, I step outside for a while to enjoy my first island sunset. I'm nearly done in what with spending several hours on a plane, and then all the excitement here on St. John. But it hasn't all been bad. In fact, I've gotten to know Cole better and so far so good. Though I'm nowhere near ready to give in and tell Paula I can see myself getting cozy with him. But I'm definitely interested.

When I return to the room, Paula looks as tired as I feel, so we agree to call it a day and I settle on my cot. I'm so tired I expect to fall asleep in an instant, but my mind is so busy that it seems like I spend half the night lying awake in the dark. And then first thing, when day breaks, I hear a twitter just outside the window.

"Birds. You'll get used to them," Paula tells me. Then she rolls over and goes back to sleep.

Even with my lack of sleep, I get up, feeling sprier than I have in some time. The cot wasn't all that bad to sleep on.

I venture out into the bar and find Tug is already here. I give him a cheerful hello, which he returns with a grunt that I take for "Top o' the morning to ya!" Which is silly, I know, but I'm in a fantastic mood. I love mornings on vacation. You never know what to expect. Everything is different. Different food, different people, different scents.

I leave Tug to his morning routine, and I go out to the top step that faces the beach. The sun has barely made its appearance, yet if I look hard, I can see hints of blue high up in the atmosphere where, later in the day, the cool peace will become fierce and bold. The sky will be full of copper, bronze, and orange—damn orange—and the color will rest on the horizon like a fire that's burning a million miles away.

So, this is paradise, I think. I can totally see why Paula is in love with this place and wants to stay. I may not like it, but that's me being selfish. And if I try to influence her to come back home just so *I* can be happy, we might both regret it. Though our mother, no doubt, would be ecstatic.

I push a hand through my hair, lost in my thoughts. I can't remember any morning in Seattle being this quiet, this hushed. It's as if the island hasn't woken up yet. Or maybe it's still stretching, getting ready for the day to begin. Even the waves seem muted as they lap the shore. Though I know, soon, tourists and locals alike will appear to spend the day enjoying themselves, the sun, this life. I know if I lived here, I'd be one of them. First thing every day, I'd get up, take a walk, find a shell or two, and only then, after I'd had my fill of all this wonder, would I get busy doing whatever it is people do here.

I wonder what Cole does. Besides look gorgeous.

I step down to the sand and walk along the shore to take advantage of the quiet. My mind wanders and I try to imagine what it would be like to be here with a lover. We'd walk hand-in-hand from one end of the beach to the other, then we'd climb aboard one of the hammocks and take a siesta, or maybe we'd roll around on a big beach towel—kissing. God, kissing. I'm not even sure I know how to do that anymore.

I'll bet Cole really knows how to kiss.

I close my eyes, can see him. His smile, so gleaming white beneath the shade of his cowboy hat, is already etched into my memory. He's so handsome. Not Seattle-corporate-world handsome—I can't even imagine him in a suit and tie—but definitely hot.

I sigh, knowing I shouldn't go there. Daydreams are for women who have yet to experience hurt. I've been hurt. No good can come of thinking about Cole this way—he barely knows I exist.

As I make my way farther down the beach, I keep my eyes open for shells. When I reach an area that is covered with them, I stop and try to find one that's perfect, but they are all either broken or have a piece missing. Even so, they're beautiful, and this beach is beyond anything I've ever seen. I think I might already be falling in love with St. John.

I think I might even feel a twinge of something for Cole. He did save Paula from that damn swing, after all.

Chapter Seven

When I get back to The Fish Shack, the place is alive with early-morning tourists, and Tug has even turned on some music. I go to check on Paula and she's in a mood—bitchy. Which means she's hungry, so I poke my head into the kitchen to see if Greenbeans is here. He is. "Breakfast about ready?" I ask.

"Was about to bring these here trays in. Figured you gals would wanna dine together, 'stead of out here with us men folk. You ladies likely still got a lotta catchin' up to do."

"Mmm, lots," I say. "Can I help?"

Greenbeans picks up one tray and hands it to me, saying, "I'll bring t'other."

As soon as we enter the room, Paula perks up. She scoots herself into a sitting position, and then she leans forward so I can stack an extra pillow behind her back.

"Wow," she says, immediately losing her frown. "I should get hurt more often."

Greenbeans sets the tray he's carrying carefully across her lap. "You gonna be a patient for but a few days. Don't get used to this."

I settle on my cot, and Greenbeans leaves us to our meal. It's some kind of hash or scrambled egg mixture, thick slices of bread with some kind of berry jam, and coffee. I take a sip and savor it all the way down. It's better than I remember. Much better than Starbucks.

"This is delicious," I say. "I think I'm in love."

"With Greenbeans?"

"Well, you did say he's the best cook on St. John. How did you find him?"

"It's more like *he* found me. Or was sent to me. By Tug. Greenbeans is a retired bullfighter. He's been here for about ten years. He and Tug knew each other in the circuit. Tug was a bullfighter, too."

"Bullfighters? You mean with the cape and the funny hat and *toro, toro*?"

Paula laughs. "No, no. *Rodeo* bullfighters. You know, the guy who keeps the bull away from the rider after he gets thrown to the ground."

"Ah, rodeo *clowns.*" I nod and smile as I say it, but what I'm thinking is, *Good for the bull.* I'd toss them to the dirt, too, if they were jamming a sharp piece of metal into my rib cage. As far as I'm concerned, bull riding is just a legal form of animal torture.

Paula gives me a serious look. "They're not clowning around. If it weren't for Tug, Cole might not be alive. He had a terrible accident his last ride. A bull named Red Jacket tried to pancake him. Cole stayed on for the full eight seconds, but before he was able to dismount, Red Jacket swung his head up and hit Cole in the face and it was lights out. Cole ate dirt."

My mouth drops open. "Wait—are you telling me that Cole used to be a professional bull rider?"

"That's right. He was good, too. He won the PBR. But like I said, he had a bad spill, and it was Tug who saved him. He dragged Cole out of harm's way. Red Jacket wanted to kill Cole. After dumping him to the ground, he brought his hindquarters down on Cole's back so hard, Tug says the earth moved." Paula shakes her head. "Lucky for Cole, he was wearing a vest."

I wince, actually feel a twinge of pain at the image I have in my head of Cole being stomped on by a two-thousand-pound animal. And I can't say I'm proud of this, but somehow I find it strangely erotic that a man could be trampled by an animal as large as a bull and survive. Even so, if Cole hadn't been on the back of that bull in the first place, he wouldn't have needed Tug to save him.

"That's terrible, what happened to Cole. But maybe someone," I say, jutting a thumb skyward, "was trying to tell him something."

"Yeah, like keep your head up and roll fast when you hit the dirt."

"What about the bulls? What advice would you give them?" I ask. Paula has never understood, or shared, my disdain for how we humans treat animals. Hell, sometimes, even I don't understand it. All I know is that if I see an animal in need, I can't resist doing something. I'm such a sucker for all animals, and I think word has gotten out because I must get at least two or three mailings each week requesting donations to help the abused or needy. It's all I can do to keep them straight. I do what I can, but it never seems to be enough.

Paula gives me an eye roll. "Look, I know you're all about saving every cute, furry kitten and every face-licking puppy, but not all animals are defenseless. Bulls are tough. Super athletes. Having a man on their back is a mere afterthought. Plus, they dish out as good as they get. Worse. Did you hear the part where I said Cole was nearly killed?"

"Mmm."

"What's that supposed to mean?"

"Nothing. Just mmm." I know Paula has a point. I've watched bull riding on TV a time or two, out of curiosity, and they're like demons, blowing snot all over the place and doing their damndest to throw whomever is on board to the ground. Still, even snot-blowing bulls deserve some measure of kindness.

Paula is quiet for a minute. I can see the wheels turning in her head. She's thinking of what she can possibly say to make it okay that Cole once took part in a sport I find cruel. She's angry, too.

Her face is darker by two shades. I've questioned her world and she doesn't like it. I sound too much like Mom. Maybe Ramone really does have nothing to do with why she's still here.

"Okay," she says at last, "I can see you're determined to think what you want. But do me a favor. Give Cole a chance before you write him off as someone who wants to put all homeless puppies to death. He's a good man. You could do a lot worse… and you have."

She's talking about Peyton. "You needn't remind me of my mistakes. And about Cole, I didn't mean to suggest he wants to put all homeless puppies to death. I just disagree with what he chose to do for a living."

"I think it's all part of the culture where he grew up."

"I'm sure."

Paula smiles a small smile. "Since he's retired, will you at least give him a chance?"

"He's your friend. I'll give him a chance."

Paula grins. "On that note, have you given any thought to sleeping with him?"

Only every minute of every hour. "No. Nor do I intend to." I try my best to sound indignant, but it sounds fake, even to me. "Speaking of cowboys, St. John seems to be overrun with them. Why do you suppose they're all here?"

"We weren't speaking of cowboys. We were talking about Cole."

"Yes, and now we're done."

"For now."

I ignore her and go back to my questions about Cole and his friends. "Why aren't they on a ranch somewhere, tending cattle or mending fences?"

"Word is, they got tired of life in the fast lane—like me."

"Do they have wives… girlfriends?" I ask, though I'm not entirely sure that, in Cole's case, I want to hear the answer.

"No wives," Paula confirms.

But what about girlfriends? I was a girlfriend at one time. To Peyton. And it hurt like hell to hear he'd found someone to replace me.

I'd like to squeeze Paula for the truth, but I see her gaze change, and I know even before I look that Cole is standing behind me. When I turn and see him, I feel all panicky inside and I'm sure it shows on my face.

"Mornin', ladies," he says, tipping his hat. He moves past me and places a gentle hand on Paula's casted leg. The look on his face is enough to make any woman's heart melt. Especially mine.

"You're here a little early, aren't you?" Paula asks. She's all smiles.

"I thought I'd stop by and see if there's anything I can do to help out," Cole says.

"A shipment of supplies is waiting for me in town. It would be great if you could go pick it up for me. And take Taylor with you. She was just telling me how she'd love to see more of the island."

My sister is the devil incarnate. I'm sure of it. But I'm Taylor Grant, woman who is good at thinking on her feet. "Can't," I say. "I was just about to head out to the beach."

Paula cocks an eyebrow at me. "You just came in from the beach, before we had breakfast."

"Yes. I know. I went for a walk. Now I need to go jogging. I hear jogging in the sand really works your calves."

"Since when do you jog? Mom says all you do is work and drink coffee."

She's got me there, but I hunch my shoulders and pick at some dog hair or something that's found its way to the front of my blouse. The less said, the better.

"I could have you back here in plenty of time to get out there before the sun sets." Cole nods toward the beach. "I need to go over to St. Thomas for some supplies myself, and I wouldn't mind the company. It's a long trip to make alone."

My stomach goes all topsy-turvy, though I've told myself over and over this attraction I have to him can't possibly go anywhere. He and I cannot get involved. I cannot take one more heartache.

"You can at least go for the Jeep ride," Paula says. "It's better than hanging around here all day, babysitting me."

Yes, I can at least go for one more Jeep ride. My heart is practically singing at the idea. So much for talking myself out of getting involved with the cowboy.

Chapter Eight

Cole and I say good-bye to Paula, and then we're off. I settle into my seat while Cole gets busy steering the Jeep around numerous big dips in the road. We make slow progress, but contrary to how I was feeling during our first Jeep ride together, I'm actually enjoying myself. I'm looking forward to seeing more of St. Thomas, too. I spent only a short time there, when I was waiting for the ferry to bring me over here to St. John, and I didn't have even a few minutes to explore.

As slow going as it is, we still seem to arrive at Cruz Bay Beach too soon, where we then depart for St. Thomas. From there, we board a bus bound for Charlotte Amalie, which Cole tells me is the capital and largest city of the U.S. Virgin Islands. I'm in total tourist mode, my eyes looking everywhere, taking in as much as I possibly can. Mostly, I see vegetation. But when we get up high, I can see the tops of homes dotting the landscape below us, many of which look like huge estates that movie stars might live in. Cole tells me that some very wealthy people call the islands home.

Before entering town, Cole and I leave the bus to walk. "The main road is always congested," he explains. "It's the locals, mostly. They're too busy swapping stories and sharing gossip to care that anybody else has business to conduct. They're on island time. I try to stay away for the most part, just come here for supplies when I need them."

"What kind of supplies?" I'm curious. I have no idea what Cole does for a living... I have no idea anything about him, except for what Paula has told me, and I doubt the rodeo circuit is big business here.

"Things I need for my sailboat."

"A sailboat. Wow. A cowboy and a sailor, too. I'm impressed."

Cole chuckles. "Don't be. Mostly, I use the boat to keep myself busy. But I also use it to take tourists out on day cruises." He glances over at me. "I could take you out one day if you have time before you go back to Seattle."

"I'd like that," I say before I even give myself a chance to think about it. I have all these feelings bouncing around inside me that have caused me to let my guard down and I'm giving in to things I might not otherwise do. But it feels good.

Cole goes on to give me a brief history about how Charlotte Amalie was once a haven for pirates such as Bluebeard and Blackbeard. He tells me, too, that the Danes built a castle for Blackbeard and it's a U.S. Historic Landmark. His enthusiasm is infectious.

"You really love it here, don't you?" I ask, though I already know the answer.

"What's not to love?"

"Being island bound. Doesn't that get old?"

Cole shakes his head. "I don't think about it like that. Besides, I can always get on my boat if I need to escape." He pauses, thinking. "I guess if I had to pick one thing I don't like, that would be all the ferries and yachts that pass through the islands every week. They double the population."

"But then they go away, right?"

"They do. But a lot of effort has been put into the preservation of buildings and homes here, to keep them looking as they did some two hundred years ago, and there are people who come to the islands who don't respect that. Sometimes, it makes me wish they would stop coming."

I know what he means. We have the same situation in Seattle. Too many people coming in because of all the high-tech jobs. It's big money that they are oh so happy to take, but not so eager to give back. It can make for resentful feelings between the lifelong citizens and people who don't see citizenship as important.

Cole and I make it to town, and I get a first-hand look at what he means by the locals causing traffic jams. Cars are stopped in the middle of the road with their drivers—who are on "island time"—talking out their windows to other drivers headed in the opposite direction. None of them care one bit about the mess they're creating.

We don't have "island time" in Seattle. People who hold up traffic are a burr under everyone's ass, and it isn't tolerated. Patience is not a virtue Seattleites own. Time is valuable, and each tick of the clock means minutes wasted that must be made up elsewhere—most likely with lost sleep or a skipped meal. If someone dares spend one second longer than necessary at a traffic light, other drivers honk their horns, shout from their windows, and maybe even give some not-so-nice hand gestures to the driver who's keeping them from their busy lives. I know this from experience. In my opinion, everyone who says that Seattle is one of the friendliest cities needs to spend a little time there during rush hour.

When Cole and I reach the heart of Charlotte Amalie, I push all thoughts of Seattle from my mind. All the brightly colored shops and restaurants are charming, with houses painted the same, in aqua, yellow, red, and lavender, and they face the bay with their intricately designed balconies that remind me of the homes I saw when I visited the New Orleans French Quarter. If I were an artist, I would set up an easel and get busy painting.

As we walk, Cole continues to point out the street names that reflect the town's Danish ancestry. His eyes are full of light while he speaks, and it makes me even more excited to be here—with him.

We make our way along, passing dozens of booths where the vendors offer a wide variety of vegetables and fruits—bananas, carrots, ackee, sour sop, and so many other food items that I can't even name them all. Some of the foods are exotically delicious-looking, while some I wouldn't try if you paid me.

I see one booth where the vendor is selling homemade jewelry, and I stop to see if I can find something for my mom. A turquoise necklace catches my eye, and I point to it. The vendor hands it to me, and I hold it up, noting how the colors match the different hues of blue in the nearby water. It's perfect so I buy it, and then I go to the next stand, where I also purchase a pair of gold earrings that I'm sure my mother will love. They're silly, just a couple of tiny pineapples, but I'll bet she wears them all this coming summer.

I catch a floral scent, and I look up ahead to a flower stand that's one of many. Cole and I stop, and he buys a single flower—a red hibiscus—which he tucks delicately behind my right ear.

"There," he says, brushing his hand lightly along my cheek, "now, you're one of us—a genuine island girl."

I blush. My crush on Cole groweth ever stronger.

All the walking and shopping has made me hungry, and I'm glad when Cole suggests we stop at a small cafe where we can share a selection of dishes. We settle at a table off in one corner that separates us from the rest of the lunch crowd, and Cole orders for both of us without even looking at a menu. I briefly wonder if he's done this before... brought a woman to this very place, to this very table. And did he also tuck a flower behind her ear?

It's jealousy I'm feeling, though how can that be? It's far too soon.

Cole and I make small talk until the first of our order arrives—a small plate of crab cakes that look meaty enough for an entire meal. They're not at all like the crab cakes back home, where it's mostly breading with a small bit of crab. These cakes are the real deal, with just a thin layer of breadcrumbs holding them together, and they're filled with sweet, delicate meat that's been seasoned to perfection. All it takes is one small bite and I'm convinced I may never again order crab cakes in Seattle.

Next comes grilled conch, drenched in white wine and garlic sauce. People here call it the poor man's lobster, though it tastes pretty rich to me. Alongside the conch is a mac-and-cheese dish that's been baked and shaped into tidy squares. The texture is smooth, like velvet, and the taste is quietly spicy. They're the complete opposite of the boxed stuff I practically lived on back when I was in law school. Cole and I stuff ourselves with so many squares I fear we might burst.

After we finish eating, we sit for a while, not ready to move on. Our waiter fills our water glasses, and we spend more time talking. I learn he has six sisters—Megan, Mandy, Mariah, Mia, Missy, and Lily, whose real name is Misty, but her teachers kept getting her confused with Missy, so she chose to call herself Lily, because that was her favorite flower.

Then there's Jared, Cole's little brother. He and Cole had a great time growing up with so many sisters, and Cole says it's how he learned about women. In my opinion, Cole's sisters did a fine job of raising him.

"Do you see them much?" I ask.

Cole shakes his head. "Not nearly enough. Poor Jared, he's back in Texas, alone with all those girls. But I think he manages all right. Our parents moved to St. Petersburg, Florida, last year. Bought a place in a seniors-only housing development. They spend their days golfing and watching reality TV. My ma has a crush on Jeff Probst. She insists that if it weren't for her need to have a firm bed to sleep on, she could be a *Survivor* contender."

We both laugh, and then I notice how our waiter keeps walking past our table. Cole notices, too. He looks around and sees that the café has begun to fill. We take the waiter's pacing as our cue to be on our way.

"Seems like we might have overstayed our welcome," Cole says.

"Seems so."

Cole looks into the sky. "This took longer than I expected. I know you wanted to go jogging on the beach."

"I'll tell you a secret. I don't really jog. Ever. I was just saying that to... I don't know, get out of coming here with you."

Cole chuckles. "I have to admit, that's the first time a woman has used exercise as an excuse not to see me."

I feel embarrassed now, not sure what to say. "It's not that I didn't want to see you. I think maybe I wanted to see you too much."

"So, you're glad you came?"

"Very."

Cole smiles big. "We better get out of here, before they kick us out."

Before we leave, Cole adds an extra tip for the long use of the table. And when we get back out to the street, he takes my hand. It's surprising and scary, but also bothersome at how quickly I've put my relationship with Peyton to rest. Two days ago, I was certain I would never get over how he said good-bye. He made me feel like I needed to get away from Seattle so that I could think straight. Men were not in my immediate future. But now... now there's this man walking next to me, and he makes me feel like there's a lot more happiness out there for me. All I need do is look.

So, was I or was I not really in love with Peyton? I'm having more and more doubts.

Hand-in-hand, Cole and I stroll, stopping every minute or two to look in a window. We make one more stop along the way at the request of a couple who informs us they're newlyweds. Would we please take their picture? Cole does, and then the couple asks if we would like them to take *our* picture. Cole tells them we don't have a camera, but thanks them, anyway, and wishes them many happy years together.

I ponder the idea of being Cole's bride, and it makes my heart feel all soft and achy. It's silly, of course, because I barely know him, and I think, too, that perhaps he's happy with his life the way it is. Plus, my life is in Seattle. There is no honeymoon in our future. But now that I've once more gone there, to daydreaming of things that cannot possibly happen, the idea of going back to

Seattle, curiously, leaves me feeling empty. I know I still have time here, but right now, I'm not sure I ever want to go home.

Cole touches my arm and releases me from such thoughts. He's listening for something. I listen, too, and then there it is... a yelping sound, like the cry of a dog. I turn, trying to decide where it's coming from, but Cole is already leading me down a narrow pathway that runs alongside a bright red building. We go all the way into an alley, where we see a truck, half-blue, half-rusted, parked at one side of a small lot. Cole quickly moves to the driver's-side window. "There's a dog inside," he tells me.

I'm immediately angry. It's at least eighty degrees in the shade. On a day like this, how can anyone think it's okay to leave their dog locked in a car? I rush to the window and peer inside. The dog looks to be a Husky mix. He's stopped crying, has seen us, but it's clear he's in trouble. His eyes are big and glassy, and he's panting and drooling all over the seat. No telling how long he's been in there.

My emotions are all over the place. I'm practically in panic mode. My heart feels like it's been punched. All I can think about is getting the dog out. I know, legally, there's not a damn thing Cole and I can do to help this poor animal, except maybe call the authorities. But would they get here in time? And would they even care enough to come? It sounds cruel, but the sad truth is there are so many places and cultures that don't value animal life, and it seems that dogs, especially, are considered disposable or expendable. I have no idea what the attitude is here on St. Thomas, but if we wait to find out, it could be too late. The Husky needs help now.

Cole checks the driver's door. It's locked. He goes around to the passenger's side. Again, locked. He swears under his breath, and I can see his jaw tightening. He's as angry as I am, which doesn't surprise me at all. Not after seeing how he is with his own dog.

"What are we going to do?" I'm frantic, practically in tears.

"You wait here. I'll see if I can find the owner of that truck," Cole says. He leaves, and I turn back to the window. A minute passes and the dog hunkers down in the seat. He won't—or can't—even lift his head now to look at me.

I wipe my eyes, watching him. He's cooking in his own skin, and I'm standing here doing nothing. I ask myself what I'll do if Cole doesn't return in time. Can I really just stand here and watch this dog die?

I press a hand to the glass, trying to comfort the dog and to, somehow, give him hope. But every second that passes seems like an hour, and I'm sick all the way to my heart. I can't keep waiting. I turn and look for something I can use to break the window. But then Cole is back, and I know he'll do something to help the dog.

"I musta checked a dozen shops," he tells me. "No one knows who owns this truck." He pulls off his hat and runs a frustrated hand through his hair. "We've got to get him out." He looks around on the ground and grabs a thick piece of wood that's lying next to a trash can. He pushes the wood into the driver's side window with a hard shove and the glass fractures, some of it spilling to the ground, but most continues to hang like a thick spider web from the frame. He keeps poking at it until enough is knocked out that he's able to reach in and unlock the door, and once he has it open, he reaches out a hand to touch the dog, speaking to him in gentle tones, to make sure he won't object to a stranger coming to his aid. The Husky looks relieved more than anything.

Cole helps the dog out of the truck, and then helps him over to a patch of shade, where he falls into a heap on the ground.

"It'll help him, being out of that furnace, but he needs more," Cole says. He spots a water hose that's hooked to a faucet at the back of the building, and the dog doesn't even balk as Cole begins running cool water over his body.

I kneel near the Husky's head, muttering soft reassurances. After several minutes, he's soaked and still panting, but he looks more comfortable and noticeably cooler. He even gives my hand a soft lick. Gratitude, I think.

I reach over to Cole and hug him. "Thank you."

"No need to thank me for doing something that needed to be done," he tells me.

"You saved him. He would have died."

Cole rubs the Husky's thick fur. "He's okay now. It's just as well his master didn't show up. He and I might've shared some harsh words."

The Husky licks Cole, and Cole roughs the Husky's head, the same as I've seen him do to Bum. He's a good man, and my heart feels full just being near him.

Each minute that passes, the dog becomes more and more alert. I'm relieved, thinking he's going to be all right.

The ground is wet from using the hose, but Cole finds a dry spot where he and I can sit and stay for several more minutes with the dog, at least until the sun moves far enough across the sky that the truck is in the shade. Then Cole helps the Husky back into the truck. It's not much cooler, but with one window gone and the other open, the kind of sun-filled heat that can kill is no longer an issue. The dog should be okay—for now.

"I wish we didn't have to leave him," I tell Cole. "We've likely only delayed the inevitable. His owner will probably see the broken glass and just think someone was trying to break in to his truck."

"You don't think he'll wonder why his dog is wet?"

"He might be dry by then."

Cole tucks a strand of my hair behind my ear. "You really do have a big heart for animals. I saw it when you met Bum. Not many people would just pull a big dog like that to their chest."

"I wasn't afraid. He was wagging his tail. You're right, though. I do love animals."

"Do you have a dog of your own?"

"Not yet. Someday."

"You'll make a good mom."

I smile. Dogs are easy. Give them love and they have no issues. Unlike human kids, who seem to be so needy. Make one wrong move and they accuse their parents of neglect or abuse or… whatever. Human kids take super human parents to get them through life.

Cole and I finally leave the Husky and we make our way back out to the front of the building, where we finish our walk through town. We end up at a large, barn-like structure that has "Yacht Supplies" in big block letters over the door, where Cole says is *the* place to get anything you need for any kind of boat. I'd wager it's the *only* place to get boat supplies.

A few minutes inside and Cole quickly locates what he needs—sealant and a can of fiberglass rubbing compound. He takes them up to the counter, pays the clerk, and we're on our way.

"That's it?" I say. "We came all this way for those two items?"

"This is important stuff," Cole tells me. He grins. "And now I have a secret to tell you. I didn't need these supplies. I have plenty back home. I just wanted to spend more time with you. I hope that's okay."

I smile at the strength of my feelings for him. He's been such an unexpected pleasure and now that I've gotten to know him, I can't imagine *not* knowing him. "It's okay," I say. And it really, *really* is.

Chapter Nine

I can't do this. I can't fall in love with a stranger. It's what I tell myself all the way back to Cruz Bay. Cole and I are both quiet, and I wonder if he's thinking the same as me. Because it would be crazy to fall in love when a few days is all we would have together. I'm terrified, though, that I might be falling for him in a big way.

It's later than I expected when we get back to The Fish Shack. We really made a day of it.

"I can't stick around," Cole tells me. He doesn't say why, just drops me off and unloads Paula's supplies, and then he's gone.

I've never bought into the notion that there is just one person for each of us, our so-called soul mate. But what if it's true, and Cole is *my* soul mate? What if, when I leave here, he's all I think about? Will he continue to think about me, or will he move on to the next female tourist who catches his eye?

I need to stop thinking this way.

I pour myself a glass of wine, then another, and then a warm and fuzzy feeling begins to grow in my stomach, and it's not long before I convince myself that I can totally handle a short-term love affair—a love trip—if that's what this thing is between me and Cole. A quickie romance is what it will be, not time enough to *really* fall in love. It might hurt for a nanosecond when Cole and I say good-bye, but it'll be like ripping off a Band-Aid. Over in an instant.

No problemo.

When I go in to see Paula, she's in a fine mood. I suspect it's because she thinks she's got her bet to me, about Cole, all wrapped up.

"You and Cole were gone quite awhile," she says. "I was thinking you might have gotten lost."

Fat chance. She knows darn well Cole knows his way around the islands. "We stopped for lunch in Charlotte Amalie," I tell her.

"Oh." Paula looks disappointed.

"What? Did you think we'd end up having hot, sweaty sex somewhere in the jungle?"

"Knowing you, no. But you obviously have sex on your mind or you wouldn't have mentioned it."

She's right. But she doesn't need to know that. I drop down on my cot and stretch out my legs. "I'm tired. Must be all that fresh air I got today."

Paula sits up straight. "Before you fall asleep, let's talk."

I yawn. "Okay, you talk, I'll listen."

Paula starts right in with, "What would you say if I asked you to extend your vacation?"

I laugh. "I'd say you've gone loco."

"No, really. What would you say? You've seen how I'm struggling with my crutches. They make my underarms sore... and I'm sure Tug could use the help."

"Tug crushes ice with his bare hands. He needs no help. And, anyway, I think you just want me to stay so you can win that crazy bet."

"That would be a bonus, yes. But I really could use your help. Plus, it would give us more time together. If you stay even one extra week, I'll probably be able to get out of here, and we could go do something fun."

"Like swing from a tree?"

"Like go over to St. Thomas for a day of shopping. I need more time with you."

"Me, too," I say. "But right now, I have wine on the brain, and it's imperative I curl up on my cot. I'll give it some thought," I tell her. And I might. An extra week in paradise couldn't hurt. Could it?

I go to sleep imagining how it would feel to have Cole's hands and lips exploring my body, and then I have a dream that has nothing to do with Cole. Some other man has his hands and lips all over me. Peyton.

When morning comes and my mind is no longer infused with alcohol, I know there is no way I can stay here for even one extra day. It's not that I'm in a hurry to get back to Seattle, to see Peyton, but I don't want to begin something with another man while I'm on the rebound. I don't want Cole to be a rebound guy.

While Paula and I have breakfast, I give her my answer. "I've thought about it and I can't stay. I need to get back to my job."

"Mom told me you recently closed a big case. She said it was a good time for you to be away."

"Mom isn't up to speed. I *lost* a big case. That makes two in a row. Which means now I have to work harder than ever to get back on track."

"But you promised," Paula says, her voice nearly going into plea mode.

"I don't think I *promised*." I'm almost sure I didn't. "Anyway, I can't be held responsible for anything I said while under the influence of alcohol."

Paula pushes her half-eaten breakfast over to her nightstand. "That's a cop-out. You weren't drunk."

"Tell that to my head. Got any aspirin?"

"So you're determined to leave at the end of next week?"

"I'm sorry, but yes. I have to get back to work." I get up from my cot and I go to gather Paula's tray. Her arms are crossed over her chest. She's not happy.

"I can't believe this," she says. "You're deserting me when I need you most."

71

Her comment strikes a nerve. I already feel like I deserted her by not being here after Ramone split with the beauty queen; I don't need another guilt trip to carry around. "I hope that's not how you really feel. And why do you need me? You have people here who can handle the workload."

"I thought I made it clear. In a few days, it'll be beyond busy here. It takes all of us to keep this place running."

I sit next to her. "But what about *my* job?"

"Your job is secure. You don't have to worry."

"How do you know?"

"You were at the top of your class. B, S, and T won't let you go until they've sucked out all your blood. You're still relatively young. You have a while to go before they're done with you."

"Great. I'm still young enough that my employer sees value in me."

"You know what I mean."

I do. And she's right. I'm still young enough that B, S, and T can get me to work more hours than I have off for having fun. That's one of the drawbacks of working for a law firm. And it's why I would love to have Paula come home, so that she and I could run our own firm. Then we could make all our employees work the long hours.

It's the end of our conversation, so I head out for a walk on the beach, where I push my feet through the silky, warm sand, just above the waterline. The waves are lapping at my feet as I walk along in the shallow water. It gives my mind quiet time, where all I have to think about is the sun, the sand, and the surf. This is perfect, I think. Maybe I *should* stay.

I continue along the shoreline, alone but not lonely. Not like I was sometimes with Peyton. I hadn't even realized how alone I was then. But then he left, was gone, and nothing in my world changed. He was just gone. So why was I so sad? Why did his leaving make me feel so crazy with need?

Thinking back, I realize it wasn't only Peyton who felt something was missing. *I* needed more, too. But the few times I considered making a change, it always came down to what was easier. I hate to admit it, but I think I may have been kidding myself about wanting to spend my life with Peyton. It was just easier to stay with him than to start over with someone new.

Like Cole.

I kick at the warm sand, laughing a little. I most definitely *want* Cole. But that could simply be a good old-fashioned case of lust. It's been a while since a man held me. Maybe I just lust for Cole.

And now I'm more confused than ever about my feelings and whether or not I should stay.

When I return to The Fish Shack, Paula has a visitor—a tiny Asian woman with spiked, short black hair and a generous smile. Paula introduces her as Ella Su, The Fish Shack's in-house masseuse. Ella Su gives me a polite greeting but doesn't stay to chat. She has a busy day ahead with a number of customers coming in for quickie massages... but I can drop in if I want and say hi. The beads and shells hanging over the door rattle in her wake.

I turn to Paula. "You have your own in-house masseuse? How metropolitan."

Paula shrugs. "I don't know about that. Hiring Ella Su seemed like a good move. People on vacation like to be pampered. So when she happened in one day, looking for work, I decided to give her a try, and it's turned out well. She's good. People even come over from St. Thomas for one of her massages."

I make a mental note of that. Sleeping on the cot isn't so bad, but I do have a cramp in one shoulder, which I'm sure is from me stressing over what might be going on between me and Cole, or even me having to make a decision about staying here longer.

It's a while before it gets busy, so I go into the bar to see if I can be of any help to Tug. He gives me the chore of lighting a string of votive candles along the bar, and when I'm done, the interior of The Fish Shack looks magical. Like it's been invaded by fireflies.

Next, Tug directs me to wipe down all the surfboard tables, and while I'm doing that, a boy carrying a basket of flowers for sale arrives. I pick several and add them to small vases that are kept under the bar. Then I put one on each table for a bit of cheerful ambiance. Paula had better watch out. If I stay, I might pick up some paint and a brush and give her place an entirely new look.

My final chore comes from Greenbeans. He's made out the day's menu, and has hand-scrawled what he's cooking on paper. He gives me a handful and I place one on each table. I'm not sure if this is the usual routine. Paula mentioned that some mornings he uses a white board to post the day's menu. I guess it all depends on his mood.

When all is done, I sit back with a tall glass of lemonade that Greenbeans has prepared from scratch. It's already hot and it isn't even midmorning, so the refreshment is a blessing. While I'm taking my break, I look around and see the boxes Cole and I brought back from town yesterday. "I can help with those if you like," I tell Tug.

"No need," he responds, and he immediately starts with the unpacking. End of conversation.

I know Tug isn't being dismissive. It's just that he's not the most prolific talker. He and I haven't shared but a handful of words in passing since I arrived. Though I can't blame his silence entirely on him. I haven't exactly been chatty myself. I think I might still be in shock thinking that he and my sister could be doing the horizontal mamba. That's a subject she and I need to delve deeper into the next time she and I are talking.

Since my services are no longer needed in the bar, I decide to check out Ella Su's massage parlor. Her door is cracked, and I can see her inside, folding towels. I tap on the door.

"Come, come," she says, beckoning me in with a wave of her hand.

I enter her domain, and the scent of lavender and sea washes over me. I'm instantly soothed.

"Would you like quickie massage?" she asks. She doesn't wait for me to answer, just gets busy lighting candles that add even more lavender fragrance to the air.

I have nothing else to do at the moment, so I get myself up onto the massage table, and I lie there, waiting for her to perform magic. "Paula tells me you're famous," I say to get the conversation going.

"Quiet now," Ella Su admonishes me. "Time to relax."

In only a couple of minutes, I see why she's in high demand. Her hands are amazingly strong, and soon my mind and body have turned to mush. I could stay on her table all day. But that's not the plan. About fifteen minutes into my massage, Ella Su slaps my ass and tells me she's finished. "You come back tomorrow if you like," she says. "My schedule wide open, like a whore's legs."

Um, okay. I thank Ella Su, wondering if I've heard her right... but why does it matter? There are no rules here, no human resources person to tell Ella Su her language isn't allowed. Anything goes here. And I guess that's why it's called vacation. So all of us who work ourselves nearly to death can once in a while just let loose and forget about all the rules imposed on us by people who don't think fun belongs in the work place.

I'm all but sleep-walking when I leave Ella Su's massage parlor, and I stay relaxed throughout the day. But when evening comes, Paula is driving me crazy. She's bored. She wants me to keep her company. And that's okay... anything to occupy my mind other than flashes of Cole lying on top of me.

I sit cross-legged at one end of Paula's cot. "How about a game of poker?" I suggest.

Paula's eyes light up. "You're on," she says, and she pulls a small, black satin bag out of her nightstand drawer and empties out the contents. Red and black chips, dice, and a deck of cards. We don't need the dice, so Paula pushes them to one side, and then she shuffles the deck.

I watch her hands. She's good, the way she handles the cards. She probably could have been a professional poker player. When we were kids, she was really into playing card games, but she also knew plenty of tricks, and she took every chance to dazzle our friends, keeping them entertained for hours. By the time she began college, I was telling her to forget about law school, that she should quit and make herself wealthy by taking other people's money. Which I guess is what some people think lawyers do anyway.

"I could see if Tug would like to join us," Paula offers. She shuffles one last time, and then waits for me to cut. "I could even give Cole a call, and the four of us could play *strip* poker."

I grab half the pile of chips and pull them over in front of me. I briefly consider her offer, but I'm not sure I'm ready to bare all to Cole. Or Tug. "How about we keep it between you and me. I'll even send you cash for your winnings."

Paula makes a face, like I've ruined everything. "Who says I'm going to win? You're giving up before you've even begun. What's happened to you? You're so cynical."

"Life has a way of doing that to a person," I tell her. Then I toss three of my cards aside and await their replacements. Which prompts Paula to give me an assessing gaze, like she's trying to figure me out. She deals me three new cards, which don't do a thing for my hand, so I end up losing with two pair, aces and tens, while she wins with three kings, seven high.

The game goes on like this for several more hands, until my pile of chips dwindles to one. I toss it over to Paula's pile, and she pulls all the chips into her lap, counting them… though I'm sure she knows exactly how many chips are in that pile.

"You owe me one hundred dollars when you get back home," she says. And then she gives me a sly grin. "Good thing we didn't have Tug and Cole join us. You'd be bare-ass naked right now."

"Yeah. Good thing." She's such a cheater.

Paula gathers the cards, dice, and chips and puts them all away, and I see this break as an opportunity for us to talk more. "Tell me about your life here," I say, practically daring her.

She looks thoughtful, doesn't immediately go into any kind of explanations or stories that she thinks I might enjoy. I'm sure she's thinking about what parts she should keep to herself and what parts are okay to share. "I've already told you everything," she says at last.

"Not *all*," I say.

"What did I leave out?"

"Why you're still here."

"We talked about that. I like the peace and quiet. The absence of stress."

"Maybe."

Paula sighs. "You and Mom seem to think I'm going through some crisis that I should be over with by now, and you want me to come home. But *this* is my home, and I don't know how to convince you that it has nothing to do with Ramone. God, why does it have to be about Ramone?"

"It doesn't. Not if it's about something, or some*one*, else." I can't let the subject go. I think it's a rule… when you're a big sister, you have to be a pain in the ass. But I am at least able to concede she no longer cares about Ramone.

"Like who?" Paula spreads her arms. "Who would it be about?"

"That's what I'm asking."

Paula's lips go tight, like she's fed up with all my questions. In a minute, she'll shut down, and I'll get nothing out of her. I can't let that happen.

"Look," I say, "I already told you, if it's something you don't want Mom to know, I'll keep it to myself. But, please, talk to me."

Paula swallows. "Promise me… and cross your heart and hope to die." Her voice is sharp and I know she's damn serious because we only use the hope-to-die promise when we have a secret so big, it can never be repeated.

I'm nervous now, and my stomach feels hollow. "Jeez, Paula, if it's that big a secret, maybe I don't want to know." What if she's about to tell me it's Cole she's in love with? But, no, she wants *me* to be with Cole.

"Do you want to know or not?"

I nod. "I do, and I promise to keep it to myself."

"It's Tug," Paula tells me. "I'm in love with him."

Tug? *Tug?* "Out there in the bar, Tug?" I point in the direction of the bar. I was only kidding when I first teased her about him. And, sure, I'd had my suspicions, but now that she's said it, I can't believe I was right.

"Yes."

"What do you mean?" I'm sure she's kidding.

"You heard me. Tug is why I'm still here."

I'm at a loss. "But… isn't he a little old for you?"

"Age is nothing. Just a number. Isn't it better to be with someone you love than to be with someone who is younger but bores you to death?" She holds up a hand, like she's anticipating my objection. "Before you say anything else, you need to know that Tug and I plan to be married soon. So there you have it. Now you know my secret. Happy?"

"Speechless. Though I don't understand why it's such a secret."

"I shouldn't have told you," Paula says, leaning back into her pillow. "Now I suppose you'll run home and tell Mom, and then the two of you will put your heads together to come up with some plot to get me to come back home."

Why does she think I'm here? The plot is already in action. "I already told you I wouldn't say anything to Mom. But, God, Paula…"

"God, what? Look, you say you want me to be happy. And I am."

"Really?"

"Mostly."

"What does that mean? Should I be worried?"

"It's complicated."

"How so?"

"Tug is married."

Chapter Ten

"You can't tell Mom," Paula warns me all over again. "I mean it. Really."

God, no, I can't tell our mom. Not after what she went through with our dad. He found someone else and he left our mom, and now he and that woman are married. That's why I can't tell her. It would send her over the edge. Paula doesn't even need to warn me. "No wonder you haven't been talking to us," I say. "Jesus, Paula." I hate it, hate that my sister is "that woman."

"It's not a big deal. He'll be divorced soon."

"Yeah. Right." I want to do an eye roll, but I won't. I need to be the grown-up here. "Does he have kids?" I ask.

Paula shakes her head. "Nope. No kids."

Well, that's something. Still, I don't even know what to say. I won't tell our mom. I promised. The thing is, though, secrets always come out. "How long do you think you can keep this from Mom? She wants to know why you're still here, and she's going to ask when I go home. What am I supposed to tell her? And what if she decides to come and visit you?"

"Mom doesn't need to know all the details. Just tell her I'm happy here, and I doubt she'll ever come and visit. Not with the way she hates flying."

"She hates putting up a Christmas tree, too, but she does it when she knows we'll be together for the holidays. She does it for you."

"And you," Paula points out, and I can't disagree. "Look," she says, "if Mom ever does decide to risk her life by getting on an airplane, I'll figure out what to tell her then. For now, all she needs to know is that I'm happy."

Happy. God. What a jumbled mess. I simply cannot believe what I'm hearing, and I'm sure I should be lecturing Paula right now. But I doubt she'd listen. She seems to have it all figured out. She's the other woman and she's okay with it.

I take a couple of calming breaths. I need to tread lightly. "Does Tug's wife know they're getting divorced?" I ask. "If you remember, Mom didn't know until she was in the midst of it."

Paula rolls her eyes, teenage-girl style, and lets out a big huff of air. "Tug's wife doesn't care what he does. They occasionally talk on the phone, and he goes to the mainland once in a while to see her. But it's all for show."

My brow furrows. "What's that mean?"

"Tug's wife is the mayor of some small town in Texas. She has aspirations to become governor one day. The election year is coming up, and she's not interested in doing anything to call attention to the state of her marriage. Once the election is over, they'll divorce."

I laugh sardonically. "You believe that?"

"I do. If Tug wanted to be married, he wouldn't be here with me."

Paula has a point there, so I suppose I should hold off on further comment. For now. For now, I'll sleep on it. Things might look different in the morning.

Morning doesn't look any different. I haven't slept. I've been lying on my cot, eyes wide open all night, thinking about my sister and Tug and how if he hurts her, I'll… hell, I don't even know what.

I feel a presence, and I look and see Ella Su standing in the doorway. She's parted the beads and shells, managing somehow to keep them from rattling, and now she's waving vigorously at me, gesturing that I should get up and come see what she wants. I join her in the bar.

"What's wrong?" I ask in a whisper, though I know I don't really need to worry about waking Paula. She's such a heavy sleeper.

"I sick. I go home now. You take care of business."

Oh. Okay. It's barely daybreak. I look around and see only one customer at the end of the bar. "What business?"

"Only one massage today," Ella Su continues. "Later. You do him."

Massage? *Him?* If I wasn't already fully awake, I am now. "What do you mean, I *do* him?"

"You give customer massage," she explains.

I take a step back and put up my hands in protest. "No. Uh-uh. I'm not a masseuse."

"You never touch a man before?"

"Well, of course I've touched a man." Plenty of men, in fact, but she doesn't need to know the details of my dating past.

"Then what problem?"

Gee, where do I begin? "Look, I'm sorry you're not feeling well, but I don't give massages. I *get* them." I fake rub the air between us, in case she doesn't understand what I'm trying to tell her.

She gives me a cool look. "I get it. You scared."

"No." I shake my head emphatically. "I am not scared. In fact, I *love* touching men. Just not strange ones." Especially if they have hairy backs. I can already feel the yuck factor curling my lips back. "I'm sorry. But no. Your customer will have to reschedule."

Ella Su frowns and gives me an impatient look. She takes my hands in hers and examines them closely. "I don't see problem.

81

You have good, strong hands. All you have to do is rub a little oil on man's back—but keep hands off noodle or he might get wrong idea," she warns me, "and thirty minutes later, tell him to get the hell off table."

God. Jesus. "No. You're not getting it. It's not that I *can't*. It's that I don't *want* to." Rub oil on man's back. Or his noodle. "And, anyway, I'm not even a licensed masseuse. I wouldn't know where to begin."

Ella Su waves a dismissive hand. "Who need license? Nobody ever ask to see *my* license. I no have one. Nobody ever complain."

Silly me. I'd forgotten I'm in a different world here.

Ella Su continues by way of walking around the room explaining and pointing out everything I'll need to be a massage master. She shows me a shelf filled with bottles of scented lotions and oils and she opens a cabinet and shows me where to find stacks of fluffy white towels. And, finally, she hands me a book titled *The Fine Art of Massage* that I can refer to, should I get lost.

Help, I'm lost!

"You can do this," Ella Su says.

But I don't want to do it. I can't. "Fine. Okay. But he'd better not be hairy," I say, shaking a finger at her.

Ella Su smiles and pats my back. Then she's gone, and I'm left alone to think my way out of this. I look down at my hands and study them. Ella Su said they were strong, but I think she was just saying that. My hands aren't strong. They're trembling. I wonder if it's too late for me to check in at the resort down the beach. I'd pay a hundred bucks to sleep in a closet.

I leave Ella Su's room, and I spend a few minutes sitting at the bar, looking at a customer who's nursing an early-morning beer. He could be Massage Guy, and he's decent-enough-looking and not excessively hairy… but I still wouldn't want to rub oil on his back.

Finally, I decide I have no choice but to skip out on my masseuse gig.

"Ella Su has gone home sick," I tell Tug as I make my way to the steps that lead to the sand. "She has a customer coming in sometime this morning, but he'll have to reschedule," I add, and then I'm off down the beach in the direction of the sea grape tree. When I get close to the log where Paula broke her leg, I see a trail off to my right. I follow it, and immediately I'm surrounded by red and yellow and white flowers—hibiscus—like those I saw on my first day here while I was riding in Cole's Jeep. The air is filled with their sweet fragrance, and I smile, remembering how Cole tucked one behind my ear when he and I went over to St. Thomas.

I put my nose to several of the flowers as I walk along, taking in their scent. I'm not paying attention to the trail at all. Before long, the flowers become scarce, and the trail narrows until all that's in front of me is green. Everywhere it's thick foliage.

I turn around and walk a dozen or so yards back, but then I'm faced with a Y in the trail that I hadn't noticed when I was coming from the other direction. Now I have a decision to make. Do I go left or do I go right?

A flicker of uncertainty passes through me. I could be lost. Though I guess not too lost, since St. John is only nine miles long, and I'll eventually find my way if I just keep walking in a straight line. The problem is the trail isn't straight. It's curvy and winding, and I'm growing more nervous by the minute. It's not distance that worries me. It's that I might end up walking in circles.

Trying hard to remember which direction I came from, I choose to go left... and the trail narrows even more. There are no flowers, nothing I recognize. I've gone the wrong way. And now there are noises and rustling sounds coming from the bushes that I'm sure I didn't hear before. I stare into the dense foliage trying to see what might be making those sounds, but all I see is a tangled mess of thick green.

The noises continue and my pulse notches up. I'm not usually afraid of wildlife, and if I were back home, I'd expect a squirrel or a dog or maybe even a raccoon to come popping out of the brush at me. But here, I can't even imagine what it might be. A monkey, perhaps? Which is silly... I think. I doubt there are any monkeys here on St. John.

But what about guerillas? And I don't mean the kind you see in a zoo. Not that I'm wealthy, or that someone would pay a ransom for me, but how would an extreme political group in the middle of the jungle know that?

The noises are getting closer. My heart is hammering in my chest, and my adrenaline has kicked into high gear. I pick up the pace until I'm running and tearing through the brush. I push it aside with my arms as I go, hoping that I won't run into something worse than what I've left behind. My strides are long, but it does me no good. I can still hear whatever it is pounding after me. Cole's words "they might bite" return to haunt me, and I imagine it's a mad donkey chasing me. So I push faster, dodging tree limbs and all kinds of plant life, some of which I'm sure I should avoid touching, but I'm scared and I'm flailing. *I have to get away.* Only now, along with being scared, my skin feels like it's on fire, and I'm itching like some tropical bug is eating me from the inside out.

My foot hits a dip, and I go down on all fours. Muck squishes between my fingers and sloshes up onto my chest. I think it's the muddy earth, but who knows what it really is. I just know it stinks, and it'd be my luck that it's some kind of animal feces.

That thought has me up on my feet and moving again. But now my pursuer is so close that I imagine I can feel hot breath slathering up the backs of my legs. With one last burst of speed, I dart forward toward a dagger of sunlight that I can see through the foliage.

My heart is practically beating out of my chest as I come to the edge of the jungle. I force my legs to carry me a few steps farther, and relief washes over me as I find myself standing in the bright sun, in the middle of a dirt road.

I toss a look over my shoulder, positive I'll finally see what's been chasing me. But there's nothing there. Nothing is after me. Or maybe my pursuer has simply given up.

I don't want to take any chances, so I keep going, pausing only briefly to catch my breath and to decide, once more, which way to go—left or right? This time, I opt for right.

I'm too tired to run anymore, but I can walk fast. And I do. Plus, I make a mental note that if and when I ever make plans to visit the jungle again, I'll get my ass in shape first… if the powers that be will only let me survive *this* visit to the jungle.

A minute passes and I hear a vehicle approaching a bend in the road. I look down at myself and see a layer of muck covering the front of my shirt. Plus, blood is oozing down my shins. But I don't care, I'm so happy to be found.

The vehicle comes into view and it's a Jeep. And then I see who the driver is. Cole. Shit—I'm tempted to jump back into the bushes. He's the last man I want looking at me right now. I don't know what I ever did to deserve this kind of karma, but it's finally caught up with me. Cole has seen me, and it's too late for me to make my escape. His Jeep is rolling to a stop beside me. I nonchalantly brush my hair back from my face in an attempt to act like I've been out having a pleasant morning walk. He doesn't need to know how relieved I am to see him, or anybody, right now.

"Hi!" I say, with exaggerated exuberance. "What's up?" *What's up?* Jeez, I'm an idiot.

"Are you okay?" Cole asks. He's looking me over and his forehead is patterned with lines.

"Of course," I say with the proper amount of indignity. "Why?" I arch an eyebrow at him, daring him to make just one comment about my appearance. He doesn't, but his gaze settles for a brief moment on the side seam of my shorts, which prompts me to glance down. The seam is ripped halfway up, exposing a lot of skin, but I shrug it off, like I knew I was hanging out all along.

"I snagged my shorts on a sticker bush," I tell him. But really? I have no idea how it happened. Plus, I'm not even sure there *are* sticker bushes here on St. John. Though if the twinkle of amusement at the corners of Cole's eyes is any indication, I'd say there probably are not. Only, right now, I don't care. The itching has taken on a new level, and I'm scratching like I'm trying to remove skin.

Cole's amusement fades and his look turns to concern. "My

boat is moored not far from here. I can take you there to get cleaned up," he offers. "I have hot running water and Fekkai shampoo," he adds… like I might need an incentive.

Cole had me at hot running water. I was ready to go anywhere with him.

Chapter Eleven

Cole and I are on the dirt road only a few minutes when we arrive at a parking area that borders a gorgeous strip of white sand and a bay full of boats. I'm out of the Jeep in an instant, eager for that shower, and I look up to see Bum running full speed, straight toward us. I ready myself for impact—he's a big dog and could easily bowl me over. But as it turns out, he also has big doggy brakes, and right before he plows into us, he manages to come to a dead stop.

Cole and I both receive a proper dog greeting that includes plenty of tongue and slobber. Though the way I see it, I'm already so yucked up from my adventure in the jungle that a little more yuck won't hurt one bit.

After Bum finishes with us, he zeroes in on a bush to take care of necessities. When he's done, Cole leads the way across the sand and down the dock to a sailboat that has the name *Destiny* printed in fancy flowing letters on its side. I assume this is the boat he uses to take tourists out sightseeing. It's nice but smaller than I'd pictured in my mind. Then I remember Cole telling me he takes couples out. It's a perfect boat for a honeymoon sail.

Cole steps wide onto the boat's deck and then holds out his

hand to me. Once we're safely aboard, he opens a hatch that leads down into the boat's cabin. "After you," he tells me with a sweep of his hand.

Down the ladder I go, with Cole right behind me. Before I even have a chance to look around, he's next to me. "You didn't have to run off," he says. "If you didn't want to give me a massage, you could have said so."

It doesn't immediately register what he's talking about. But then it does and I'm at a loss for words. I feel the flush of embarrassment fill my cheeks. *He* was the man coming in for a massage? "I didn't know it was you," I tell him.

He laughs. "Should I be flattered? Does that mean you would have stuck around if you'd known it was me?"

I practically cringe, not knowing how to answer. "I know nothing about giving massages," I say. "I was afraid I wouldn't give you your money's worth."

Cole's eyes are twinkling in the dim light. "What's to know? You pour a bit of oil on a person's back, rub it around, and call it good."

"Now you sound like Ella Su. Like it's so easy."

"Would have been… for me. All I had to do was lie there and take it."

I blush again and turn my head, pretending to peruse the interior of his boat. It's elegant with dark wood and cushy seating. There's even a kitchenette that looks like it gets some use but is clean. "So, this is the boat you use for your business?" I ask by way of changing the subject. I'm concerned that if we continue on with our discussion about my skills as a masseuse, our conversation will be anything but benign. As it is, I can see Cole's mind working, like he has something to say.

"What are you so afraid of, Taylor?" he finally asks.

His words hit me—almost hurt. Because he's right. I am afraid. Of him. And of ever falling in love again… if I was, in fact, ever in love with Peyton. The past couple of days, I've decided I'm not sure I even know what real love feels like. "Who says I'm afraid?" I ask, smirking slightly to keep things light.

"Aren't you?"

"Of some things, I suppose. I think you already know I'm afraid of sharks. And let's see… dogs that bite."

"That's it? Sharks and dogs? What about the Husky? You didn't seem to be afraid of him."

"Dogs that *bite*," I correct him. "The Husky needed our help. He wasn't going to bite us."

He grins. "If you say so, Taylor Grant, attorney at law."

"Why do you always use my full name? Why not just Taylor?"

"I like your full name. It fits. Sounds good coming out of my mouth." He takes my hand and leads me to a tiny bathroom that's off the bedroom and points out a tube of cream that he says will help with my itching. Then he gestures to a tan-colored bath towel. "That's clean. The shower is small but it works. Take all the time you need."

As soon as Cole is out of sight, I step under a stream of warm water and I lather myself up until the itching begins to subside. I feel like I haven't had a proper shower since I arrived here in St. John. Paula has what *she* calls a shower, but it's on the outside of The Fish Shack in a small, makeshift area—surrounded by vegetation for privacy, of course—that someone put together, complete with shower head and that's about it. Oh, and a small ledge for soap and shampoo. But for me, I prefer a shower that isn't exposed to anyone who might be interested in looking.

Cole's shower has plenty of warm water, so I take my time getting clean. And when I've finished, I dry myself off and I spread the cream in a thin layer over my arms and legs, hoping it will be the end of my misery.

In moments, I feel like new. I step out of the bathroom, into the bedroom, and I see that Cole has laid some clean clothes out for me—a blue tank top and a pair of shorts. They're nice and girly, but a bit on the young side for my taste. Especially the shorts, which are too short. They don't leave a lot to the imagination. But since Cole has already seen me in my own that were ripped all the way up one side, I don't imagine I'll be showing him anything he hasn't seen.

When I go to find him, he's in the kitchen area. He and Bum are having a master-dog moment. Cole is giving Bum commands in trade for treats, and I stand back and enjoy the show. This goes on for a couple of minutes, and I'm impressed with the way they work together. I can see they have a serious bond. Of course, I could see that the first day I watched them together on the beach.

Cole senses my presence, and he looks over at me and smiles. "You look great."

"I feel stuffed into these shorts," I say and I pull at the hem to try and cover more skin.

Cole comes over to me, pushes a strand of hair behind my ear. "It's all good. I promise."

I struggle for a response, but all I can come up with is, "I rinsed my clothes and left them hanging." I gesture in the direction of the bathroom, nervous of how close—touching close—we are, and now I want him to kiss me so bad it's like a rogue wave swelling inside me, about to topple me over. I'm practically willing the kiss to happen.

And then it does, and it's the kind of kiss you might see on the big screen, the kind that makes a girl's toes curl. It doesn't even enter my mind that I should resist, that I should run away as fast as I can to protect my heart. Instead, I keep my toes planted, enjoying every second of Cole's lips on mine. He's a master at kissing, and with every touch, he's sending a clear message—he wants me.

His kiss goes on, and my head begins swimming with all kinds of thoughts and possibilities... and questions. Such as *Can this really be happening? Am I really doing this?* And, too, *What comes next?*

Cole takes a break from kissing me and he whispers against my cheek, "I'll stop if you want."

"Don't," I whisper back. But my voice is ragged and quiet and I'm not sure he even hears me. I want him so bad, I can hardly think. And I don't want any more talk about it else I might come to my senses.

In my next breath, Cole is kissing his way down my neck and pressing himself to me. I feel hard muscle everywhere. And I mean *every*where... which only makes me want him more. I am all but quivering beneath his touch.

Before reason hits, Cole is relieving me of my clothes and we leave a trail—a bra here, panties there—all the way to the bedroom, where he and I quickly become tangled in his sheets. I know I should be thinking about this, but his kisses have become even more demanding, and I'm right there with him. My hands are on his back and my nails are raking his skin, urging him on.

He kisses me over and over again until the sweetness of his lips feels like it's breaking me. His hands move over me in a slow, purposeful way that makes me want to cry out. I want to tell him that I don't want slow. Or purposeful. I want *now*. *Right* now!

"Please," I say, gasping. But I'm too embarrassed to tell him to just get on with it.

He locks gazes with me. "You're beautiful, Taylor Grant," he says, his voice low and strained. "You excite me to hell and back, and I'm not sure I'll ever want to let you go after we do this."

I stare into his oh-so-blue eyes and I can see he means every word he's said. "Me too, you," I whisper.

Cole captures my hands and pushes them over my head until my need turns into an ache. But it's an ache I desire. I can't wait for him to do whatever he will. Every muscle in my body is full of tension, full of the need for release. It's been too long since I felt a man's arms around me, loving me. I am his completely. I draw a breath. "Now," I say. "*Please.*"

And then he's inside me and we move together in motion and spirit until I've escaped, gone to a place I've never been. I close my eyes and let the world fade around me. I don't want him to see how emotional I am. I don't want him to see that I'd all but given up on love, that I wasn't even sure I'd recognize it when it happened. I think it could be happening now. That I barely know him is irrelevant. I feel loved. Loved by a man I've only just begun to know.

Chapter Twelve

Cool air washes over me and I feel good, at peace. I want this moment to last forever, or at least until I go back to Seattle. Then I'll be able to get on with my life and I won't hold back. I'll eventually meet someone who won't leave me a good-bye note on the back of a coffeehouse napkin. But… I'll never forget Cole. Making love with him has been unbearably beautiful. Still, as beautiful as it was, there's also pain swelling inside me. At some point, he and I will say good-bye and it makes me feel like I'm being ripped apart. My hand goes to my chest and I take in a deep breath to try and relax.

"You okay?" Cole asks.

"Perfect," I whisper. I'm such a liar.

"You're thinking about what happens next, when you go home," he says.

"I am," I admit.

"Are you sorry we made love?"

I manage a smile. "Not at all. In fact, I think we should stay here all day, making love." And I mean it from the bottom of my heart.

Cole kisses me, and I can feel the stubble on his chin and the heat of his body against mine. It feels so right, like this is where I belong. Like this is the man I am meant to be with. So where does that leave us? I can hardly ask him to come and be with me in Seattle.

I push the sheet aside, need to get up and out of Cole's bed before I say something he might not be ready to hear. "I should go," I tell him.

"What happened to us staying here in bed all day?" he protests.

I hunch my shoulders and continue on my way. It's the only thing I can do if I want to avoid turning his bedroom into a flood zone.

Once I'm away from him, and behind the closed bathroom door, I gain control of my emotions. I scold myself, feeling stupid and reckless. It was a mistake for me to let things go so far between us.

I stay in the bathroom until I'm sure I can hold myself together. And by the time I go back to the bedroom, Cole is talking to someone on his phone. He clicks off when he sees me.

"That was Tug. I told him you were with me and that you wouldn't be home for a while."

I force my lips into an impish smile. We've just made love. I don't want to ruin the memory of it by bringing us both down. "And where will I be?"

Cole moves close and puts his arms around me. "I know what you're thinking. That I'm going to hold you to your promise and make you stay in bed all day."

"Hmm. I hadn't realized I made a promise."

"Oh, you did. I heard it. But, sorry, I'm going to have to disappoint you."

I raise my eyebrows, curious.

"I'd like for you to meet one of my friends. Toby Dunn. He lives not far from here. What do you say?"

I put a finger to my chin, like I'm giving it considerable thought. "Hmm, let me see. Back to bed, or meet one of your friends?" I shrug. "That seems an easy choice. I'd love to meet your friend Toby."

Cole half frowns. "I'm not sure if I should be happy or upset.

Did I do something wrong? Were you not happy with my performance?"

Ecstatic, actually. "Don't worry, cowboy," I say, patting his chest. "I'm sure you'll have another opportunity before I go back to Seattle."

Cole grins. "I like the sound of that."

Before we leave the marina, Cole fills a bowl with fresh water for Bum. Plus, he leaves a fan and a radio on, and then he and I are back in his Jeep, bumping along the North Shore Road that I've become so acquainted with. I no longer pay attention to the birds or their chatter. I stay quiet, lost in my thoughts. I can only imagine what Paula is thinking—that she's made herself a quick hundred bucks, I bet. No doubt, extensive questioning will ensue when I see her later tonight.

We drive past Trunk Bay, Cinnamon Bay, and Maho Bay, and then we turn off onto another road that winds through the island's interior. I know the names of all the beaches only because I've spent a fair amount of time staring at a large map that's pinned to one of the walls at The Fish Shack that highlights every road and trail here on St. John. Funny, I don't remember seeing the trail where I got lost.

On the way, Cole tells me that Toby is from Texas, too. Another ex-bull fighter. I'm glad for our conversation. It takes my mind off me having to leave here in a couple of weeks.

"How did you all come to be here?" I ask. "Is there something special about the islands, or St. John, that made you all want to say good-bye to your lives and leave everything you know behind?"

"Look around," Cole tells me. "Everything about this place is special."

My lips form a thin line. "That's what Paula tells me." I consider asking him what he knows, if anything, about why Paula stays here, but I need to hear it from her. Anything Cole could tell me would only be second-hand information.

We make one more turn, and that takes us off the main dirt road and down a long driveway lined with palm and sea grape trees. Sea grape trees are everywhere.

At the end of the driveway, we come to a modest ranch-style house that features the Caribbean Sea as its backyard, which is the same as Paula's place. Except there's also a barn.

I'll admit, I'm envious. I'd love to have an ocean or a lake to look at when I step out my back door. Mostly, I have buildings to look at. Lots and lots of buildings.

I absentmindedly begin to scratch at my arms. And then my legs. I'd almost forgotten about the bug bites, but now the itching is back in full force.

Cole and I are out of the Jeep in a flash. "Toby will have something for that," he tells me. "He keeps a supply of lotions and potions on hand that can cure just about any ailment."

As we reach the front door, it swings open, and a large man with a lot of blond hair and a scruffy beard appears. He reminds me of a big pup, all exuberant to have someone new to play with. Cole introduces us, and Toby is quick to see my discomfort.

"You bug bit?" he asks.

"All over," Cole answers for me, and I guess he should know.

"Jeez, Louise, let's get you inside, get some ointment on you." Toby takes me by the hand, leads me into his house, and steers me to a bathroom, where he hands me a small, plastic tub full of medical paraphernalia. "You'll find something in there that'll help. McKenzie and I will be over at the barn when you're finished."

I'm hardly listening. All I want is for him to leave so that I can dig through the tub and find the ointment. As soon as the door is closed and I'm alone, I strip down to my bra and panties to survey every inch of my skin. Angry bumps cover my legs and arms, and even my torso. I look gross. And now I'm horrified that the first time Cole and I made love, he saw me looking like this. Though, at the time, he didn't seem all that horrified.

I smile, remembering how his eyes lit up when he saw me lying naked in his bed. With only a small mirror and a very dim light to look at myself, I had no idea the full state of my appearance. And now I swear it'll be a cold day in hell before I let him see me looking like this again.

I get busy pushing things around in the plastic tub, finally finding a tube of anti-itch *cream*. It's different than what I used at Cole's—prescription strength—and I imagine it will take care of the problem for good. I certainly hope so.

I waste no time in smearing a good amount all over me, covering every bump I can find, and the relief is almost instant. In no time, I'm back to feeling human.

I get dressed again, still hating how short the shorts are that Cole loaned me, but nothing I can do about that right now.

I go in search of the men, stepping out the front door and down to the driveway, and then I make my way over to the barn, where it looms big and daunting, the color of fireplace ash. Bits of red paint remain, probably from when it was first built, but it has clearly taken a beating from the weather many times over.

The barn door is tall and splintery, and as I approach it, I can hear the men talking inside. I hear my name mentioned, so I wait, don't want to interrupt. But now I feel like I'm eavesdropping, so I step a few feet away. I don't mind one bit waiting outside for a few more minutes to enjoy the scenery and the sun.

I turn and look across the wide pebbled driveway, back to the house, where I see splashes of bright blue color. It's the same as the barn, showing abuse from the weather. Though, unlike Paula's place, all the window frames have glass. And of course, there's a bundle of bananas hanging from a twine at one corner of the front porch. My guess is that hanging bananas from the front porch is a tradition here.

I look farther out and see endless coconut palms, and then the Caribbean Sea. It makes me feel so small and insignificant. I tilt my face to the sky to take in the healing rays of the sun. I don't give a damn right now what lecture my dermatologist might have for me on the subject of the sun and its harmful rays. I'm on vacation. I'm free to misbehave.

Though I think I've already misbehaved—with Cole.

Laughter spills out to me, loud and hearty from inside the barn, along with bits of conversation. I don't mean to listen, but

Toby has a booming voice, and I'd have to walk to the other side of the driveway to escape hearing him.

"Did you see Ariel? She blew out of here like she was on fire," he says. "That woman drives me crazy. She don't understand. A man like me has needs. Hell, I can't wait forever."

I smile. Spoken like a true man. But then, that's how I felt a few hours ago, until Cole had his way with me. I don't think I've ever had my needs so well taken care of.

I hear a tinny pop—the top of a beer can, I suspect—then nothing for at least another minute. Then I hear Cole.

"Paula got hurt, broke her leg."

"Serious?" It's Toby speaking. I can almost see his brow drawing tight. "Anything I can do?"

"Taylor will be here another week." A few seconds of silence, and then Cole continues. "I've been worried about Sophie. It's good you called."

Who's Sophie?

The men don't elaborate. They move on to another subject. Toby is speaking again.

"So, Taylor's a city gal. And a lawyer. Are you and she—"

Cole cuts him off. "She's complicated. That's about all I'm going to say."

Complicated? Me? At least Cole doesn't come right out and give his friend a play-by-play on how he and I spent the morning.

"She's a woman," Toby says flatly. "Pay attention to her signals... all those things a woman does to pretend she's not interested in a man's sorry ass."

I smile. If he only knew.

"Signals?" Cole asks.

"Yeah, you know, all that lash fluttering and hair tossing. Plus, the looks they give a man that say they can't stand the sight of him, but what they really want is for him to jump their bones. It's serious business, man."

"Sounds like you got it all figured out," Cole tells him.

"Boy howdy," Toby responds.

I smile again. Men are so clueless. When it comes to women,

they have nothing figured out.

"Seems to me, her being a lawyer and all, you got you some trouble," Toby continues.

"How so?" Cole asks.

"She been around too many bad men. She can't trust a one of us."

Cole responds, but now there's a bird twittering in a nearby bush, so I can't hear. If I had a rock, I'd throw it at the little feathered noisemaker.

The twittering lasts only a minute, and then I hear Toby again.

"I hear tell those Seattle women got a real wild streak in 'em."

This elicits a sharp laugh from Cole. "Where you been gettin' all your facts about Seattle women?"

"Hell, Paula's a Seattle woman, ain't she?"

A few minutes pass and both men remain quiet. They've finished talking. About me, anyway. So I guess it's settled… I'm a wild Seattle woman. And I don't trust men.

I've decided I like Toby. He's rough around the edges, but he keeps it real. Even if he is seriously misinformed about women.

The men have had their time, and I'm tired of ogling the scenery. It's time I join them. I pull on the barn door, and as I step inside, I'm met by a pungent mix of odors that can only be described as barn. Leather, hay, grain… horse dung. Which is not nearly as offensive as other kinds of animal dung.

Cole smiles, seeing me, and the look on his face makes me wish we were back in his bed. I pretend to be oblivious and I step forward, where I hear footsteps crunching on straw in a stall that's directly in front of me. I peer over the top of the gate and I see a horse with big, glossy eyes and a coat the color of cool fire. It's a mare with a belly on her that looks about ready to burst.

She looks at me, snorting air through her nostrils. I don't know what it means, but I hold out my hand and she comes over and allows me to rub her neck for a minute. She's warm under my hand, and slightly damp with sweat. I breathe deeply of her scent. I've always loved the smells associated with horses. When I was a little girl, I had a dream that one day, for my birthday, my mom would surprise me with a horse of my own. Of course, that was silly. Mom had only enough money for what we needed. Not luxuries, like owning a horse.

Cole steps up beside me. "This is Sophie. She's about ready to become a mama with twins. I expect she's feeling plenty uncomfortable."

Ah, so *this* is Sophie. And pregnant with twins. Yikes.

"If you don't mind, I'd like to stay and give Toby a hand," Cole continues. "You don't have to stay and watch. You can go to the house and wait if you like. Might be a while, though." He rubs a hand over Sophie's face. "She's been through this once before, and neither foal made it. One was stillborn and the other acted out, like he was on a constant drunk binge. Ran into trees, stumbled around. It wasn't good." He keeps rubbing Sophie, murmuring softly, letting her know that she and her babies will be fine this time.

I'm touched seeing so much tenderness from him. "I'd like to stay," I say quietly. No way am I leaving now. I may not have any desire to go through the birthing process myself, but I wouldn't miss this magnificent animal giving birth for anything.

Cole continues speaking to Sophie, his voice low and soothing, until Sophie gives him an eye roll and goes to stand by herself in one corner of the stall.

Toby unlatches the gate and goes in. He smoothes a hand over her swollen belly, takes a look under her tail. "Won't be long," he confirms.

I'm tense and excited at the same time. I've never experienced a miracle such as this. But after several minutes of watching and waiting for something to happen, I'm getting impatient, so when I hear a loud thud, like a hoof hitting wood, coming from three stalls down, I wander in that direction.

"Careful," Cole warns. "That's BTO. He's not too friendly, unless you bring him a bribe."

"BTO?"

"Big Time Operator."

When I reach the gate, I get a look at this horse, BTO. He's a big, beautiful, snorting sorrel, and he looks like he could breathe fire. His eyes go wild when he sees me. He doesn't seem impressed. I back up a step to give him his space, but he continues to disapprove of my presence, tossing his head high into the air and looking like he might rear up. He's all taut muscle. I step back even farther, concerned that he might come through the gate.

Cole comes and stands beside me. He reaches into his pocket and pulls out a piece of candy. "Here," he says, handing it to me. "It's peppermint. He loves these. It's about the only way you'll get his interest."

I'm tentative as I reach over the gate. My palm is open; the candy is in sight.

BTO has been watching us. His eyes are locked on my hand and he's quick to act. Before I can chicken out, he's up to the gate, and his velvety nose is at my hand, taking the candy. When he's finished, he lets me know he wants more with a hard nuzzle to my shoulder and a tug at the collar of my shirt.

"That's all I have," I whisper to him, but all he does is blink his big eyes at me.

Since I've shared, I'm hoping he'll let me closer. I reach out to touch him, and he quivers but stays put. I rub his neck for several minutes, completely enthralled. I could spend all day watching him… if it weren't for the mare giving birth a few yards away. A couple of pats, and then Cole and I return to see what's happening with Sophie. She's on her side now, glistening all over, and straining hard for each breath. The straw around her looks wet. Her water has broken. But Toby is at her side, stroking her and speaking softly, so I'd say she's in good hands.

"Is a vet coming?" I ask Cole.

Cole shakes his head. "Both me and Toby have been through this enough times we could open our own practice."

I'm amazed at Cole. Toby, too. Men in Seattle can barely change the oil in their car, let alone participate in the birth of a baby horse. Sometimes, Seattle men don't even seem like real men anymore. They spend all their time on their electronic gadgets, even when they're out to dinner with a woman. And the woman, too, might be on her phone, texting or checking messages.

I hate to say it, but I miss the good old days, when men used to stare longingly at a woman who catches their eye, and then somehow he'd work up the courage to talk to her. Sadly, I think those days might be gone for good. But not here, not when men like Cole exist. So maybe there's hope after all.

I stay still, watching Toby tend to Sophie. After a minute, he looks up at me and Cole. "It be time," he tells us. Short and sweet, Sophie is about to become a mom.

Chapter Thirteen

Sophie's side is heaving, and the veins in her face and beneath her slick coat are protruding like thick, knotty cords. Each contraction causes her body to ripple, bringing with it more pain. I can't even imagine being in her place right now.

Cole joins Toby in Sophie's stall. He glances over his shoulder at me. "Care to get a closer look?"

He doesn't have to ask twice. I immediately unlatch the gate and step inside. Even in her state, Sophie is aware of all intruders. She raises her head and gives me a brief look that I take to mean *Don't bother me, I'm busy.*

I hear BTO snort and kick at his stall, like he, too, can feel the excitement in the air, like it's been charged with electricity. Something lovely and magical is about to happen, and I can hardly believe I'm here to see it.

But when I look at Sophie, her eyes are wide, and she's not having one bit of fun. Her body is like a huge contracting muscle that's gone into cramp mode, while the men are completely fixed on what's happening south of her head. They're all business and seemingly oblivious to her pain. I doubt they'd notice if an earthquake happened right now.

I watch Sophie struggle, wishing I could do something to make her more comfortable. Then, all at once, something spindly and gooey, and not at all what I expected it to look like, squeezes out her back end.

"Holy shit!" I gasp and topple back on my heels. I'm sure that what I'm seeing is a leg, but it is *so* not pretty. Not that I didn't know it was coming, but good God! Someone call the Men in Black.

I want to look away, but I can't make my head turn. It's like watching a train wreck. All I can do is stare and wonder what happens next. I've never witnessed such a thing… though I know for sure that one gooey leg does not a baby horse make.

"Where's the rest?" I ask.

The men ignore me. They don't seem nearly as bothered as I am that Sophie has just one spindly leg sticking out of her.

Another minute ticks off and I'm growing concerned. It seems to me the baby is stuck and that maybe someone should do something to help things along.

"Whaddya think, call Doc Emerson?" Cole finally asks Toby.

Yes, *please,* call Doc Emerson. I know the men have done this before, but for God's sake, call Doc Emerson.

"Let's give her another minute," Toby says.

I silently vote let's not.

We all continue to watch and wait while Sophie blows huge puffs of air and groans like she's all but fed up with this nonsense. As for me, I'm amazed she can even survive giving birth to something the size of a baby horse. Though I've heard how once it's over, it's over. No more pain. No more screaming. Life goes on.

Hard to imagine. Even harder to believe. Which is why I intend to keep the doors to this baby factory closed—permanently.

One last groan and Sophie's head collapses onto the straw. She looks defeated and weary. I'm weary *watching* her. But then another torturous minute passes, and she's back at it again, doing all she can to help her babies enter this world. Her belly tightens, rippling once more, and Cole gets into position, kneeling in the straw, ready to assist with the birth of baby number one. He and Toby both have beads of sweat running down the sides of their faces.

I want to help, too, but I don't dare get in the way. I settle for sending Sophie positive vibes. *C'mon, girl. You can do this.*

Again, Sophie stiffens. She gives another big push, and then at last more body parts arrive. They squish out in a big, brown, slimy mess, and it's one of the grossest things I've ever seen, but it's also amazing and beautiful and it nearly drives me to tears. Sophie has had a baby!

Toby goes to work on the foal, tearing away the gooey film— the placenta—and then he uses a towel to clear the foal's mouth and nose. I wait to hear something, but there's only quiet. I look to Cole. He's busy waiting for baby number two to arrive.

The foal's silence has me on edge. Toby is massaging him, doing all he can to help the poor thing come to life, but there's practically no sound in the barn. "He ain't breathin'," Toby says. Sweat drips off his brow. The barn is stifling. "C'mon, junior," he urges.

Fear pushes away all my happy feelings as I remember what Cole told me about Sophie's other babies. I can't bear to think of that happening again.

Several miserable seconds tick by, and then I hear a quiet snuffling sound. My eyes focus on the foal, and I think I even see him move. It's only a twitch, but yes, I'm sure he moved!

Toby continues rubbing the foal's coat until he appears to just "wake up." His big head bobs around some, and Toby comments, "Look at that big ol' head. We oughtta call him Bobblehead, Bobby for short."

Cole and I laugh, but I think Sophie's baby is beautiful. He's going to be a genius horse with a head that big. "What about baby number two?" I ask Cole.

"Old Doc Emerson was wrong. Just one this time," Cole tells me. He nods at the foal. "This little guy is it."

We all step back and let Sophie be a mother. She nuzzles him, making sure he's okay, and she does a great job of cleaning him until he's all fuzzy and new and oh so perfect.

Not long after his first bath, Bobby is already trying to stand, which is no easy task with such long legs that don't seem to work in unison. He gets to where he's kneeling, but when he tries to push himself all the way up, he falls back onto the straw over and over again. After making dozens of attempts, I think he might be frustrated and ready to give up. Then, finally, he gets it right and he's standing and looking around like he's not sure what to do next. I'm so happy for him I want to clap my hands and cheer. But I don't, because I wouldn't want to do anything to startle either Mom or Baby. So, I just continue watching in silence with the men.

Once Baby is really solid on his feet, we all smile big and laugh. What a sight! What a great big beautiful baby Sophie has delivered!

I can't say I'm disappointed she didn't have a second foal. Relieved is more like it. Poor girl looks like she's been through hell. As do the men. As do I, I'm sure.

Toby is the first to mention needing a shower. After he makes sure Baby "Bobblehead" knows his food source, we all leave the barn so that Mom and Baby can be alone. Toby is quick to go to the house, and then it's just me and Cole.

Standing in the bright sun, I breathe deep of the fresh air. I hadn't realized how stuffy it was in the barn. I'm also aware of how much my cheeks hurt from smiling so much. And when I look over at Cole, he's smiling, too. At me.

"I'm afraid we could use another shower ourselves," he tells me.

I look down at myself. I'm not as big a mess as the men, but I'm not against going back to Cole's boat… for another round of lovemaking perhaps? My heart is pounding at the idea, and I don't know what else to do, so I look down at the sand. It's white and beautiful at my feet. I slip off one of my flip-flops and sink my toes in deep. I can't believe how lucky am I right now, to be here, on this island, with this man. Seattle men do not deliver baby horses. Seattle does not have men like Cole McKenzie. I am completely smitten.

"Parrotfish," Cole tells me.

I look up. "Pardon?"

"The sand. Parrotfish feed on the algae by munching on coral, then they spit out what's left. That's what makes the sand here so soft and white."

I wrinkle my nose and slip my foot back into the flip-flop. "Remind me not to go barefoot on the beach anymore."

We both laugh, and then Cole picks a piece of straw from my hair. His hand lingers and he draws me to him. He kisses me, and I relax against the fence, against a knot in the wood that's digging into my back. It's uncomfortable, but I couldn't give a damn. I wouldn't care if an entire plank were sticking through me right now so long as Cole never stops kissing me.

Chapter Fourteen

Back at the boat, Cole and I get clean. That's all. It's all we have room for in his tiny shower. And then he takes me into his bed for more lovemaking, and it's even better than the first time. He satisfies me completely—twice—and I don't even care if Paula finds out she's won her bet.

Afterward, while Cole and I lie together, I wonder what happens next for us. Though I already know—I go back to Seattle, and Cole goes back to his life here.

And therein lies the pain I'd hoped to avoid.

My eyes fill. Life seems so impossible right now.

Cole squeezes me to his side when I've been silent too long. "You spend too much time thinking," he says.

"Yes," I admit.

"Do you ever get any rest… mentally?" he asks.

"When I'm asleep."

He's quiet for a minute and then says, "We should talk."

I'm caught off guard. Men usually pull the silent act after having sex, and beginning a conversation with "We should talk" tends not to bode well for the other party.

"I had a wife once," Cole begins. "I thought that was

107

something you should know."

It's not the conversation I was expecting, but I'm glad he's willing to share his past with me and I'm eager to hear more.

"Her name was Janine," he goes on. "I thought she was the love of my life, and I hers. We had our lives all planned out. She was going to be a stay-at-home mom, while I brought in the money and flowers to her every day."

I laugh softly. "Sounds simple enough."

"It was. Until I got it into my head I wanted to compete in the PBR."

I shift slightly at his side, uncomfortable with staying quiet. I feel like I should tell him that I at least know part of his story. "Paula mentioned that you were hurt during your last ride."

"I was. Pretty bad." He pauses, and then continues. "All Janine wanted was a man who came home to her every night. Which was fine by me. But then the PBR became a passion and it was like a fire I couldn't put out. I was convinced I could win. Which I did. But by that time, Janine'd had enough of my disappearing act. She'd found someone else to keep her warm in bed."

Cole goes quiet for a minute, and the only sound is the slapping of water against the sides of his boat, along with the occasional cry of a seagull. "I hate that I did that to her—to us," he says at last. "And I probably deserved to have my head kicked in by a bull."

"We all make mistakes," I say, wanting to give him some small measure of comfort.

"We do, but sometimes we don't recover. I wasn't a good husband."

I have no idea what to say, so I just squeeze myself tighter against his side. After a few minutes, I'm hoping we can change the conversation to something lighter. "Did you always know you wanted to be a cowboy? Was that always your dream?" I ask.

He chuckles. "Cowboys are born, darlin'. But as far as dreams go, my family was poor. With eight kids, if we had enough to eat, that was a dream. My ma stayed home to make sure we didn't burn down the house, but my pa, he worked two jobs for a lot of years. That is, until he had an accident that took him out of the oil fields. After that, my ma had to take over as provider."

A quiet sadness settles into his eyes, and then he takes my hand and kisses the backs of my fingers. "Me and my brother had a knack for gettin' ourselves into trouble. We spent all our time raising hell." His lips tighten into a sour line. "It wasn't until I heard one of my little sisters crying one night, because she was hungry and couldn't sleep, that I decided it was time I become responsible and get a job.

"It took a while. Folks all around the area knew me and my brother. They wouldn't give us the time of day—at first, anyway. But we kept on asking for work and offering to do just about anything, until, eventually, it paid off. Things were better after that. We were even able to enjoy a good steak dinner every now and again." He chuckles. "That was then. Now, I'm into fish. I eat so much of it, I think I might grow fins one day."

We both laugh. I'm glad he's been honest with me, and I love hearing about his family. But I feel like there's more. "Do you ever plan to go back to Texas?" I ask. "I know you must miss all your sisters and your brother."

Cole puts his free arm behind his head and continues holding me close with the other. "I do miss them. But St. John is my home, now. Everything I need is right here." He looks at me and smiles. "What about you, Taylor Grant? Do you miss Seattle?"

Oh boy. Where do I begin? But before I can answer, we hear Bum moving around, probably in dire need of a potty break. I don't remember Cole letting him out when we got back.

Cole rolls over on top of me and kisses me before getting up to pull on his jeans. And it's not just a quick peck. It's lingering and it makes me smile. No man has ever kissed me the way he kisses me. No man has ever made me feel the way he makes me feel. I think I would like to be kissed by him every day for the rest of my life.

While Cole and Bum are outside, I get up to go check on my clothes. They're dry, though far from clean. But they smell much

ALEXA DARIN

better than the clothes I wore to the barn. Once the goo from me getting close to Baby Bobby dried, I couldn't wait to get them off, they reeked so. If they were mine, I'd seriously consider tossing them out. But they're not... mine.

And now that I'm thinking about it, I wonder who they belong to. I should have asked, but I didn't, and now I think I might have to live with my curiosity.

I hear a noise at the door, and I think it's Cole, but then I'm surprised when a girl who can't be more than fifteen or sixteen opens the door and is standing before me. She takes me in, her eyes blazing, while I'm just plain embarrassed because I'm not yet dressed.

I try to cover myself with my clothes that are still in my hand, and I wait... for the shit to hit the fan, I suppose. I don't know who this girl is, but if looks could kill...

Her glare burns over me, moving from my face all the way to the floor, where the clothes I wore to the barn lay. She narrows her eyes and snatches the shorts up off the floor. "He let you wear my *clothes*?" she says, shaking them at me.

Jesus. I inch back as far as I can go. Was this the "more" that I was worried about? And I guess that answers my question about whose clothes I was wearing.

"Lacy!" Cole shouts behind the girl. I've never heard such anger in his voice.

The girl turns and shoves the shorts into his hands. "They stink. Thanks for asking my permission." She looks back to me and gives me the death glare—I know the death glare, as I've seen it plenty of times in court—and all my good feelings fizzle away. All I want to do now is get out of here.

The girl—Lacy—pushes past Cole, leaving the bathroom door hanging open, and now Cole and I are looking at each other like we're strangers, like neither of us knows what to say or do.

Cole speaks first. "Sorry 'bout that. I didn't know she was going to show up."

Obviously. And now I feel vulnerable, like every part of me is exposed, including my emotions. My eyes are all warm and

110

misty. "Do you mind?" I say, and I shut the door in his face. I press my back to the door while I try to think. Only I *can't* think. My heart feels like it's about to explode, and my mind isn't far behind.

I've been wondering who Cole spends his time with when he's not with me, and, well, I guess now I know. But, *God*, is it possible Cole has a taste for girls who are young enough to be his daughter?

No. I refuse to consider it. But now my heart is aching, and I'm so flustered it's all I can do to get dressed.

Tears sting my eyes while I slip my tank top over my head. I pull on my underwear and shorts, and then I look at myself in the mirror to see if I'm presentable. But that's hardly the case. My eyes are all red-rimmed and my mascara is smudged, so it's obvious I've been crying. And not only that, but I look damn old. Not young like that girl, woman, *person* who just walked in on me.

The ache in my chest builds, and I press a hand over my heart. I feel like a wild storm is growing inside me. Men. Shit. I told myself I'd never let myself feel this way again.

Yet, here I am, feeling this way again.

I wait for what seems like forever before I even think about leaving the tiny bathroom. Cole hasn't knocked or said anything through the door. He must be soothing the woman-child. He's not doing anything to soothe me. That's okay. I don't feel like talking… or being soothed.

But somehow, I know Cole is out there waiting for me. The woman-child must have left. I've heard no screaming or shouting. She has to be gone.

I don't want to talk to Cole right now. I need to get out of here. But how?

I swing my gaze to the ceiling. No escape hatch.

Figures.

I settle against the door, can practically feel Cole's presence in the other room. But I could be wrong. He and the young woman may be off talking on dry land, keeping their discussion private.

My stomach tightens as I touch the door handle. I want to peer out… enough to see into the bedroom, but I'm afraid. Even so, I gather myself and look anyway… and I was right. Cole is in the bedroom, waiting for me.

"Can we talk?" he asks as soon as he sees me.

My forehead wrinkles into a mean frown… because I'm so tough… because I don't want him to see me cry.

"I need to go," I say. "You should see to your friend." My words come out sharper than I intend, but I'm not about to apologize. I'm so glad I never told him how I felt—*feel*—about him.

I try to step past him, but he blocks my way. "Don't leave. Let me explain," he says. His hands are on my arms, and I feel the warmth of his touch, but I'm no longer sure I want his touch anywhere near me. I'm angry and I'm afraid I might say something I can't take back. I need some time alone.

"Maybe later," I say, and I try to push past him again, but he stands firm.

"Now," he says. "We need to talk now. I don't want you to walk away feeling like this."

I hate having to defend what I want to do. *Hate it.* "What makes you think you know how I'm feeling?"

"Maybe I don't. But I have a good idea. You're about to leave without hearing me out. That tells me whatever you're feeling isn't good."

I feel a pinch as the realization hits that even if I do stay and listen to what he has to say, in the end, it's still going to hurt. I'll be leaving here soon. That's our end. It might as well happen right this minute.

A lump forms in my throat and I swallow it away. I'm determined not to fall apart. "You don't need to explain. But rule number one," I say, "if you're going to see two women at once, keep them from running into each other." I'm being flippant, sarcastic even, but I don't care.

Cole catches my chin in his hand and forces me to look at him. "It isn't what you think, Taylor. The only woman I want to spend any time with is standin' right here in front of me." His voice is like a soothing balm as he tries to pull me to him, but I'm determined to refuse his comfort. I'm damaged, an emotional mess, and the only thing I want right now is to *not* be with him. I can't ever let him kiss me again. Or touch me. If I do, I won't have the strength to say good-bye.

"It doesn't matter what I think. In a few days, I'll be going home, and then you and your *girl*friend can get back to... whatever."

Cole looks frustrated, maybe even slightly annoyed. "That *girl* is my daughter. I was about to tell you about her. I would have told you sooner, but I wanted to find the right time. That's why I told you about Janine. Paula mentioned how you don't like kids. I was afraid my having one would scare you off."

I can't believe what I'm hearing. Cole has a *daughter*? My throat feels full. I can barely breathe. But one thing I know is that my sister has some explaining to do.

Chapter Fifteen

I can't believe Paula has done this to me. She's known my position on motherhood since we were kids. If she didn't already have a broken leg, I would wring her neck.

When I get back to The Fish Shack, it's not late, but it's Monday, and Paula closes early on Mondays. I find her on her cot painting her toenails. She can barely reach the foot on the leg that's broken, and she's making a mess, but I don't think she cares. When she sees me, she immediately recaps the bottle of red polish.

"Where have you been all day?" she asks. "Tug said you took off after Ella Su got sick, and then Cole was left with no one to give him a massage."

"Which is interesting, because I know Cole called Tug. And I'm sure Tug talked to you," I tell Paula. "So you know I've been with Cole. He just dropped me off, and he seems to be doing fine without his massage." Better than me, actually. He and I talked on the way back here, but it was him mostly, apologizing for the way Lacy spoke to me and also for not telling me about her.

I sit on my cot and roll to my side, exhausted from the day. "You could have told me. That day on the beach, you could have told me," I say.

Paula draws her knee, on the leg that's not broken, to her chest. "You met Lacy," she says.

"Jesus, Paula, did you really think I was never going to find out that Cole has a kid?"

"Not a kid. A teenage daughter," Paula corrects me.

"Fine. Teenage daughter. That's even worse."

Paula holds up a hand, stopping my speech from becoming a full-blown rant. "I'm well aware of the horrors you've witnessed in family court. You don't have to remind me."

"It's not just what I've witnessed in court. I've *never* wanted kids. You know that. I don't want to be a mom. So why would you set me up with a man I'm not compatible with?"

Paula arches an eyebrow. "I didn't set you up with anyone. I merely suggested you give him a look. And who said anything about you being Lacy's mom? How about just being her friend? She doesn't have many of those here."

"That's not going to happen. She already hates me."

"C'mon. She doesn't even know you."

"Cole loaned me some of her clothes, and when she found them on the bathroom floor, stinking like horse afterbirth, she looked at me with death in her eyes. I thought she was going to go all *Exorcist* on me."

Paula's eyes light up. "Sophie has given birth? Are they just beautiful?" She claps her hands together. "I can't wait to see them!"

"There was only one. And yes, he's beautiful, with a head big enough for two foals. But back to Lacy. She wasn't at all happy about Cole letting me wear her clothes."

Paula looks confused. "Why were you wearing Lacy's clothes?"

I sit up, on the edge of my cot. "Mine were trashed. Cole gave me something clean to wear after I had a shower on his boat."

Paula's eyes are positively gleaming. "You were *naked* on Cole's boat?"

My face warms. I don't care to discuss me being naked with

Cole. And I'm not about to admit she won her bet. "Don't make a big deal out of it. This isn't about me and Cole or whether or not I was naked with him. I needed a change of clothes." I wave a dismissive hand. "You should have warned me he had a daughter."

"If I'd warned you, the two of you would have never gotten together."

"That's just it. We're *not* together. We were never going to *be* together. I live in Seattle. He lives here. Get it?"

Paula looks annoyed. "Of course I get it. No one said you had to *be* together. Not like you're talking about anyway. I just thought you'd make a good couple—for a couple of weeks. And about Lacy. She's been having a lot of trouble adjusting to island life. You know how it is being a teenager. She had to leave all her friends behind, and Cole says she's not even trying to make new ones here."

I stand and begin pacing. "That's exactly my point. Teenagers have issues that take some kind of psychiatric therapy to resolve. I'm not equipped to handle those kinds of issues."

"Good God, Taylor. It's not like you'll be spending the rest of your life with her. You'll be leaving here soon, remember?"

"Exactly. So why would I want to get involved with Cole if I might never see him again?"

"Forgive me, but I thought it would be good for you to spend some time with another man so you would know how much better you could do than Peyton."

"Leave Peyton out of this. He and I are over. Cole has a daughter. I don't want to have kids." I pace some more, needing to do something, but I don't know what.

"Again, no one is asking you to be Lacy's mom."

"But what if Cole and I… what if…"

"The two of you were to fall in love?" Paula finishes for me.

"You haven't been listening. We live an ocean apart."

Paula looks thoughtful. "That could change."

"No. It can't." But even as I say it, I dare to imagine a life with Cole. Of course, it would have to be one of those long-distance relationships. Which would mean a lot of traveling, which makes me cringe. I'm not fond of all that touchy-feely security stuff, not to mention the long lines I'd be forced to endure. No, a relationship with Cole, beyond what we have right here and now, isn't feasible. "You should have told me," I say, and I turn to leave Paula to her nail polishing.

"Where are you going?" she asks.

"Out for some fresh air."

I hear Paula mumble something, but I continue on, walking past the bar, looking at all the bottles on the shelves—I still don't believe anyone drinks all that neon-colored crap—and as I stop to contemplate grabbing one of the bottles from the middle shelf that's full of amber-colored liquid, the back door swings open.

It's Cole. Nervous bubbles fizz in my stomach, looking at him.

"You're back." I say. "I wasn't expecting to see you again."

"Ever?"

I smile a small smile. "No. Tonight."

"After I dropped you off, I realized I forgot to tell you something."

"That you have another kid?" I wince as I say it, though at this point, nothing would surprise me.

"No. Lacy is it." He steps closer to me, and he smells so good—like fresh air and sea—that I'm taken back to our time in his bed. I'm hardly listening to what he's saying. And then he takes my hand and leads me out to the front of the bar, where I feel like I'm standing on the edge of the universe, like nothing can hurt me as long as I have him next to me. But why does he have to have a kid?

"I like the way I feel when I'm with you, Taylor," he says. "You're important to me. I know you'll be leaving here soon, and that it might be a long time before I see you again, but I need you to know that you'll be missed. Not forgotten. And I know I should have told you about Lacy… it was wrong of me not to."

"You've already apologized," I say. "And it's okay. I get why you didn't tell me about Lacy. But the truth is, Paula was right. I've never wanted kids. I'm not patient enough to be a mother."

Cole smiles thinly. "Sometimes I'm not patient enough to be a father."

"But you are."

"I muddle through, somehow."

I feel even worse now because I'm not even interested in muddling through. "I've never felt ready to be a mom," I say. "Motherhood takes time. I've seen so many kids end up in trouble because both parents were too busy to pay attention. Kids need attention. I'm afraid I wouldn't be able to give them enough of my time."

Cole smiles. "Because you want to make partner."

He's been talking to Paula. "Yes, I've worked hard for it. Until Paula came here, she and I had discussed opening our own law firm one day. But now… well, she's chosen to live on a beach." I sit on the top step and he sits next to me.

"So, now, it's make partner or bust?"

"Something like that."

"What about opening a law firm with someone else?"

"I could. But it wouldn't be the same. It was supposed to be me and Paula. We were going to have the name *Grant Law Firm* in big, bold letters on the side of a building in downtown Seattle."

"Instead, you have to work your butt off, so that others can have *their* name plastered on the side of a big building."

"Mine, too, if I make partner."

"What about your personal life?" Cole asks. "When do you make time for that?"

"Someday."

Cole shakes his head. "Seems like people live life backwards. They work hard while they're young, so that when they're old, they can do all the things they'd like to have done when they were young."

"That sounds about right," I agree.

"Doesn't seem like much fun, waiting to be old to live."

We both go quiet for a minute and just listen to the sound of the waves lapping the shore. The water is glistening under the moonlight. The wind is barely blowing and the sea is calm, at peace. So unlike how I feel at the moment.

"I'm sorry," I say at last.

"For what?"

"That I've never wanted to be responsible for raising a child. That I got so worked up about you having a daughter. I wish she and I hadn't met the way we did."

Cole takes my hand. "No need to apologize for who you are. Kids are a lot of work. Like you said, they need time. I'm not sure I do any better than you would. Seems like you understand more than most what it takes to raise them." He chuckles lightly. "My mom could tell you stories that would scare you off motherhood for good."

"But that's just it," I say. "I'm already scared off motherhood. I can't imagine a life filled with the worry and challenge that comes with parenting. I'd probably end up in the court system with all the other poor parents who don't have a clue what to do with their kids." I pause, hesitant to ask. "Do you think your daughter will ever forgive you for letting me wear her clothes?"

"It'll take a while, but she'll get over it. What she may never get over is me making her live on this island. She feels trapped and doesn't much like living with me."

"She can't live with her mom?" I ask. But then I immediately wish I hadn't. I don't want to sound like one of those women who want the man but not his kids. I may not be in love with the idea of being a mother, but if Cole and I were to actually become a real couple, I would never expect him to send his daughter packing. I know how vital it is for a girl to have a father, a man in her life she can look up to and respect. Someone who will stand at the door and give any boy who dates her the evil eye to let him know he expects his little girl to return home happy and in one piece.

"Lacy's mother is dead," Cole tells me.

And don't I have a knack for stepping in it? "I'm sorry. I didn't mean to bring up bad memories."

"You didn't know. I never mentioned Janine's passing. It was a car accident. My marriage was long over when it happened. That's why Lacy is here. I had to force her, but I thought she should at least give island living a chance before I let her go live with her grandparents—Janine's parents. I always wanted Lacy to come and visit—summers, spring breaks—but Janine wouldn't allow it. She thought I'd keep Lacy. And now Lacy blames me for being absent from her life."

"Don't you think she knows you love her and wanted to see her? Didn't you ever go visit her?"

"I went. But it wasn't like I had a home where we could spend real time together. After a while, we became disconnected. And, yeah, I suppose I could tell Lacy about everything that went on between me and her mom, but what good would it do? Tarnishing the memory of her mother isn't how to make her happy living with me."

I admire Cole for keeping his daughter out of the mess that went on between him and his ex-wife, but I hope Lacy at least knows how much she's loved. I rest a hand on his arm. I want him to know I'm here for him. "From what I've heard, being the parent of a teen does get easier."

"When?"

I shake my head. "I'm afraid you'll have to ask someone else about that."

Before we can continue our conversation, a loud groan comes from Paula's room, and I'm off the step in an instant. Cole follows and when we get to Paula, her eyes are hazy with tears.

"It's my leg," she says. "It hurts."

I look and see that the skin on her leg, including her foot, has a bluish tint. Plus, it's swollen. I know immediately what the problem is; her circulation is being cut off by the cast. "We need to get her to the medical center right away," I tell Cole.

Chapter Sixteen

Dr. Dyhr informs us that Paula has developed a blood clot, a deep vein thrombosis, and I can't even wrap my head around it. How did I let this happen? Paula and I were supposed to be having fun, catching up, being crazy, forgetting about everything in our lives that doesn't make sense. Now here she is once again lying in an antiseptic bed, in a place that's too far from home for my liking, and there's nothing I can do about it.

Dr. Dyhr explains everything, saying what he can to reassure us, but I'm barely listening. I'm fighting to keep my tears in check. Paula is not the first person in our family to develop a blood clot. Our grandfather had one. And then he died.

It takes everything I have to keep up a brave front. But I have to. Especially when I go in to see Paula. I don't want her to know how scared I am. If I were to lose her, I think my heart would stop beating.

"Will she be okay?" I ask Dr. Dyhr. "Will she be able to get the help she needs here?" My bottom lip trembles as I speak. I'd feel much better if she were in Seattle's Virginia Mason. I'm sure they could fix her right up.

The good doc takes it in stride that I've just suggested St.

John's medical facility might not be the best place to handle something as serious as a blood clot. "We can help her," he says. His voice is gentle, and he sounds much older and wiser than he looks. He has the kind of bedside manner we all hope for in our physicians, but I wouldn't care if he were the devil himself so long as he could fix my sis.

He continues explaining, while Cole and I nod our heads as though we know exactly what he's talking about. But I still have doubts about Paula being treated here, and my mind is working a plan.

"Would it be better to take her somewhere else? To the mainland?" I ask. Somewhere where all the doctors have a thousand medical certificates and diplomas on their walls to prove, without a doubt, they can damn near play God.

"She should do fine here," Dr. Dyhr reassures me once more. Then he pauses, like he's choosing his words carefully. "Your sister is stubborn. She wants us to let her go home tonight."

I start to protest, but he puts up a hand, stopping me. "No need to worry. I'm not ready to let her leave. She needs to stay put for at least three, four days. We've taken off her cast and replaced it with a soft cast, which will keep her leg immobilized yet still accommodate the swelling. We've also started her on a blood thinner. But until we get the dose right, she'll be our guest."

"So she can come home in a few days?" I ask.

"Barring any complications," Dr. Dyhr says. He squeezes my arm gently. "Let's not worry about something that probably won't happen." He looks at his watch. "I have a few other patients to see before my shift is over. You can go in now and see her. But don't stay too long. She's tired, and she'll need all the rest she can get between blood draws."

I'm cold all over. Shivering cold. I don't know if it's from fear or if the medical center has upped the air conditioning, but I have goose bumps all over my arms, and not only that, but I'm feeling like I might vomit.

"You okay?" Cole asks.

"I'll be fine," I tell him. But I'm not fine. Not only am I afraid for Paula, but I'm awash with anger. I want to scold her and tell her that this is not the time for her to show everyone how independent she is. I'll hog-tie her if I have to, to keep her from doing something stupid. Though the time to hog-tie her would have been when she wanted to swing from that damn tree.

Tug has arrived, and he joins me and Cole as we go through the same double doors that Dr. Dyhr went through. A nurse directs us to Paula's cubicle. She's not even in a room yet, but we find her in good spirits. Plus, she's still breathing. My chills slowly ebb away.

I stand at the foot of her bed, looking over every square inch of her leg. It's propped up on a pillow and is wrapped in a heating pad. None of this seems to bother her in the least. She's busy joking with some young intern, telling him that if he ever decides he doesn't want to work in medicine anymore, she'll hire him to tend bar. I don't think she's aware of the gravity of her situation. Either that or she simply has no intention of taking it seriously. My guess is it's a little of both.

"The bartending job's taken," Tug grumbles. He sits next to Paula and gives the intern a stern look that says he'd better shove off—which he does. Then Tug settles his gaze on Paula. "You aimin' to get rid of me? 'Cause I gotta tell you, I ain't ready to retire yet." His voice is gruff, but his eyes are soft and flanked with concern. He may already have one pinky in the Rest Easy home for seniors, and a wife on the side, but it's clear that Paula owns his heart.

My fears subside the longer I'm with Paula. She looks good, healthy. Not at all in any kind of distress. Soon, the four of us are visiting and talking like we're a group of old friends, catching up on the past. The time goes by quickly. I hear some great stories about Paula's adventures here on St. John, like when she was walking along the beach and a rogue wave came along and toppled her over. When she rose up out of the water, she was sans her bikini top, and Tug was among the onlookers. That's how they met. He gave her his shirt, and it was instant attraction for both of them.

Paula's eyes sparkle as she tells the story, and I can see that Tug owns her heart, as well.

I'm happy for Paula, though I'm not sure our mother will accept him into the family as easily as I have. It might be best if our mother never hear that Tug and my sister were involved while he was still married. That is, if he does indeed ever get divorced. I've learned from experience that it's best to take a wait-and-see approach with life.

Eventually, the nurse assigned to Paula pokes her head inside the cubicle and admonishes me and the men for keeping Paula from getting her rest. Paula scolds us, as well, for slacking off. There's work to be done at The Fish Shack, and if we don't all get back to it, we're fired.

Cole and I laugh, but Tug pulls his keys from his pocket. He hands them to Cole, saying, "Take my truck. I'll be staying a while longer."

On day three of Paula's stay at the medical center, I'm hoping I'll be able to take her home. Visiting her there hasn't been fun for either of us. I saw her as often as possible and even managed to learn my way over all the bumpy roads, so that I could drive myself. And thank God for her pink Mini Moke. It's a girlie car, but it's functional and that's all I cared about.

As soon as I walk into Paula's room, I can tell she's in a mood. I sit on the edge of the bed next to her. "What's wrong?" I ask. She looks healthy, and the swelling in her leg has subsided substantially, so I'm not ready to panic.

"I spoke with Dr. Dyhr. He says I have to stay one more day. He wants to make sure about the blood thinner dose. Plus, now he's telling me I should keep my leg elevated as much as possible for a few weeks—at least."

"Slacker," I say.

Paula doesn't see the humor. She rolls her eyes so far back in her head I'm sure she can see her pillow. "I am so not a slacker."

I cock an eyebrow at her. "Okay. Just kidding."

"You're not taking this seriously," Paula admonishes me.

"I want to, but now that I know you're going to live, I can't help but be happy about it." Though I do intend to check with Dr. Dyhr about Paula's delayed release. I want to make sure she isn't hiding some terrible truth from me.

"If I can't work for a few weeks," she goes on, "I'll have nothing left of my business. The Fish Shack will go under. Everyone will go over to the Duffy's on St. Thomas. They're my biggest competitor."

If it were me, I'd have already started to worry. The Fish Shack is a morgue right now. Though from what Cole has told me, it's simply the calm before the storm.

Paula's face brightens. "I have an idea!"

I'm afraid to ask. Over the years, Paula has had a lot of "ideas," and they don't always include a good time for me.

I don't say anything. I just wait to see if she'll continue. I notice a nice arrangement of flowers, and I lean to smell them. Gardenia, sweetly fragrant.

"They're from Tug," Paula tells me. "So, here's what I'm thinking."

I'm still not asking.

"I know you said you had to get back to work, but now that I'm nearly an invalid, would you reconsider?"

"We talked about this."

"That was before, when I was only on crutches." She continues, "This is now. I need you. And since you tended bar for a while when you were in law school, you probably remember enough that you could help Tug."

"We talked about that, too. Tug won't need help."

"He might."

As much as I'd like to stay and help out, I don't know how I can with all that's going on at B, S, and T. Still, Paula's request is more of a plea. But I need more details. "How long? How long would you need me to stay?" I ask.

"A while," Paula says.

"Define a while."

"Five or six weeks. Maybe. Dr. Dyhr says every patient recovers at their own pace."

I almost choke. "*Six weeks*? You want me to stay here for *six more weeks*? Are you *insane*? If I stay here that long, I might as well stay forever. I'll have no job to go back to."

Paula just stares at me, so I continue my rant. "You've been stuck on this island too long. You're out of touch with reality. I can't take an unplanned, six-week vacation from my job and expect to have it waiting for me when I return."

Paula stays silent.

"Look, there's absolutely no way B, S, and T will understand my needing a sudden, extended vacation. They'd have to completely rearrange my schedule, call all my clients..." I'm thinking out loud more than anything. I chew my lip, wondering about possibilities. There's this fresh-out-of-law-school intern who might be able to fill in for me. Though that could be risky. If she's good, B, S, and T might decide to keep her on... for less pay. That settles it.

"I can't stay," I tell Paula. "Taking six weeks of unplanned time off would be the end of my career at B, S, and T." Not to mention spending six more weeks here with Cole, and then leaving, would be hell of the worst kind. Instead of it being like having a Band-Aid ripped off, it would be more like going through open heart surgery, and I'm not sure my heart could survive an ache of such magnitude.

I see a tear make its way down Paula's cheek, and I feel like a shitty sister. Again. Like I should stop worrying about myself and my job, or how I'm going to keep myself from falling even more in love with Cole. I need to be here for Paula.

"Fine," I say. "I'll stay." B, S, and T wouldn't dare give my office to the intern.

Chapter Seventeen

Before I leave the medical center, I ask to see Dr. Dyhr. He's off making rounds, so I ask the nurse about Paula. She assures me nothing is wrong, that sometimes it takes longer than expected to get the blood thinner dosage right. Which is what Dr. Dyhr told me the day we brought Paula in. So I can relax.

Then I call B, S, and T. They tell me I should stay and be here for my sister. But Mr. Stockwell's tone isn't all that reassuring. I may not have a job when I return. He doesn't come right out and say it, but… life happens. And I don't think he means it as a good thing.

As I leave the medical center parking area, I consider being here on this island another six weeks with Cole. I don't know how I can go that long without telling him how I feel about him, how my heart practically leaps from my chest at the mention of his name. The only reason I haven't yet is because I don't want to complicate things between us… though I'll admit his admission about his feelings for me has made me very happy.

I hadn't planned it, but I take a detour off the main road, which takes me in the direction of the bay, where Cole keeps his boat. He and I have no more secrets. He has a daughter, and he knows how I feel about kids, so we should be able to handle our feelings, now that we both know the situation.

The sky is hot and blue when I arrive at the marina. As I approach the end of the dock, where Cole's boat is moored, I see him kneeling on the deck. He's working and sweating, and all I can think is how good he looks with his bronzed skin glistening under the hot sun. That and sex. The memory of our last time in bed together quickly fills my mind.

When he looks up and sees me, his face lights. He stands, his blue eyes focusing on mine. He kisses me, and I feel unexpectedly and utterly happy, and now I can't even think of a thing to say. I look down and see a box of supplies and the square of sandpaper in his hand. "Boat problems?" I ask.

"Nothing big. Maintenance mostly."

I tuck my hands in the back pockets of my shorts, anything to keep from fidgeting. "I could help if you like."

Cole smiles. "It's a boring chore that I don't much think you'd enjoy." He looks me up and down. "Plus, you're not really dressed for the job. You'd likely need a shower afterwards."

My stomach does a little flip. Another shower together. Then lovemaking. It's becoming a routine with us. I shrug. "I don't mind."

Cole hands me a sheet of sandpaper, and then he points to a small area. He gives me some brief instructions—Boat Repair 101—and then watches me for a minute before going back to his own sanding.

It's not hard at first, and Cole makes it look easy, but it's only a couple of minutes before I begin to really feel it in my arms. My muscles aren't used to this type of work. They're used to pushing a pen around paper.

I force myself to continue sanding, but after only a few minutes more, my muscles are on fire and I'm completely done in. I need to do something about that when I get back home. Join a club maybe. There's one down the street from my condo.

I sit back on my heels to watch Cole work. He doesn't appear to be in any distress at all. I'm not, either. Anymore. In fact, I'm quite happy to sit here and enjoy the view. It's spectacular. I could watch Cole and his muscles work all day long.

I see a cooler at the end of the bench, and I move down and flip the lid. It's full of beer and water and I take a beer and pop the top. It goes down easy in this heat.

Cole continues to sand, and my mind wanders. To Paula, mostly. And to everything that's happened to her since I came to St. John. Somehow, I feel like my coming here has been bad luck for her. I don't know how or why, but it seems like some sort of karma. Like maybe something she did to me in our childhood is coming back to haunt her. Which is ridiculous. I was just as big a pain in her ass when it came to childhood antics.

Cole notices me taking a break and he wanders over. He pulls a beer of his own from the ice chest and uncaps it. He sits with me on the bench and I lean into him. "Have you noticed how Paula has practically become an invalid since I arrived?" I ask.

"Now that you mention it, I guess I have noticed. But accidents happen, darlin'. It's not anyone's fault, and I know Paula wouldn't want to hear you talkin' like that. I don't know about you, but I can think of at least one positive thing that's come of this whole mess."

"What's that?"

He grins. "You'll be sticking around a while longer."

I smile tightly. "Paula told you."

"She did. I saw her last night. I think she's plotting against you… so you probably shouldn't feel too bad about causing her to break her leg."

I laugh and feel somewhat better about my sister's stroke of bad luck.

"You know I'd change places with Paula if I could," Cole continues. "But I don't think that'll be necessary. She's a tough gal. She'll be back to her old self in no time." He smiles gently, and then kisses me, and the warmth of his lips make me want more. But I'm afraid of the hurt that will follow.

"Cole," I say, putting my hands to his chest. I can feel his heartbeat. "I'm not sure this is a good idea."

He pushes his hands into my hair and forces me to look at him. "Aren't we past that stage where you run and I chase and then you let me catch you? I have real feelings for you, Taylor Grant. You don't have to like it, but you need to hear it. And for as long as you're here, I'm going to be in your face." He kisses me again and our lips linger hotly together, after which he continues holding me.

"You're making me cry," I say, my voice thick with emotion.

"Okay, I wouldn't want to ruin your mascara, so let's change the subject." He squeezes one of my arms, like he's testing it for ripeness… or something.

"What are you doing?" I ask.

"I'm wondering why you've already quit sanding."

I scoff. "Sanding is harder than it looks."

Cole laughs, and it sends warm feelings through me. It's so nice to feel happy again.

Bum joins us and sits at Cole's feet. Cole gives him some attention, and he rolls over in doggy pleasure. All is well in his doggy world.

Cole stands and stretches. It's getting late. He looks tired.

I stand, too, ready to leave. "I should be getting back to The Fish Shack."

"I think you should come with me, back to my place."

"Isn't this your home?"

"This is where I work. I have a house a mile or so inland."

"Hmm. Is this another secret you've been keeping?"

Cole laughs. "No secret. It just hasn't come up."

I have to agree. We've been so busy that I guess there hasn't been a reason for him to tell me he has another place he calls home besides this boat. And now I'm eager to see the rest of his world. I leave Paula's Moke at the marina, and I ride with him a short distance to a house so beautiful I think I must be hallucinating. It's large and looks like a hacienda, sitting atop a small hill, up from the beach. And it's got a stunning view. Though I have yet to see any view here that isn't stunning.

Cole takes my hand and doesn't even let me stop to enjoy the scenery. He leads me through a magnificent set of double doors that have horse heads carved into them, and then we stop inside a large foyer, where, to my left is a dining room and on my right, the living room. Straight ahead is a long hallway. Cole continues with my hand in his, and we keep going until we come to a room that has another set of double doors. The master suite, I presume. Cole opens both doors, and I'm not at all surprised when I see a saddle sitting in one corner, next to a big cushy, leather chair, and then a king-size bed that's suspended from the ceiling by thick, tan ropes.

I swallow, feeling nervous and excited at the same time. "Does it swing?" I ask. But what I'm thinking is *Oh my God,* and I can already envision me and Cole lying atop the bed, going at it for all it's worth… until the rope breaks.

I gasp a little and put a hand to my throat.

"You all right?" Cole asks.

"Yes, I guess I'm just… slightly overheated."

Cole grins. "It's the air conditioning. It needs work."

It is *so* not the air conditioning.

Cole reaches behind me and releases the tie that holds my red silk halter top around my neck. I'm still processing the bed when my blouse falls to the floor. Cole takes a moment to gaze at my breasts, and then he fills his hands with them. "Is this okay?" he asks. "I don't want to do anything you're uncomfortable with."

I look down at his hands. "Yet you're already holding my breasts."

"I didn't want to waste any time, in case you gave me the go-ahead."

"Go ahead," I whisper. And as he pushes me onto his bed, I look up to see a fan, in the shape of a wagon wheel, hanging from the ceiling.

Cole sees me looking and tells me, "It helps keep the room cool."

I'm sure.

The bed is not at all what I anticipated. It rocks gently, with only a slight swing… and now I'm wondering what's the point.

But then Cole kisses me and it's the perfect distraction. Kiss after kiss after kiss makes me feel like I'm floating, falling deeper in love with him. I don't ever want this to end. But it will. And that's when the pain begins. No matter how I try to convince myself that I can walk away when the time comes, saying good-bye to Cole is going to hurt like hell.

Why didn't I think ahead to this part? How could I let myself in for this kind of heartache? My emotions get the better of me and I begin to cry.

Cole kisses me again. Kisses my tears. "I'm going to assume your tears are because you're happy," he says.

I smile. "It's something new I'm trying… for sympathy."

"For what?"

"Everything."

Cole laughs and rolls over to pluck a tissue from a box on his nightstand. But something catches his eye—a piece of paper—and his face turns dark as he reads it.

He turns back to me, his jaw tight. "It's Lacy. She's gone. Run away." He gets up immediately and begins to pace, like he's not sure what to do. "There's only one way off this island," he says. "I'm sorry, but I have to go after her."

I get up, too, and I put my blouse back on. I no longer feel the warmth of his touch. It's lost, like it never was. I feel like I should say something… or maybe leave. But I can't because I left Paula's Moke at the marina.

"You can stay here if you want, and wait for me," Cole continues. "Then I'll take you back to get your car." He gestures around the room. "You could read or watch TV—or you could go with me."

My non-mommy gene raises its hackles. I'm not equipped for this. But the way Cole is looking at me… he needs me. "Are you sure? Wouldn't that make things worse?"

Cole holds out his hand to me. "It couldn't get any worse."

The ferry terminal in Cruz Bay is small. There are few places to hide. But it doesn't matter, because Lacy is in plain view. She's sitting sideways on a bench, leaning against a small sports bag with a piece of paper next to her, which, I presume, is a ticket to the mainland. Her hands are folded in her lap, her legs are stretched out, and her eyes are closed. She looks fine, like she has no worries. It's almost as if she didn't think her dad would even bother to come looking for her.

I mentally shake my head. The teenage mind is a mystery to me. I don't know how people do it—raise them without killing them.

I glance at Cole. He doesn't look like he's in a killing mood. He looks hurt. I want to say something that will help, but having no experience in such matters, I can't.

Cole walks over to Lacy and stands silently, facing her, until his presence makes her open her eyes. They look at each other for a long minute, and then he speaks. "Hey, Angel Face."

"Hey, Cole," Lacy responds. Not "Hey, Dad." Her slight makes the muscles in Cole's jaw tense.

"Been here long?" he asks.

"Not so."

His brow softens considerably, concern settling into relief. "You ready to come home?"

Lacy glances at me, then back to her dad. She bites nervously at her lip, and it makes *me* nervous. "I want to go back and live with Gamma and Gamps," she says. And before Cole can respond, she goes on. "It's not like I won't ever see you. I will. School breaks... summers..." She speaks quickly, making her case, like she's practiced it a hundred times, like she's desperate.

Cole waits. He's being polite, allowing her to have her say. Then, when he's sure she's finished, he tells her, "We've talked about this. You live here now."

"But I hate it here," Lacy says. Her voice is raised, and people are beginning to look.

"Stop," Cole says, matching her tone. "I won't keep doing this, coming after you, wondering where you're off to." He picks up her bag, but she jumps from her seat and grabs it back.

"You don't have to wonder. I'll be back in Texas, where I belong!"

Several people are watching now, and I give them a reassuring smile. Though I'm not at all reassured. I feel awkward standing here, witnessing and being a part of something that's so personal between a father and his daughter. They should be alone in a room where they can talk freely, without an audience.

Cole takes the ticket from Lacy's hand. "You're not leaving. This is where you live. And it would be so much easier on both of us if you could give it a try without all this drama." His voice carries, and nearly everyone in the terminal is looking at us.

Lacy's hands are fisted at her sides, like she's ready for battle. I can only imagine how far this domestic squabble will go. It's nothing I haven't seen many times in the court room, child against parent and vice versa, but it rarely ends well for either party. Hurt feelings, and sometimes even worse, come from heated words not held back when silence would be so much better. And though I can't pretend to know anything about parenting, I do know, from my experience as an attorney, that someone needs to step in here. A mediator of sorts.

"Hey," I say softly, touching Cole's arm. "Let me talk to her. I used to be a young girl once." I smile, but my hand is firm. He needs to let me try.

He looks relieved and, surprisingly, steps away.

Lacy glowers at me, but she follows, and we go around the corner, out of her dad's view. I'm happy that she's showing a willingness to talk with me, so I intend to use the time wisely. I shoot the remaining onlookers a glance. I don't need the prying eyes. Thankfully, most have gotten bored with the parent-teen ordeal and are busy again with their magazines or cell phones.

"He's an asshole," Lacy starts right in.

I draw back. It's hard to imagine her being an "angel face" right now. She's in a fighting mood that's pretty ugly. "That may be," I admit. "I can't say yet."

"Seems to me if a woman sleeps with a man, she should at

least know that much," Lacy comments. Her anger is as much directed at me as it was at Cole a minute ago, and she has a point, but I'm not about to discuss my sleeping with her father. Nor am I about to back down.

"I may not know your dad all that well, but I've known a lot of men, some of them really bad, and I have to say, your dad doesn't seem like one of the bad guys." I smile a little smile, feeling clumsy and out of place. I can see in her eyes that I'm failing miserably. But I'm not ready to give up. "He's just a big, dumb boy," I continue, trying to lighten our conversation. "Can't you give him a chance?" I dare to touch her shoulder, and it's no surprise when she moves away.

"My relationship with my dad is none of your business." She glares at me for a minute. "I still haven't gotten the stink out of my clothes that you borrowed."

"Sorry about that. It might take a couple of washes."

Lacy stares at me for another minute, like she's trying to figure me out. Eventually, she looks away. "Whatever."

Whatever. Teen speak for *I'm done listening, now leave me alone.*

"Look, all he wants is to be your dad."

Lacy's mouth twists with a mix of anger and fear. "I can't stay here," she tells me.

"Why not?"

"Because." She looks at me, her eyes hazy with tears. Her hands are shaking. "I'm pregnant. And when my dad finds out, he's going to kill me. And then he'll kill my baby's daddy."

Pregnant? Dear God. This is so not how I expected to spend my vacation. I shouldn't even be here. I should be back home in Seattle, sitting at my desk, in my own little miserable world. Not here, where the deceit of blue skies makes all seem well. All is not well. A half hour ago, Cole and I were lying on his bed, and it was all happy, happy, swingy, swingy. Now… this.

I shove a hand to my forehead. I feel dizzy. If ever I needed something to hold on to, it's now. Cole is going to be a grandfather. A *grandfather.* And here I thought my life was in the crapper. Ha! My life is all butterflies and moonbeams compared to this.

"You don't look so good," Lacy tells me.

"I think I'm going to be sick."

"Maybe you're pregnant, too."

"What? No!" I give my head a vigorous shake and swallow hard as a cold layer of sweat forms at the back of my neck.

Lacy waits a minute, then asks, "Are you going to tell my dad?"

Pressure… pain… like someone is driving an arrow through my brain.

"Well?" Lacy presses me. Her eyes are liquid. She's even pulled a tissue from her pocket.

Hell. *Hell.*

"I'll stay quiet, for the time being," I say. "But you need to tell him." As the words leave my mouth, it's like I've waved a magic wand. The haze clears from Lacy's eyes, and the corners of her mouth lift. It's like she was just waiting for me to give her the go-ahead. I feel like such a sap. I've been worked by a teenager. Which more than confirms I should never have kids. They'd run roughshod over me.

Cole pokes his head around the corner. "Everything okay?" he asks.

Both Lacy and I jump, like we've been caught committing a crime. We give each other a look, and Lacy's eyes once again plead for my silence.

"Everything is fine," I tell Cole. "Lacy has decided to go back home with you." I give Lacy a smile, letting her know she owes me big time. "Isn't that right, Lacy?"

"Yeah, right," she says sharply. I don't think she wants to test me yet.

Chapter Eighteen

Paula is home and I'm happy. But now that I'm going to be here awhile, I have to push the rush of Seattle living to the back of my mind and settle into a routine. Which I do. First thing each morning, after my shower, I busy myself with chores. There are always tables that need wiping down, Tiki torches to be filled, and sand and debris that needs to be swept from the front steps. After that, I'm free to walk the beach to let the warm ocean breeze finish drying my hair. I haven't used a blow dryer once since I got here, and my hair, once straight and polished, is now full of free-flowing waves. I've grown to like it, but I doubt it will work in Seattle. Not in my job. I need to be polished and professional. We're not the granola types everyone thinks we are. I'd even go so far as to suggest we've joined civilization. We have Neiman Marcus, Tiffany's, and Gucci. We have it all. Including an ever increasing population that makes me glad I'm here at the moment.

But now it seems The Fish Shack is getting busier every day. Tourists have begun to arrive in swarms, just like Paula warned me they would. But I don't mind it so much and when I have time, I sit with them and make small talk. It's a nice change of pace from my life in Seattle, which has every hour taken up by scheduled meetings and appointments. But here, I just take things as they come. Plus, I get to meet some great and interesting people, such as Darlene and Carlene, twins who've come to St. John to celebrate their twenty-first birthday. Then there's Thomas and Colleen, who are here to celebrate thirty years of the old ball and chain. Plus, so many others. But my favorite couple so far is Carter and Bailey Davis. They're here on their honeymoon from Las Vegas, and they stop in every morning on their way down the beach. Carter sings, does a great impression of the late Elvis Presley, and it's always a lively time when he shows up. He's every woman's dream, and all I have to say beyond that is, "You go, Bailey." She's one lucky woman.

But I have no reason to be envious of anyone. Cole is every bit the prize. Though I am constantly aware of the monumental secret I'm keeping from him, which could very well be the end of us. I don't believe a relationship can be built on lies. Or secrets. But I guess there's one thing I won't have to worry about. When all hell breaks loose and he kicks me out of his life, I won't be running into him at my local Starbucks. In fact, I haven't seen him but once since we found Lacy at the ferry terminal. He's been booked solid, taking couples out on his sailboat. Even so, every time I hear a Jeep pull up out back, I hold my breath, thinking it might be him coming to tell me how he wants nothing more to do with me. It's what I deserve for keeping Lacy's secret, but there's not much I can do about that now.

For the third day in a row, my mood is much like a typical Seattle winter day. Dreary. Cold. Bleak. I could use a soothing touch, so I go to Ella Su's door, thinking I can check her schedule to see if she might have an opening. I haven't seen her yet, but it's still early, so I don't even knock. I just push open the door and *surprise*! Not only is Ella Su already here, but she's got a naked client on her table.

"Oh, I am so sorry," I say, and I start to close the door. But Ella Su calls me back.

"It okay," she says. "This is Karyn, with y. She need

emergency massage for bad case of jitters. She getting married tonight to man she sleep with after she get drunk at office party. After wedding, everybody come back here to get drunk and happy."

Karyn with a y flutters her hand in a hello gesture. She doesn't seem at all put off that Ella Su has informed me about her office affair. I think it's possible that Karyn with a y has already begun working on getting drunk and happy.

I leave Ella Su with her client, and I stand with my back to the door remembering that I was told about this. I knew there was a wedding reception here tonight. I was supposed to hire a band. I forgot.

When I tell Paula, she's very accommodating. "It's okay," she says. "There's always karaoke."

Karaoke! What a great idea! Mostly because it gets me off the hook.

After a full day of preparation, I'm eager for the festivities to begin. But I'm also exhausted after decorating and making sure every dish in the place is clean. With people arriving soon, I need some alone time. I step outside, but I'm out on the front steps only a minute when I hear a commotion coming from Ella Su's room. I poke my head back inside just in time to see her door swing open and a man with only a towel around his waist and a dozen hairs atop his head appear. I've seen him before, but I've no idea who he is. Everyone gives him a glance and then looks away, like he's part of the atmosphere. He has to be a local.

"You must be Taylor," he says when he sees me. But Ella Su is quick to show her face, and she curses a red streak in Taiwanese—I think—as she swings a towel at the odd little man. Her dark eyes look like they could spit fire.

"*Out!*" she shouts as she snaps the towel at the man's back. But he's already scooted out of her reach and is headed for the door.

"Is there a problem?" I ask Ella Su, only half thinking I might actually need to step in to help.

Ella Su turns to me. "That nasty man. He push the towel to the floor on purpose. Next time I show him what happens to his nasty penis. I put hot rocks on it." Then back she goes into her massage parlor.

I have no idea what to think, but when I check in with Paula once more, I bring up the subject of Ella Su and the little bald man.

She laughs. "That would be Hector Clay. He's got a thing for Ella Su. Everyone knows it, and so does she, but she likes to pretend she doesn't. She claims he has a nasty penis." Paula shakes her head. "If you ask me, she shouldn't be so choosy. There isn't a lot of prime male flesh here on St. John."

I would agree but for the cowboys.

Guests begin to arrive, and some of them—two men and one woman—do not seem at all interested in waiting to begin celebrating the occasion. They park themselves at the bar, and the men commence playing a game of horse, using olives for basketballs and the woman's cleavage for a hoop. They try to get me to join in, but as much as I enjoy the idea of having my breasts smell like martini garnish, I politely pass.

An hour later, The Fish Shack is at capacity, and everyone is well on their way to that crazy place where people go when they've had too much to drink. And Tug, with his heavy-handed pouring, isn't helping matters any. Myself, I still don't think the shark on the wall is funny, and I'm worried someone might wander out front and become shark bait.

Another hour and, finally, Tug turns off the overhead speakers and sets up the karaoke machine. Everyone seems eager to participate. I've been hoping to see Cole, but so far, he hasn't showed, so I claim a barstool next to a man who's been nursing a beer for the last half hour. I have a great view of the room, and I'm eager to see all the fun. Paula is prone with leg up, per doctor's orders, over in one corner.

The newlyweds go first. They pick out something by Faith Hill and hubbie, Tim McGraw, and their singing is so bad the best man and maid of honor are booing and throwing pineapple chunks at them by the end of the first chorus. The groom responds with an enthusiastic hand gesture, and everyone laughs. It's good times all around.

Next up is a guy in khaki shorts and a brightly colored Hawaiian shirt—no reason to put on your Sunday best for a beach wedding, right? He chooses a silly song called "Lime in the Coconut," which turns out to be a huge hit. And when he's done, everyone cheers for more, but I don't see that happening. Khaki shorts guy is done. I watch as he stumbles back into the crowd and heads for the open front, where I keep an eye on him until I see him climb into one of the hammocks. He immediately stops moving, and I make a mental note to check on him later, to see if he's still breathing.

Singer after singer croons to the tunes, most of which are pretty awful, but then comes a woman with flowers in her hair. She can barely walk, let alone stand, so she camps on the floor and someone hands her the microphone. A couple of false starts later, she finally gets going, belting out Shania Twain's "Any Man Of Mine" like she's an honest-to-goodness country star. It's crazy and good and everyone goes wild. But then, without warning, she falls over backward and it's song over. I don't think she's dead, but she may wish she was in the morning.

The festivities go on without her. The singing continues, the drinking continues, and I keep hoping Cole will show up. The longer he stays away, the more anxious I become. Each hour that passes, I'm more and more convinced Lacy has told him everything, and now he doesn't want to ever see me again.

Dammit, I should never have agreed to keep Lacy's secret.

But as afraid as I am of the outcome, I try to believe that Cole cares enough for me that this thing with Lacy won't be the end of us. It can't be. We love each other... don't we? Neither of us has come out and said it, but I think we're both aware the feelings are there.

The party winds down around midnight, and just when I think we've served our last drink, The Fish Shack comes alive again with at least two dozen men and a handful of native beauties who have all come over from St. Thomas for a different experience than what they get on the bigger island. The men are construction workers, looking for a good time, and the women are here to provide them their pleasure. Pleasure is allowed here on St. John, or so I'm told.

Tired as I am, I keep my eye on everyone. Some of the men look like they might be in the mood for trouble, and with as much alcohol as they're consuming, I'd be surprised if they didn't find some. I guess that's where Tug would step in.

For the most part, everyone is on their best behavior. The men are ogling the women, and the women are ogling them back. My only complaint is the place reeks of beer and sweat and perfume, and I'm ready for the evening to be over. But then the back door swings open and a guy who looks to be more boy than man walks in. He angles his way to the bar, looking shifty the way he keeps his head down, almost like he's trying not to be seen, so I keep him in my sights.

My lawyer antenna is up. I'm sure this guy is too young to frequent a bar. But then things are different here. Maybe he's not too young. And maybe I need to stop being an attorney and let things be. Drinking and letting loose is part of the island experience, and I don't want to do anything that will give Paula's place the reputation of being St. John's most not-fun place to party.

I turn my focus back to the island women and the construction workers. One table in particular catches my attention. Three men seem to be vying for one woman's affections. She's an exotic-looking creature with long black hair and a lot of curves that back in Seattle would be considered zaftig. Too heavy for most men's taste, but here, she's the cream of the crop, and it doesn't surprise me when she and one of the men disappear out the back door.

I'm a million miles away from the city, but when it comes to the man-woman thing, some things never change. Sex is sex, and at any given time, several million people are doing it somewhere in the world.

Sex.

Cole.

I miss him so much I can hardly think about anything else, and I vow, the next time he and I are together, we'll stay in bed all day long and make love until I'm too sore to walk.

But for now I'm back to watching the young man. A girl has joined him, and they're real cozy, with their heads pressed together and their chairs as tight as they can possibly be. I can only see the back of the girl's head, but she's blond, and something about her makes me uneasy.

I continue to watch and wait for the girl to turn so I can see her face. When she finally does, I'm sick. It's Lacy.

In a bar and *pregnant*? What could she be thinking?

I see red as I push my way through the crowd. When I reach her, I ask, "What are you doing here?" I get an eye roll in response, so I take her by the arm and usher her toward the back door. The young man doesn't follow.

I get Lacy outside, away from the smoke and toxins. Heavy wind blows stiffly in our faces, like a fan that's turned on high. I have to shout to be heard, which is fine with me. I'm in a shouting mood. "Wait right here," I say, and then I go back inside.

I face the young man head on. I grab his keys from the bar and shake them in his face. "That girl out there is only fifteen years old. You could be charged with statutory rape, as well as contributing to the delinquency of a minor." I'm only guessing, as I have no idea what the laws here in St. John are, but it sounds more than reasonable to me.

I stare at him for a minute, and he stares back. Finally, his lips spread into a sneer, and he pops off the barstool so that we're standing chest to chest. I estimate his height at a couple of inches taller than me, and his weight probably tips the scale at a good one-seventy. Which isn't all that big. Hell, I've been around men who weigh three-hundred-plus and have murdered people. This guy is nothing but a gnat. But that doesn't mean I'm going to be stupid. He could be a monster with a kid's face. I need to be careful.

"Who are you to tell me who I can or can't see?" he asks. His eyes are cold and I'll admit it puts me off. But the truth is, I've learned to be good at bluffing, and I don't back down.

Tug steps over to where we are. "Easy, boy. Show a little respect for your elders," he says from behind the bar. He gives me a reassuring nod.

The boy's mouth twists into an even nastier sneer, but he heads for the door, like he's had enough. I follow him to make sure he doesn't take Lacy with him, though by the time I push through the door, he's gone and his taillights are a blur in a haze of dirt and dark.

Little turd.

I turn on Lacy. "What are you doing with someone like that? And here? You're pregnant and a minor. You should be home in bed, not here with some jerk who doesn't give a damn about you."

Lacy steps back to put some distance between us. Her eyes are burning, and I can tell she and I are about to get into it. "Get away from me. You're not my mom. It's none of your business what I do. You can't even touch me." She gives me a smug smile. "I could have you arrested if you do."

Silly child! Does she really think she can intimidate me with threats? "And I could tell your dad that he's about to become a grandfather," I shoot back.

Lacy raises her chin. "You wouldn't dare."

"Wouldn't I?"

It's a standoff. Neither one of us is willing to back down. We're looking into each other's eyes and the seconds are ticking off and I'm beginning to think I've lost this battle. But when I see her flinch—just a blink, and then tears form in the corners of her eyes—it's enough to let me know I have the edge. Only now I feel like I'm playing the role of wicked stepmother, and I don't think I like it very much. If—and this is so farfetched I don't even know why I'm considering it—Cole and I were to get married, I'd hate for Lacy and me to get off to a bad start. She doesn't have to love me, but if she could at least tolerate me, that would be nice. I would never want Cole to feel like he had to choose sides.

My mouth softens into a weak smile. I don't want to lose the ground I've gained, but I'd like for her to feel I am friend. "Look," I say, "I'm only concerned for your baby. You don't want to do anything to hurt your child, do you? And what about the father? How would he feel if he knew you were out with another man?" Then I'm hit with a thought. "That guy"—I nod in the direction of the jungle—"he's not the father of your baby, is he?"

Lacy shakes her head. She places a hand over her belly. Her eyes are wet, her anger gone. "I love him. And I miss him. And I just want to go back home, so he and I can be together."

Mixed feelings push through my own stubbornness, and I gather her to my chest. She needs someone, and right now, God help her, she's stuck with me.

"You have to tell your dad," I say.

Lacy is quiet for a moment. But then she stiffens and pulls her emotions back to a place deep inside, where no one can touch them. "I can't. You don't have a clue what's going on with me and my dad. He wouldn't listen. He'd just be angry."

I feel as though I've lost the advantage and now I'm back to step one. I have no idea how to proceed from here.

I think back to my own teen years, back to a time when I had been out with a friend and we got caught stealing from the local mini-mart. My mom had to pick me up from the police station. But that wasn't the worst part of that day. It was the look on my mom's face. She was disappointed, and it haunted me for weeks. I never wanted to see that look again. A beating or being grounded would have hurt less.

I stare at a palm frond. It's fluttering, free and easy in the warm wind, which is so not me right now. St. John may not have busy streets and crowded sidewalks, but the people here still have problems, and I'm one of those people. If I weren't an attorney, if I didn't care so much for Cole, I'd go to him and tell him about Lacy. But Lacy's pregnancy is a private family matter, something shared with others only if Cole wants it shared. I need to give his daughter time and hope that she comes to a decision we can all live with. So much for me thinking I should never have agreed to keep her secret. But maybe I can minimize the damage.

"I'll give you a week. One," I tell her. "And then you have to tell your dad. Plus, you have to promise me you won't touch a drop of alcohol while you're pregnant." I shake a finger at her, the same as my mother used to do to me when she meant business.

Lacy nods, but it means nothing. I've nodded plenty of times just to shut my own mother up. I'm about to repeat myself, but then Greenbeans appears. He's done for the night and is ready to go home.

"Evenin', ladies," he says. He looks at me, then at Lacy, and he seems to know he's just missed the shit hitting the fan. "Need a ride home, young lady?" he asks Lacy.

"That's a great idea," I say, and I'm so thankful I could hug him. "One week," I mouth to Lacy as she follows Greenbeans to his truck.

Chapter Nineteen

The following morning, I finally see Cole and he looks rested and happy. I'm relieved when he talks with me for a minute, and then kisses me like he hasn't seen me for a lifetime. Then he's off to the bedroom to see Paula. A few minutes later, he reappears and he has Paula in his arms. He takes her out to the beach and sits her at the water's edge. This is usually Tug's job, but The Fish Shack is beyond busy this morning, so Cole steps in to do what he can to help. I'm just happy my concern about Lacy is over. And in one week, her secret will be out in the open. Cole will know everything.

I watch him on the beach, sitting close to Paula. If one didn't know better, they might think Cole and Paula were sweethearts. Paula is splashing her one good foot in the water, and Cole is looking out at forever. I wonder what he's thinking about. Me, perhaps? Or maybe not. Maybe he's just enjoying the beach. He never seems to tire of it. Bum is out there with them, too, splashing in the surf and chasing waves. I'm envious. I want more than a few words and a kiss. Though I should be glad for that much.

I never thought I'd feel this way, but I've become jealous of the life Paula has here. She lives on this beach without a care in the world, while I have so many cares that sometimes I think they may very well drag me down and drown me. I need to find a way to change that. One way that instantly comes to mind is to never agree to keep a secret from any man I'm falling in love with.

Several minutes pass, and I need more time with Cole. Plus, I need to remind Paula that she's supposed to keep her leg elevated. I step out onto the porch and call to her and Cole, but neither of them hear me, so I step down to the sand, and as I approach, I can hear them talking. About me. I heard Paula mention my name, and what she's saying must be amusing because Cole lets out a hearty laugh. She looks over her shoulder and sees me, and then she goes silent. I can only imagine the tales she's been sharing.

"Tug has made us all something cold to drink," I say, pretending to be oblivious to her gossiping about me.

Cole helps Paula to her feet and then swings her back into his arms, which is exactly where I'd like to be right now. But that can come later.

When we're back inside, Tug has a table prepared for us with snacks and our drinks. It's beer for Cole, something fruity with a kick for me, and something nonalcoholic for Paula. Paula narrows her eyes and takes one sip from her glass before she wrinkles her nose. "This isn't a *drink*," she says. She looks over at my glass. "I want one of those." She reaches, like she's about to give mine the taste test, but Tug stops her.

"Two words," he says. "Pain pills. You won't be mixing them with alcohol while I'm around."

Paula gives him an icy glare, which he returns, and both Cole and I stifle a laugh. I no longer have any doubt about Tug. He loves my sister. He'll take good care of her when I'm gone… whether she likes it or not.

After Cole and I finish our drinks, it's the moment I've been waiting for—alone time. We head out to the hammocks and choose the blue double-wide that will accommodate both of us. I have a warm buzz going from the drink Tug concocted for me, and I'm eager to be close to Cole, this man who has me feeling so surprisingly in love.

He and I board the hammock and lie quietly for a few minutes, enjoying the simplicity of our time together. I have my head resting on his chest and I'm smiling so big my face feels stretched. Cole can't see how happy I am. That I am truly and completely happy.

I close my eyes and let my mind drift once again to the impossible. Only now, nothing seems impossible. A lot of people manage long-distance relationships. Why not Cole and me?

As I begin to envision life with Cole, I hear his breathing change. I think he's drifting off. I might too, I'm so comfortable here next to him. I tuck myself tighter to his side, ready for a long stay. Then a voice comes from the side of the hammock.

"Can we talk?" the voice says. I know who it is—Lacy. I consider pretending to be asleep, that I don't hear her, but she probably has something important to say or she wouldn't be here.

I open my eyes, and Cole raises his head, though he looks like he isn't sure what's going on. "Lacy, honey," he says. "Do you need something?"

"I want to talk," Lacy tells him.

"Can it wait?" he asks.

Lacy blows out a huff of teen disapproval. "No."

"All right then, I'll meet you up at the Jeep in a minute," he tells her.

"Not *you*," she says, sighing in that exasperated way teens do when we adults don't seem to get it. "*Her.* Your *girl*friend."

Cole's brow furrows as he looks over at me. I'm sure he's thinking the same thing I am. What the hell is going on?

"Lacy, if you have something to say to Taylor, maybe—"

"It's okay. I don't mind," I say. And as I slip off the hammock, I whisper to him, "Don't worry, I'm tougher than I look."

Lacy and I head down the beach leaving Cole, I'm sure, with plenty of questions. I look back and smile to let him know I'm really okay with his daughter wanting to talk with me. But who

149

knows how this will turn out. I can only guess the topic of conversation.

Lacy gives me a wide berth as we walk, which doesn't give me a lot of confidence. Her body language suggests she'd like me to keep my distance. Which is fine. I don't intend to push myself on her. I know it's a stretch that she and I will ever be friends. There isn't enough time for her and me to get to know each other, or for us to build any kind of relationship.

It's sad that Lacy lost her mother at such a young age. I can't imagine not having a mom, and I think maybe she doesn't know how to deal with it. So she shows anger. Toward her dad—especially her dad—but toward others, too. She isn't so different from all the other teens I've seen who come through the court system. She feels the world has done her wrong, and she wants everyone to know it. She wants to keep everyone at arm's length, so that no one else can hurt her. The problem is, she's so busy trying to keep herself safe that it's hard for others to show they care. And sometimes, they just plain give up.

I'm not ready to give up on Lacy. I care about her. She matters to me. If she needs to talk, I'm willing to listen.

"I'm sorry you keep finding your dad and me together like that," I tell her, though I'm not sure I *need* to apologize. Cole and I are adults, after all.

Lacy waves a hand. "Yeah, whatever. I couldn't care less what you and my dad do."

I glance over my shoulder and see Cole walking back up to The Fish Shack. Bum is trotting by his side. "Okay, so what did you want to talk about?"

Lacy looks over at me through thick lashes. She's a pretty girl. Youthful glow. Blond, silky hair. Big eyes. Poor Cole. Every man on this island will be after her one day. Though I suppose her condition might keep them at bay for a short while.

"I think something might be wrong with my baby," she tells me. Her voice is tight, and she's speaking so low I have to get closer to hear her over the surf.

"What do you mean?" I ask.

"I've been having pain."

"What kind of pain?" I'm alarmed and I'm sure it shows on my face.

Lacy looks away, like she's uncomfortable talking about this with me. "Cramps," she says at last. "Not real bad. But I was wondering if it means I'm going to have a miscarriage."

My heart thumps. I'm all but a stranger to her, and here she is asking me such an important question, which I'm not sure I'm qualified to answer. I've never been pregnant, and I've only had one friend who's had a baby. She had some pain, but everything turned out fine. "I'm not sure," I say. "Is there anything else going on besides the pain?"

Lacy shakes her head.

I'm not encouraged. If she were to have a miscarriage, Cole would never forgive me for keeping this from him. *I'd* never forgive me. "Lacy, honey, I know you're afraid, but your dad needs to know about this."

"No! No way!" Lacy backs away from me. "If you tell him, I swear I'll run away. He'll never see me again. I trusted you! You can't tell him anything!"

"He can get you help if you need it," I say, trying to reason with her. But she keeps backing up, her arms tight at her sides. Finally, she turns around and runs back down the beach. I call to her, but she keeps running.

Great. That went well. What now? What am I supposed to tell Cole? That his daughter wanted some fashion advice?

When I get back to The Fish Shack, Cole and Lacy are gone. Most of the customers are gone, too, and Tug is serving up drinks to a couple of locals. Paula is at the end of the bar, looking over some papers. She's supposed to be lying down, but I'm not in the mood to nag.

"Did Cole say anything before he left?" I ask anyone who might be listening.

"*Adios, amigo,*" Tug answers.

Paula gives Tug a hard look. It's likely she hasn't gotten over his no-drinking-while-on-drugs policy. "He said to tell you he'd see you later," Paula tells me. "What was all the drama with Lacy? She blew in here like a hurricane and told Cole she wanted him to take her home, pronto."

"That's it?"

"A smart man knows not to argue with an angry woman," Tug says as he wipes a spill off the counter. He tosses the dish towel into the sink and makes his way down to the other end of the bar to take an order from another customer who has come in off the beach.

"What was Lacy so angry about?" Paula asks.

"She's a teen. Everything," I say. I sit on one of the barstools, feeling defeated, not having a clue what I should do. I really need to speak with Cole. I can't just sit back and go about business as usual when Lacy could be in the middle of a crisis. But maybe she's telling him what's going on this very minute. I should give them some time.

By mid-afternoon, I haven't heard anything from Cole, and I'm practically going crazy. I suspect Lacy has told him nothing.

I look around The Fish Shack. It's all but empty, which isn't helping one bit. At least if I were busy, I wouldn't keep imagining the worst.

Paula has gone back to her room, and it's been quiet with her, too. I look in on her and she's asleep. I could leave. Tug doesn't need any help, and Paula will be fine without me sitting at her side. This might be my one and only opportunity to talk with Cole before all hell breaks loose.

"I'll be back in a while," I tell Tug as I head out. He tosses me a wave.

I don't know whether I should go to the marina or Cole's house, but I'm not entirely sure how to find his house again, so I drive to the marina and when I arrive, he's standing on the deck of his boat holding an armful of rope…and he's naked from the waist up. Okay, so maybe all hell isn't about to break loose.

I'm always in awe when I see Cole naked. He's exactly the type of man you might imagine in a calendar of hot men. He could pull off an entire calendar himself. Plenty of muscle to get a woman's imagination going about what he might have hiding inside his jeans, and a face that can melt even a frigid woman's heart. But I'm not here to satisfy my lustful desires. I need to stay focused.

Cole drops the rope as I approach. "Sorry I had to leave so abruptly," he says. "Lacy was in such a state when she came in off the beach that I thought I should get her out of there." He chuckles. "Teenagers are a confusing bunch."

He has no idea.

He helps me onto the boat deck, squeezing my hand firmly as he pulls me toward him. We're face-to-face and I'm tucked tight against him. It would be easy to forget why I'm here, with him holding me like this, but I can't take the chance when Lacy might need help.

"Is she all right?" I ask.

He shrugs. "Right as a teenager can be, I guess. Did she give you a hard time? I didn't ask what the two of you talked about. I thought if she wanted me to know, she'd have said. I've learned that if I want to keep the peace, I need to give her a measure of privacy."

My mouth is dry as I contemplate how much information I should give him. Should I tell him everything, or should I keep my promise to Lacy? I'm worried about her. If only I could see her to make sure she's okay. "Is Lacy here with you?" My mind has gone to the worst possible place. I am so not prepared to be a parent.

"I took her home. Is there a problem?"

"I feel bad about what happened on the beach. I think she hates me."

"She hates everybody these days. She wants to go home, back to Texas, and I won't let her. That makes me enemy number one." He's quiet for a beat. "Seeing me with you likely makes her think I'm trying to replace her ma." He shakes his head. "I'm not. It's just time I get on with my life."

"It's hard, I'm sure, for her to see us together. It hasn't been the best of circumstances."

He laughs a quiet laugh. "She'll eventually have to allow me to start dating. But finding you naked on my boat, and then today, us in the hammock together probably didn't help."

I feel a flush of warmth remembering how he and I spent our time in bed the other day on his boat. Thank God Lacy didn't show up and find that scenario. And I don't blame her for being upset about me wearing her clothes. But today, in the hammock with Cole was innocent. It wasn't like we were making out or doing anything distasteful. "She was so upset when she ran off down the beach," I say. "Maybe we should go check on her."

"Why? I don't think you need to be worried. Her feathers were ruffled, but we talked some once we got back home, and she calmed down and said she felt better. When I left her, she was in her room. Sometimes it's better to leave her be."

I'm on the verge of panicking, not sure what to do. I know if Cole thought something was wrong, he wouldn't be here at the marina. Maybe I'm overreacting.

"You're sure?" I ask.

"Absolutely." Cole pulls me close and changes the subject by way of gesturing toward the open water. "It's about as perfect as a day can get for sailing." He tucks a strand of my hair behind my ear and kisses me on my forehead. "You interested?"

I smile up at him, feeling like this is how life should be. Simple. No worries. Just sailing on the water of life. "Very," I tell him.

Cole pats me once, twice on my butt and tells me to relax on the bench while he gets the boat ready. I do as I'm told, managing somehow to stop worrying about Lacy, but then my thoughts go straight to B, S, and T. I wonder how things are going… wonder if I still have a job. If not, then what? I could go to work for another firm. There are a lot of law firms in Seattle. Or I could stay here.

I could stay here.

With Cole.

My stomach does a little flip. The idea is crazy, but I think I could really see myself becoming an island girl. I might even wear flowers in my hair once in a while.

Cole maneuvers *Destiny* away from the marina, and when we're out where he doesn't have to do anything more, he comes over to the bench and settles next to me.

"Did you know it used to be bad luck for a woman to board a ship?" he asks.

"Why is that?" I'm honestly curious.

"They were considered a dangerous distraction."

"Mmm. Do I distract you?"

"Only every time I look at you."

I know the feeling. It's the same for me when I look at him. Especially when he's not wearing a shirt.

"I hope you have sunscreen. You could get sunburned," he tells me.

"I didn't think to bring any."

Cole grins. "What do you think we should do about that?"

I consider his question for a brief second. I know, by the twinkle in his eyes, what he's getting at. "Maybe we should get out of the sun."

"I agree," Cole says and he pulls me from the bench. I don't resist one bit, just follow along as he leads the way down to the cabin. Before we're even to the bedroom, he's removing my clothes, and by the time we reach his bed, every bit of stress I'd been feeling over the situation with Lacy has melted away.

"I'm falling in love with you, Taylor Grant," Cole tells me as he begins making love to me, and it's so unexpected that I can't find words to respond. I just take a breath, hoping that this is not just a dream. It can't be, not with the feelings I've allowed myself.

"Did I say something wrong?" he asks.

"No." My voice is barely a whisper. What Cole and I have feels right and perfect, like he and I are meant to be. And, somehow, I've managed to convince myself that this can really happen, that no matter what, we'll get through it. But when he finds out about Lacy, what we have may very well come to an abrupt end.

"Want to talk about it?" Cole asks when I stay quiet.

I shake my head, afraid to speak. I might give in and tell him everything.

"I'm a good listener," he says.

My chest is so tight I can barely breathe. "Just make love to me," I whisper.

It's a request that Cole gladly obliges, and as his tenderness fills me, I feel somewhat healed, like maybe I don't need to worry that he'll stop loving me when he finds out about Lacy. That he'll understand, and then he and I will go on as if nothing has happened. Though I think that might just be wishful thinking.

By the time we get back to the marina, the sun is going down, and I'm weary from the run of emotions I've been through. But then Cole checks his messages and Toby has left a text, asking if Cole and I would like to come for dinner. He has something important he wants to share.

Chapter Twenty

Ariel is at Toby's when Cole and I arrive. She's an exotic-looking woman with long, straight black hair that hangs nearly to her waist, and her nose is pierced with a tiny diamond that makes her look as though she has a shining star on her face. She seems older than Toby, mostly in manner, but she's so stunning that it's not hard to imagine any man taking more than a decent glance in her direction.

After a few minutes of introductory talk, Ariel takes me into the kitchen with her so that we can continue to visit while she finishes preparing dinner. We're having fruit salad, steamed Chilean bass, and roasted potatoes… and the smell is killing me. After spending the afternoon making love with Cole, I feel like I could eat an entire boatload of fish.

Ariel asks me to set a small wood table that's sitting over in one corner, and I begin by spreading a tablecloth that's been finely embroidered in seascape colors of turquoise, royal blue, and mossy green. Then I finish with white place settings. It's all very cool and Caribbean, and I vow to spend more time on the beach when I get back home, though Seattle and surrounding area beaches can in no way compare to beach life here. Alki is a favorite hangout, but you have to fight traffic to get there, and then fight again for a parking spot.

As a final touch, Ariel lights a couple of candles, which she tells me are more for insurance purposes, in case the lights go out, and then she uncorks a bottle of white wine. Then we're ready for the men. I call them to the kitchen, and Toby ignores the wine and, instead, grabs a can of Coors Light from the refrigerator. "Been tryin' to cut down on calories," he says, patting the swell above his belt.

Cole joins him, though I doubt he's counting calories. A couple of hours ago, he was lying naked on top of me, and I felt not one extra ounce of flesh anywhere.

Both men take a seat at the table, but Ariel remains standing. So do I. Ariel looks from Toby to Cole and back. It takes them a moment, but then they get it, and they're on their feet in an instant, waiting for me and Ariel to sit.

I spread my napkin on my lap, feeling so at home it's like I've always been here. I look around the table and am filled with a quiet contentment as we all fill our plates. After the four of us settle, ready to eat, Toby begins the dinner conversation. "I know we didn't have much time to get acquainted last time you were here, what with Sophie giving birth and all, but I hear tell you're an attorney," he says to me.

"I am," I say.

"It's always handy to have an attorney in the family. I might even have a question or two for you."

"Oh. Okay," I say. Though I can't imagine what kind of question a cowboy might need answered on a Caribbean island by a Seattle attorney. I don't even have legal privileges here.

"She's on vacation," Cole reminds Toby.

"It's okay," I say. "I don't mind. What did you want to ask me?"

Toby looks sheepish, like he wasn't prepared to be put on the spot. "Nothing in particular," he says.

I smile. Whenever he's ready to talk, I'll be ready to listen.

An hour passes and when our stomachs are full, the four of us sit back in our chairs, ready to relax. Except for Toby. He gets up, looking like he might be sick. He's shifting from one foot to the other, and I think I even see perspiration beading on his forehead.

"I want to share some news with y'all," he says at last.

"Okay, let's have it," Cole tells him. "You're making all of us wonder if we need to get you a bucket."

"Mule's ass," Toby mutters, and then he continues. "As I was sayin', I got somethin' to tell y'all." He looks at Ariel, still shuffling his feet. She smiles, and it's clear that this is an important moment for both of them. I'm excited to hear what Toby has to say. I sit forward in my chair, waiting.

Toby clears his throat. "I wanted y'all to be the first to know," he says, looking at me and Cole. "Me and my sweetie, Ariel, are finally doin' it. We're gettin' hitched." He looks straight at Cole. "And I'd like you, you doggone son of a bitch, to be my best man."

Cole smiles broadly, like the sun has landed on his face. He tips his chair back on two legs and looks as though he might be thinking of a proper response for such an announcement. "I have to admit," he says at last, looking straight at Toby, "I never thought I'd see the day when you'd get any woman to marry you. Especially this lovely woman right here." He places a hand on one of Ariel's. "Only thing is, I can't figure out what she sees in you."

Toby gives him a stern glare. "Why you gotta do that? Why you gotta make this harder for me than it already is?"

Cole laughs, but Ariel has her lips pressed together, and she's looking at Toby like she truly feels his pain. Then she looks at Cole with her eyes lit up like fire, like she might call him a son of a bitch herself if he doesn't give Toby a break.

Cole backs off, but only slightly. "What do you think, Ariel? Do you think a son of a bitch should be the best man at your wedding?"

Ariel's face turns into a beam of happiness. "Only if that son of a bitch be you, Cole McKenzie."

In an instant, Cole and Toby are up and out of their chairs, and they're slapping each other on the back so hard it makes me wince. And when they finish with each other, Cole pulls Ariel from her chair and kisses her. Then he turns to me and pulls me out of my chair and kisses me, too. Toby gets in on the action by hugging me, and then I hug Ariel, and it's like we're one big happy family, celebrating. And I guess if you're lucky enough to find that special someone who makes you happy, then that's plenty of reason to celebrate.

When all congratulations are finished, the four of us continue with more talk and plenty of laughs. Then, finally, the subject of Sophie's baby comes up.

"He's a big one," Toby says. "I might have to knock down a stall wall so he has room to move around." He looks at Cole. "Maybe you could take him home. I bet Lacy could do something with him."

"I can't get Lacy to clean her room these days," Cole says. "Better if you keep Sophie's foal here for now. We'll figure out what to do with him later."

I don't know what that means, but I haven't seen Baby Bobby since he was born, and I can't wait to go to the barn and see for myself how big he's grown. Cole and I excuse ourselves, and we take a walk across the driveway. I'm hunched against the night air, taking quick strides. I'm not cold, just excited.

We enter the barn, and I'm taken aback when I see that Baby Bobby has practically doubled in size. "My God, he's so big," I say to Cole.

"He eats well, from what I've heard."

I look to Sophie and she's gone back to her pre-baby weight days, looking sleek and elegant. Motherhood seems to suit her.

I watch her for a minute, but I don't think she remembers me. She continues munching on hay and isn't the least bit interested in saying hello to visitors.

I call to Bobby, and he trots over, kicking his back hooves out behind him. He immediately nuzzles my hand, looking for a treat, but I have nothing, so I just rub the soft velvet of his nose. Cole opens the stall gate, and Bobby immediately races out. He's all legs, bucking and kicking from one end of the barn to the other in what can only be described as pure joy. I watch, amazed at his energy.

After several trips back and forth, Bobby needs a rest, and he comes over to me once more, to see if I've changed my mind about giving him a treat. Cole reaches into his pocket and hands me a peppermint, which I give to Bobby, and he sucks it like he's found heaven.

Our visit to the barn ends when we hear the wind begin to howl. Cole doesn't appear to be bothered, so when we're back at the house, I go inside to help Ariel with the dishes while Cole joins Toby on the porch for one more beer. Ariel and I talk more, but it's small talk, because we're still getting to know each other. Though, as our conversation continues, it turns more personal. Ariel is a smart woman, very much in tune to other people's feelings, and she senses I have something on my mind.

"You ever need to talk, you know where to fin' me," she says.

I don't think Ariel is being nosy, but I can't share what I know about Lacy. I steer our talk elsewhere. "How long have you lived here?" I ask.

"All my life," Ariel tells me. She smiles. "And dat is a very long time."

"You were born here?"

"I was. And you?"

"I was born in Seattle." The words coming off my tongue don't seem nearly as glamorous as being born on an island in the Caribbean. Still, I've always been happy to be a Pacific Northwesterner.

"And now you are here," Ariel says.

"Yes, for a short time. I'll be leaving once my sister is back on her feet."

Ariel nods. "Paula."

"Yes."

"You don' wish to stay?"

Her question catches me off guard. I'm not sure what I wish anymore.

She pats my hand. "Cole be a good man. He take care of you, if you let him."

A lump forms in my throat. I know Cole is a good man and that he would take care of me. But as long as I'm keeping secrets from him, nothing is for sure.

I continue helping Ariel with the dishes, and when they are dried and put away, I wander into the living room to see what's become of the men. They're still out on the front porch, talking and drinking beer, and they've even lit a couple of cigars. I can smell the acrid, sweet scent as it blows in through the screen door.

I hear their voices over the wind. They're talking about Lacy.

"She's angry," Cole says. "I don't know if it has something to do with Janine or if it's that she has to look at me every day."

"I'd say it's that she has to look at you. I know if I had to look at your mug every day, I'd be mad, too," Toby tells him.

And back and forth it goes.

I smile. Cole has a good friend in Toby. He seems like the kind of friend who'd be there whenever he was needed.

As the men puff on their cigars, the smoke is quickly sucked away by the wind. It's fiercer now, and as I look out, I can see the fronds on the palm trees that line the driveway whipping sharply about.

An unexpected clatter from a loose shutter on one of the windows catches me by surprise, and it makes the hair on the back of my neck feel all prickly and full of electricity. Ariel walks into the room and sees me rubbing my arms.

"You get use to dat in a hurry," she tells me. "Hurricane season is nigh on us. Don' matter if one come or not, the wind goin' make a fuss, anyhow. It just be warnin' us not to get too comfy."

Hurricane? The idea of being caught in one makes my arms even more prickly. I've got goose bumps all over. "Do you think one might be coming?" I ask.

"Don' be botherin' yoself, thinkin' 'bout dat. If one was a-comin', we'd have heard," she reassures me.

I'm not at all reassured. I want Cole to come inside, where I can be closer to him. I want *him* to tell me not to worry. But when I look out, he and Toby don't seem to be paying any attention to the wind's fierceness. Toby is puffing on his cigar, and Cole is watching the smoke disappear into the night.

A flash lights the sky, and I count the seconds until I hear the connecting boom. I get to seven. The wind howls even louder, like a shrill scream. I shudder and continue to rub my arms vigorously. "It sounds angry," I say to Ariel.

"If it be, not much we can do to change it," she tells me, and she wanders back into the kitchen.

Cole keeps staring into the sky. I step closer to the window and look, too. I can see the moon and shadows from low-hanging clouds that look heavy and full of weather. They're moving quickly, rolling into one another to form new, even more ominous shapes. Ariel may be taking this change in the weather in stride, but I'm beginning to wish I were back home in Seattle. We don't have hurricanes or tornadoes or other extremes in the weather. Maybe a minor earthquake every fifteen or twenty years, but that's about it.

The men come inside, and Cole tells me we need to leave, that we need to go—*now*. I waste no time saying thank you for dinner and good-bye to our hosts, but before Cole and I even get to his Jeep, plum-sized drops of rain are coming down on our heads. And before we get to the end of the driveway, visibility is so poor and the night so dark that it feels like we're barely moving. The road is unlit, and along with the usual bumps and ruts, we're now dealing with thick mud that makes it seem like we're standing still. I'm holding my breath, as well as the edge of my seat. I'm used to the rain, but in Seattle, even if the weatherman dubs it the "storm of the year," we can all rest easy knowing that when morning comes, our homes will still be standing.

I'm shivering. I want to be out of this rain. But I'm not so sure I want to be back at The Fish Shack, waiting for another wall to be torn away and blown down the beach. If this gets any worse, I'd like to be inside a house that's structurally sound.

"You okay?" Cole asks.

"We don't have hurricanes in Seattle," I say. "We have rain." Lots and lots of rain.

"This ain't no hurricane, darlin'. We wouldn't be out here if it was." He puts a hand on my knee for reassurance. "Paula tells me your lowlands get flooded each year. Sometimes so bad livestock needs to be moved."

"That's true. We do flood. Not in Seattle, but in other areas. Near the rivers," I tell him.

"You don't get much wind?"

"Some. We have a few trees come down." I know what he's doing. He's making conversation to take my mind off what's going on outside the Jeep. But I can't pretend I don't see the chaos that's going on all around us. "It isn't anything like this. Our homes don't get ripped apart and carried down the beach."

Cole laughs lightly. "We'll be all right," he tells me. But as he says it, he moves his hand from my knee and back to the steering wheel. And it's just in time. There's a tree branch in the middle of the road, and Cole has to wrench the Jeep to the right to avoid hitting it.

The wind is screaming ever louder. I'm all but deaf. I just want it to stop. I clutch the front of my seat with both hands, afraid if I let go, I might get blown away.

"We need to try to make it to my house," Cole shouts. His voice is barely audible over the wind and rain. "The Fish Shack is too far. With all the debris that's flying around, we could get hit. Something could come right through the windshield."

I know he's right, but I'm terrified for Paula. "Do you think The Fish Shack will hold up to this?" I ask.

"Don't worry about your sister. Tug wouldn't leave her alone," Cole tells me.

A large object comes at us and cracks hard against the windshield. My breath hitches. I don't know how the glass held. I'm almost in a panic. I know this isn't a full-out hurricane, but with the wind screaming and the sky raining trees, it might as well be.

Another large palm frond blows directly in our path, and Cole jerks the Jeep once more to one side. He gives me a comforting look, but I'll be glad for this ride to be over. I grip the door and brace myself and pray we'll get through this. My life can't come to an end on this island.

I keep my eyes closed, hoping we'll reach safety and hoping, too, that everyone else here on St. John is in a secure place. I don't want to wake up in the morning and find out someone I know has been injured.

After a million scary minutes, Cole and I arrive at his house. The wind has died down some, too, enough that my stomach is no longer in my throat, but I won't feel completely safe until I'm inside. Cole takes my hand and we run like crazy for the door.

As we near the porch, a figure appears and scuttles toward us. It's a man, I think, and I strain to see his face through the rain. When he gets close enough, I know immediately that it's the guy who was at The Fish Shack the other night with Lacy.

He shoots past me and Cole without saying a word, and Cole only gives him a passing glance. As soon as we enter the house, I know something is wrong. I can feel it.

The first thing we see is the glow of a candle. And then I see Lacy. She's curled up on the sofa and has a washcloth pressed to one cheek. Even in the dim light, I can see she's been crying.

Cole moves quickly, kneeling beside her. "Lacy, honey, what's wrong? Who was that boy? Did he hurt you?"

Lacy shakes her head. "He's a friend." Her breath comes in quick, painful gasps.

Cole looks confused. "Are you sick?"

Lacy says nothing at first. But then she whispers something that neither Cole nor I can make out.

"I can't hear you, honey," Cole tells her. He leans his head near her mouth, and in another moment, he raises his head and looks over at me. "I can't have heard right. She's not making any sense. She's saying something about a baby."

Fear whips through me. A promise or not, Cole is about to find out he's going to be a grandfather. "We have to get her to a doctor," I say. I look around for a blanket but see nothing, so I tell him to get one from the bedroom.

Once Cole is out of earshot, I ask Lacy, "How are you doing? Tell me what's happening. Are you still having pain?"

New tears fill her eyes. "I think I'm having a miscarriage."

Chapter Twenty-One

Cole comes back with a blanket and covers Lacy. She cries out. Her face is written with fear. I step back, away from her, so that I can talk to Cole.

"What's going on?" he asks.

I feel hollow. This is it. I have no choice but to tell him everything. I know it could mean the end of us, but that seems such a small thing right now. I touch his arm, feeling his warmth. "Lacy is pregnant. We need to get her to the hospital."

Cole is taken aback. I see shock in his eyes. It's exactly the reaction I expected. "What the hell are you talking about?" he asks.

"Dad," Lacy calls to Cole. He goes to her side and takes her hand. "It's true," she says. "I'm pregnant. I made Taylor promise not to tell you. I was afraid."

Cole looks at me. "You knew?"

"I'm sorry... so sorry," I tell him. I move closer, but he's not having any of it. He recoils like he's been kicked. Like I knew he would. But it's not something I can help right now. He and I can talk at the hospital. "We need to go," I tell him.

When we get Lacy out to the Jeep, the weather has calmed

considerably. I'm no longer afraid, just concerned and worried as hell about Lacy. The road is still thick with mud and debris, but the water has begun to soak into the ground, so we're able to go faster now.

We make it to the medical center and we get Lacy checked in. Then Cole takes a seat in the waiting room. His arms rest heavily on his knees, his head is bent, his eyes are on the floor. I can see he's trying to process everything. I know if Lacy had been injured by the storm, the medical staff would not have been able to keep him out of the exam room. But Lacy isn't injured. She's pregnant. And hospital personnel thought it best he wait out here. With me. I'm two chairs over to give him some space, but it feels like two miles.

After a lengthy silence, he shoots me a sharp glare. "So, you knew about this? And you didn't think it was important enough to tell me?" His tone is clipped, angry. It's possible he hates me right now and I can't blame him.

"I wanted to," I say. "I gave Lacy my word that I'd wait… give her the chance to tell you herself."

"She's a kid. She doesn't get to call the shots. You've seen firsthand what I've been dealing with. Did you really think she ever intended to tell me anything?" He sits up and releases a long, resigned breath. "I suppose you also know who the father of her baby is."

I feel like I'm on the witness stand. I hate that I know who the father is, but nothing I can say right now will make this better, so I stay quiet.

Cole is looking at me, waiting for an answer. "Do you?" he presses me.

"Wouldn't you like to wait and talk with Lacy about this?" I ask. I'm dying inside. I'd like nothing more than to take him in my arms and to let him know I'm here for both him and his daughter, but I'm not sure he'd allow it. I'm surprised he even let me come here with him. As it was, I sat in back with Lacy, and every time I looked, I could see him staring back at me in the rearview mirror. He never said anything. He didn't have to.

Whatever I could imagine he was thinking, it was probably worse.

I don't blame him for the way he's feeling. But I'd at least like the chance to explain. Because that's what guilt does. Makes you want to explain away your actions, as if that will somehow make everything better.

Assuaging my guilt isn't what I want, though. Or maybe it is. I'm not sure of anything right now. Forgiveness might be a lot to ask for. So I'll wait. Cole needs time to process what's happening with his daughter, and I need to let him be.

I'm processing, too. Meeting Cole and getting to know him, growing to love him, is more than I could have ever imagined with my wounds still so fresh from what happened between me and Peyton. But keeping Lacy's secret was quite possibly the stupidest thing I've ever done, and now I have to live with the consequences.

Twenty minutes tick off the clock that's hanging on the wall above the emergency station. Cole remains quiet. He has nothing else to say to me... I guess. I'm just another person in the waiting room.

Three other people are in the waiting area with us. They're quiet, too. Not a one of them protested when hospital staff took Lacy in right away. As I look from face to face, I can see how weary we all are from sitting and wondering what happens next.

And what does happen next?

Another half hour passes, and at last, the on-duty attending physician pushes through the swinging doors at the side of the waiting room. His face is a proper mask of sympathy as he walks over to me and Cole. We stand, Cole with his hands on his hips and far enough away from me for the message to come through loud and clear that he and I are a separate entity. Still, the doctor looks from me to him as he speaks, as though he assumes he's speaking to both mother and father of the pregnant girl.

"She's had a miscarriage," the doctor explains, focusing on me.

"Sweet Jesus," Cole all but gasps. He edges a few inches

169

farther away from me. "How on earth…"

"Sometimes it's nature's way when something is wrong. It's nothing she did," the doc says. "She'll be fine in a few days, but I'd like her to spend the night here. The nurse will let you know when you can go in and see her," he tells us, and then he disappears through the swinging doors.

I turn to Cole, ready to answer any questions he might have, though I know it's doubtful he wants to hear anything from me right now. I could try to explain, but he won't hear a word. He's completely closed himself off.

And anyway, what could I say? That I'm sorry? No. He's not ready for that. Even so, I need to say what I can before he walks away.

"I wanted to tell you. When Lacy told me she was pregnant, we were all at the ferry terminal and I didn't think that was the time—"

"You've known since then?" he asks, incredulous.

"I wanted to give her the chance to tell you herself. I didn't think it was any of my business—"

"You didn't think it was your business to tell the man you're sleeping with about his pregnant daughter? Jesus, Taylor." He rubs both his hands over his head.

I wait, but nothing more comes. I don't think he has anything more to say to me. But then he starts in again, continuing with words that hurt, but that I have to take because I know he needs to get them out if he and I are ever to get past this. "You're not a parent. You don't know what it's like to raise a child. If you did, you'd have come to me immediately and told me what was going on with Lacy."

"You're right, and I'm so sorry." I'm near tears now. "Like I said, I wanted to give her the chance to come to you herself."

"Did you really think she would?"

"I was hopeful."

"And if she didn't?" He shakes his head. "Christ, Taylor, how can I trust you or believe what we have is real if you're already keeping secrets from me?" He stares down at the floor for what seems like forever and then says, "I need to be with someone I don't have to wonder about."

I feel like the wind has been knocked out of me. My wounds have barely healed where Peyton is concerned, and now this. But it's exactly how I'd feel if the roles were reversed. If I had a daughter and Cole had kept something as serious as this from me, well, that would likely be the end of us. Even so, if I could just make him understand...

"Cole, you have to know I never meant to keep secrets or do anything to make you not trust me, but I wanted your daughter to trust me, too."

"Why?"

Why? Because I've fallen in love with you, and you've fallen in love with me, and I want Lacy to accept me. But I don't get to say it because the nurse interrupts us to let us know we can go in and see Lacy.

Cole immediately walks away from me. Without so much as a parting glance, he disappears through the double doors and I'm left alone. I don't belong in there with father and daughter. Not now. Maybe never.

Tears prick my eyes and I wipe them away. I feel like I'm suffocating, I'm so hurt. I don't want this to be the end of me and Cole. I want to believe that after this is over, he'll consider that I truly am sorry, that I really did feel stuck between my feelings for him and keeping my word to his daughter.

I go outside to call Paula, and I make an attempt to explain things without going into too much detail. She tells me she'll send Tug to pick me up—I thought things couldn't get any worse—and I manage a feeble, "Okay."

The wind has died down, like it never was, and the air smells clean and fresh. It's as though nature has had a heated argument, but now it's over, and all is well. If only we humans could clear the air so easily.

The moon is out, but the clouds keep the night dark. I see a stone bench in the pale glow of a frail-looking lamp post, and that's where I sit, waiting for Tug. I can only imagine what he'll think of me once he hears about this. Though it'll have to be Cole who tells him.

I feel unsettled, like I need to go for a run to rid myself of the stress I'm feeling. But I don't want to miss my ride, so I stay put and kick at the sand. My toe hits a rock and I curse repeatedly. My mother would threaten to wash my mouth out with soap, but some situations call for cursing, so I curse even more.

Tug is taking way too long. It's giving me time to ponder my life and Cole and my previous three boyfriends—Peyton, Cliff, and Nick. I surmise that too many boyfriends in one lifetime are not good for a woman. Though Cole and I have known each other such a short time I'm not entirely sure I should even classify him as a boyfriend.

So, how do I classify him? A one-night stand? No. Technically, he and I have been together three times. Lovers? Not anymore. So what is—was—Cole to me? Which column do I put him in?

My toe continues to throb, so I bend over to examine it. I don't see any blood. Guess I'll live.

I reach up and rub my chest, where I've had a dull ache ever since we found Lacy. A tear rolls down my cheek. I feel broken and so very alone.

I see Tug's truck come around the bend, and I stand and wait for him to pull up next to me. I manage to put on a brave face, and I hope it'll be enough to keep him from asking too many questions.

"Everything okay in there?" he asks, nodding at the front door of the medical center.

I climb into the passenger's seat. "Lacy had an issue. She'll be fine in a day or two."

"What kind of issue?" Tug asks.

"She's fine," I tell him. I won't go into details. I won't do anything else to make matters worse.

"You sure you don't want to stay here with McKenzie? He's been having a hard time of it lately with Lacy. I'm sure he could use a little support."

Yes, but not mine. "He didn't want me to stay." Another tear slides down my cheek—*dammit*—and I turn my head and wipe it away.

Tug raises a skeptical eyebrow. "He told you that? He told you to leave?"

"Can we just please go?" I say. Of course Cole didn't come right out and tell me to leave. But he said enough that I know he doesn't want me anywhere near him. Or Lacy. I'm not an idiot, for chrissakes. I don't need to read any fine print to know what Cole's harsh words meant.

Tug slides me a sideways glance, grunting. He's probably thinking that if I don't change my tone, he'll put me over his knee. Though I seriously hope he wouldn't dare.

Tug's reaction to my non-explanation isn't a surprise. As Cole's friend, I fully expected him to be concerned for Lacy. But dammit, I don't think I should be expected to explain everything that happens between me and Cole. Besides, everyone will find out everything soon enough… because there are no secrets on this damn island.

Chapter Twenty-Two

Despite Tug's deft hand at guiding his truck around all the storm debris, the drive is slow and torturous. Tug is quiet for the most part—for once I'm glad he's a man of few words—but he steals quick glances in my direction every few minutes, which makes me feel like I should say something. But what? I'd rather jump out and walk back to The Fish Shack than get him involved in this mess I've made. The only thing keeping me in my seat is the memory of what happened the last time I ventured out on my own in this godforsaken jungle. That and the fact that I'm not fond of being out alone at night on a dark road.

After Tug and I have traveled in silence long enough, I come to a decision. I need to go home. I don't belong here. So there it is. More proof that I'm a coward. About a lot of things—change, new things, to hope for a love that's real. Peyton did that to me. Bastard. He did such a number on me and now I'm afraid to see what comes next. And, too, I'm afraid to stay here, even for Paula, because Cole is here. Though I should stay. Because the reality is Paula has only been home a few days, and she still needs me. But what about *my* needs? I've had about all the fun I can stand. I need to go back to my comfort zone of work, work, work and sleeping in my office chair.

I lean my head against the window and contemplate how long it will take me to pack. One or two minutes, at most. A lot of what I brought with me—fool that I was for thinking that silk and cashmere were suitable fabrics for island living—has seen better days, and I see no reason to allot it any suitcase space. I could just… leave.

"You two have an argument?" Tug asks, breaking our silence.

He means Cole. I open my mouth to give him a half-baked answer, but all that comes out is a sob. I hate it. I hate being a fragile, sobby woman and showing it to others. It's so not who I am… or was. Though I'm beginning to think I no longer know who that person is.

Tug quickly pulls the truck over to the side of the road, and we sit there while he watches me cry. I hope he's not thinking about being nice. That would only make things worse. I'd prefer he slap me and tell me to woman up.

He doesn't slap me, but he does give my shoulder a reassuring squeeze. "Cole's my friend, but Lord knows he can be stubborn," he says. "Hell, you're both stubborn. But I see how you are with him and he's different now that you're here. Whatever's happened, it'll pass, like tonight's storm."

Ha! He has no idea. This wasn't an ordinary storm. It was a hurricane, and it blew whatever Cole and I had away. And as far as being able to agree or disagree on Cole's stubbornness, I still don't know him well enough to comment.

It's not often that I let the floodgates open, but right now, I can't help myself. I'm hurt and feeling like I've just lost my best friend. No, not a friend. Someone I think I could see myself with forever, and God, does it hurt.

Tug lets me cry for a minute. Just sits across from me and stares, while my eyes begin to burn from my mascara. I'm sure it's all over my face. I must look like the bride of Frankenstein. And for some reason, that strikes me as funny, so I begin to laugh. I'm laughing and crying at the same time.

"You okay there, missy?" Tug eventually asks. He hands me a

tissue. "You haven't gone loco on me, have you?"

I take the tissue and wipe my nose, and it's enough to distract me from my current state. I'm feeling better. Not good but better. "I'm all right," I say. I shake my head. "It's just been one hell of a bad day."

"Far as I can see," Tug continues, "the two of you deserve each other. You both have a lot of crazy in you. Maybe you should think about that." He rolls the truck's engine over and once more we're on our way. Fifteen minutes later, we're back at The Fish Shack, and he drops me off, sayin he'll see me in the morning.

If I'm still here.

I'll be here. I have no flight plans, and I'm sure it'll take a couple of days to arrange something.

I stand in the red dirt at the bottom of the steps and stare up at the plank door. I don't feel like facing Paula yet. She'll have questions, and I don't have any good answers. I could take a walk on the beach—the wind is gone, replaced by calm—but I don't have the energy. Today has kicked my ass... Lacy, Cole, the weather. But at least The Fish Shack is still standing. The back of it, anyway. When Tug and I drove up, I saw a few pieces of bamboo strewn about, but I won't know until morning, when I can get a better look.

As I stand at the back door contemplating my next move, a cat I call Bananas—because he likes to eat them—approaches me. He leaps up, putting his front paws on my leg, with his tail twitching and his eyes blinking. He's happy to see me, or maybe he just wants a handout.

I pick him up and rub his head affectionately. "You're a good friend," I tell him. "In fact, after tonight, you might be my *only* friend." Which sounds pathetic, even to me.

I leave the porch and go to the front of The Fish Shack. The moon's glow reveals the storm's aftermath, where palm fronds, bits of wood, and unidentifiable debris litter the beach. But Paula's home and The Fish Shack still have three walls. The wood and debris must have blown here from somewhere else.

I put Bananas down and I go up the front steps, being as quiet as possible so I don't wake Paula. I see several small candles still burning on the bar, their flames dancing in the dark, casting ghostly shadows across the walls. But it's also nice and would make for a romantic setting under the right circumstances.

I leave the candles burning. They, along with the moon, provide enough light that I can see what I'm doing. I plan to cozy up with an open bottle.

I choose a bottle that's full of Cruzan rum, plus I find a shot glass to go with it. Then I make my way out to the beach and I sit in the sand and pour myself a shot. The rum goes down my throat with a smooth warmth that I feel all the way to my toes, so I pour myself one more. Two shots and I'm done. I don't need any more. My morning will be hellish as it is.

"I was worried about you," a voice says, coming up behind me. It's Paula.

I turn to look. "Hey," I say. "I didn't wake you, did I?"

"No. I couldn't sleep." Paula drops her crutches and sits next to me. She's brought her own shot glass. "Are you okay?" she asks.

I nod, because I'm afraid if I talk I'll start to cry.

She takes the bottle of rum from me, pours herself a shot, and downs it.

"Aren't you on painkillers?" I ask.

"I'm painkiller free," she says. "Some storm, huh?"

I manage a tight smile. "Yep. Some storm."

"I was worried you'd be caught out in it."

"I was. But I was with Cole and we made it to his place safely."

"I'm not sure I understand. When you called for a ride, you said you and Cole were at the medical center with Lacy. You said you'd explain later. I assumed it was nothing serious... a sliver of wood in her toe or something. This is later. Please explain."

"No sliver. Worse."

"Okay, what?"

I'd wanted to leave it to Cole to tell whomever he wants the news about what happened to Lacy. But now Paula's eyes are wide and she wants answers. "I kept a secret from Cole."

"What kind of secret?"

"One I shouldn't have kept."

"About Lacy? The fact that she's pregnant and he's going to be a grandpa?"

My mouth falls open. "You knew?"

Paula shrugs. "I heard you talking to Lacy the other night, when you and she were out on the back porch." She rests back on her arms. "Wow, Lacy pregnant. I can hardly believe it. But why was she at the medical center?"

"That's just it. She isn't pregnant. Anymore. She had a miscarriage."

Paula sits up straight. "Jesus."

"Yeah, Jesus. I need to go home," I say.

Paula's eyebrows arch. "Right now?"

"As soon as is humanly possible."

"Why?"

"Because. Cole is mad at me."

Paula gives me the mother look. "You screwed up. It happens. But that doesn't mean Cole wants you to go home. Give him a few days. He'll come around."

My throat feels like it's closing. "I'm not so sure about that. You didn't hear him, the way he was talking. The things he said."

Paula scoffs. "What did you expect? Of course he's mad. But you don't need to run back home at the first sign of trouble."

I put my hands to my face. "I didn't come here for this. I can't do this."

Paula pours herself one more shot and downs it. "You can certainly go home, but I think you're just afraid you'll be hurt again." She rests back onto the sand once more. "You're in love with Cole."

"I am," I admit. And then I sit back and I listen to the surf, while Paula looks into the sky at the full moon. My heart aches so, I think it might rip me apart, but somehow I manage to hold myself together.

Paula tosses her shot glass aside and holds my hand. "I think I might be drunk," she says.

"Me, too," I say, and we both laugh. I feel better with Paula sitting here with me. Not good but better.

Chapter Twenty-Three

The following morning, I take Paula's Mini Moke to the medical center to see Lacy. It's early, but I want to get there before she goes home. I'm sure once she's under Cole's protective care, he won't allow me to visit.

I pass the nurses' station, and no one says a word to me. Which doesn't mean a thing except that Cole probably hasn't gotten a restraining order or instructed hospital personnel to keep me away from Lacy yet.

Outside her room, I stop and listen. I hear nothing. If I slip inside and wait quietly, I can sit with her for a while. Maybe I'll leave before she wakes. Or maybe I'll stay and chance having Cole show up.

I slip into her room, but I don't have to worry about Cole. He's already here. I stop short and look at him sitting in a chair beside her bed. His head is slumped to one side and his eyes are closed. He's sleeping, was likely here all night.

I consider leaving. It would be so easy to tuck my tail between my legs and run away. But I won't. Even if Cole has more harsh words for me, this is where I want to be. I look over at Lacy. She's resting comfortably. Her forehead, usually creased with angst and anger, is now smoothed in slumber. But sure as the sun will rise high in St. John's big blue sky today, her frown will return. How could it not? She's just lost her baby.

As I stand in the doorway, looking from dad to daughter, I think maybe I *should* leave. Lacy doesn't need the stress my being here may cause if Cole were to wake and see me. And chances are it's not only Cole who doesn't want to see me. Lacy and I aren't exactly friends. I just happened to be available when she felt like spilling about her pregnancy.

Yes, I should leave. I turn and reach for the door handle.

"What are you doing here?" It's Cole, his voice barely a whisper.

My throat immediately tightens. My heart lurches as I face him. Last night seems a lifetime ago. Already I miss him. Miss his tenderness. Before we went to his house and found Lacy, I was beginning to think he and I might really have a shot at being a couple. But now, as I look at the grim set to his mouth, I hardly recognize him. He's become hard. Distant. Off-limits.

"I wanted to see Lacy. I didn't mean to wake you," I whisper. I'm shaking, not ready to hear again how much he disapproves of how I handled the situation with his daughter.

Cole glances over at her, his face softening as he takes her in. He studies her for a minute, love shoving away all the hurt that was there only seconds before. "The last time I stayed by her bedside all night, she had the chicken pox," he tells me. "If she woke up, I didn't want her to feel alone or afraid." He smiles with genuine tenderness. "Her face looked like it'd been pounded by gravel. But she was my little girl, and to me, she still had the sweetest angel face ever. From that day on, that's what I called her… Angel Face."

A lump grows in my throat. I remember Cole calling Lacy that at the ferry terminal when she ran away. His sharing is more than I expected, probably more than I deserve, though I'm not even sure he's talking to me. I think he'd be saying the same no matter who was standing in the doorway.

"The boy next door was responsible for her getting sick," he goes on. "Too much close contact." He takes a heavy breath. "Too much close contact caused this, too, I expect." He lets out a short, angry laugh as though he's just realized the humor in his words.

I nod. I don't want to speak, because I'm afraid he might realize who he's been sharing with, and then he'll stop and ask me to leave.

His gaze roams over every inch of Lacy. The covers rise and fall as she breathes. I can only imagine what he must be feeling right now. It's hard for me, as someone who's known Lacy for such a short time, to picture her as a small child. But if I really look, I can see traces of that girl Cole is talking about. Only she's no longer a child. She's a young woman. I wonder if Cole will be able to accept that.

He's quiet for a minute, and so am I. As I look at him, my thoughts are scattered. It occurs to me that he looks way too young to be a grandfather. His hair has grown out some since I arrived here on St. John, and it makes him look younger. Incredibly sexy.

"What am I supposed to say to her when she wakes up?" he asks. "The doc said she was just over two months along. That means she was already pregnant when she got here." He looks confused. "I didn't have a clue. How could I not know?"

My heart jumps painfully hearing him talk like this. I want to reach out and touch him, but I doubt it's what he wants. And frankly, I don't think I'm up for the rejection.

Cole gets up from the plastic chair he's sitting in and walks over to the window. The morning sun is out in full force. No wind. No dancing palm fronds. Everything is still. Back to normal.

Only everything is not normal. It's all shot to hell.

"I wish it were still storming," he says, "and that I was out there on my boat, fighting the sea. It would give me something to think about other than the jumble of thoughts that are mixing around inside my head right now." After a minute, he faces me. "Dammit, Taylor, how could you not tell me?"

"Dad?" a quiet voice comes from the bed.

Cole and I both turn. Lacy's eyes are open. She looks frightened. Cole steps over and takes her small hands in his. "Hey, Lacy girl, how're you feelin'?"

"I'm okay." She skirts me a look and scoots herself up to sitting.

I smile and move closer. I can feel Cole's eyes on me. I know he wants me to leave. "I came to see how you're doing," I say. "But I should go. I'm sure you have things you want to discuss with your dad."

"Don't," she says, and then she looks to Cole. "You don't want her to leave, do you?"

"You need your rest," he tells her. "The doctor will be in later this morning to release you. I just wanted to be here when you woke up."

"So I wouldn't be scared?" Lacy asks.

"Something like that," he answers, smiling solemnly.

"I'm not a child anymore. I stopped waking up scared that there might be a bogeyman in my closet a long time ago."

I feel like an intruder. I should leave so they can talk, but Lacy wants me to stay and so I do. I gaze around the room, trying, somehow, to give them a moment, until I catch Cole looking at me.

"We should both go," he tells me directly, and then he goes to kiss Lacy on the forehead, but she turns her head enough to let him know she's not ready to go back to being his little girl.

"Don't be mad at Taylor," she tells him. "I made her promise not to say anything to you. I told her if she did, I'd run away. That's why she kept quiet. She gave me a week, and then she was going to tell you everything."

Cole presses his lips tight.

"I thought the two of you were hot for each other," Lacy continues, looking from her dad to me.

My face warms. I don't know what to say. Speaking for myself, I *am* hot for her dad. More than hot. I'm in love with him. But I can't speak for him, and I'm not sure I even want to hear how he's feeling about me right now.

"Let's just say we've cooled off," Cole says.

"Since when? You were together last night." Lacy looks like she doesn't understand.

"A man has a right to know what's going on with his child," he tells her.

Lacy's frown grows deep. "I'm not a child." Her jaw is tense, like her dad's. She looks so much like him. No doubt about it, she's her father's daughter.

My heart is pounding, but it's clear Cole isn't about to be swayed by anything Lacy says. He's not interested in hearing anything in my defense.

"So, you're breaking up because Taylor kept her word to me?" Lacy asks. "What about all the times you broke your promises to me? You must have told me a thousand times how I'd get to see you, and then it never happened."

"Lacy," Cole says, "it wasn't that simple."

"Yes. It was. It was just that simple. You walked out of my life and never looked back. You obviously never wanted me. *Or* Mom. You're probably glad she's dead."

"You know that's not true," Cole tells her.

Lacy folds her arms over her chest and stares straight ahead. She's shutting down. Nothing Cole can say will get through to her right now.

I hate that I've had any part in causing this friction between a man and his daughter. I move to the side of Lacy's bed. "Your dad loves you. He may not be perfect, but things aren't always as they seem—"

Cole holds up a hand, stopping me. "I don't need you to defend me."

I back off, wondering if he thinks I might say something about Lacy's mother. Which I wouldn't, but I guess he doesn't know that. He no longer feels he knows me.

Lacy is crying now. Her tears spill faster than she can wipe them away. "You left Mom and me behind. And look what happened. She's dead. *Dead.* I'll never see her again. And now I have to live here on this stupid island with you."

"I saw you as often as I could. You were too far away—"

"No! *You* were too far away. *You* left *me*."

Cole's lips are tight. It would be easy for him to lash out and tell Lacy the truth about her mother. But he won't, and I understand. He wants to spare her. Even if it means sacrificing himself.

I'm at a loss. I hate this. I want to go back to making love with Cole. I want to go back to how things were before Lacy told me she was pregnant. I want for Lacy to know what a great guy her dad is. I have no idea how his wife could have thought what she did about him. The Cole I know would never keep a child from her mother.

The door swings open and a nurse enters the room. She looks from Cole to Lacy to me. "What's going on in here? It's too early for loud voices, Mr. McKenzie. Have you been here all night?" she asks, her tone a clear accusation.

"Me and my daughter are having a private conversation," Cole tells the nurse. He gently ushers her from the room, ignoring her protests and threats to call the doctor.

"Bully," Lacy mutters.

"I'll be back in a while to pick you up," Cole tells her. "We'll finish this discussion at home."

"Don't you even want to know who the daddy of my baby was? So you can go beat him up?"

Cole's eyes flash with anger that quickly turns to tenderness. "You can try to hurt me all you want, but you're still my daughter, and I'm always going to love you, Lacy girl." And then he's gone. I suspect to punch something. That's what I'd be doing.

Lacy looks at me. "Well?"

I notch an eyebrow. "Well, what?"

"Aren't you going after him?"

"I don't think so."

"Why? Don't you care about him?"

"Of course I care about your dad. But… I'm confused. I thought you hated me."

"Since when does anyone care about how *I* feel? Go after him."

My insides are churning. I look at the door. Cole is probably on the way to his boat. "I don't think he's in any mood to see me right now."

"He may not want to talk, but he'll listen to you if you make him," Lacy says.

At this point, I guess I have nothing to lose.

I was right, Cole was marina bound. I see his Jeep in the parking lot when I drive up. I walk the dock and don't even call out when I step onto his boat. I just open the hatch and climb down into the cabin. I can hear water running at the back of the boat, and I know he's in the shower. My mind flashes at the memory of our last time together here, making love. I'll never forget that day, how the heat of our desire erupting into one of the most pleasurable moments in my life, made me feel whole again. Long after we'd made love I could still feel his breath on my cheek, his mouth on mine. Just thinking about it makes me want him. I want his warmth and his touch and... everything.

I stop myself mid-thought. I can't do this. I'm just torturing myself, and I should be ashamed that I'm even thinking about sex at a time like this. But I can't help it. Sex with Cole was so unexpected and beautiful and healing. And I know I could stay here in St. John a while longer to continue trying to make things right between us. But back at the medical center, when I looked in Cole's eyes, I didn't see love or anything close to love. I saw betrayal.

I turn and go back up the ladder. I need to let Cole decide if he wants to talk. He knows where to find me.

Chapter Twenty-Four

In the morning, when I try to arrange a flight out of St. Thomas, Delta is booked solid, and it looks like I might be stuck here for another couple of weeks. Which is unimaginable. I feel like every part of me is fractured, and I need to be back home where I can lounge around in sweats and not have to smile and pretend all is well in my world.

I end up speaking with one of Delta's helpful associates who offers me a smokin' deal, if I would like to pay an outrageous amount to be put on standby.

"I have to warn you, though," she tells me. "Even if you are able to get on a flight, you'll have to travel through four airports to get home. That puts you back in Seattle about thirty hours after you leave St. John. Will that do, ma'am?"

Hmm… let's see. That would be a no.

The operator understands my plight. She tells me that if a better deal comes up, she'll call me back, and that's that.

It's barely daybreak o'clock and I need something to take my mind off Cole. I go through my usual morning routine—shower and chores—then I'm ready for my morning walk. It's earlier than I typically head out, but I'm glad for that. With any luck, I'll be able to avoid running into anyone I know who might want to stop and chat. I'm in no mood to chat.

As I head for the steps, I hear the back door swing open and I look, hoping to see Cole. But it's not Cole. Not even close.

Peyton?

"Hello, Taylor," Peyton says as he walks toward me. His arms are outstretched as he reaches me, and he tries to gather me to him, but I resist, sure I'm hallucinating. Peyton can't possibly be here in St. John.

Peyton ignores my hesitation at throwing myself into his arms. And since he didn't get an enthusiastic hug, he plants a light kiss on my cheek. "It's good to see you," he says.

I think I'm in shock. "What are you doing here?" I ask. I'm aware of Tug behind the bar, glowering at us.

"I came to see you," Peyton says. Then he takes me by the arm and leads me over to the open front of the bar. "Is there somewhere we can go and talk privately?" he asks.

Most definitely. I take the lead and we step down to the beach. As soon as my feet hit sand, I stop and turn to look at him… because I can still hardly believe my eyes.

"Surprised to see me?" Peyton asks.

Stunned is more like it. "Why are you here?" I ask.

"I needed to see you."

"Why?"

Peyton sighs. "You haven't been checking your messages, have you?"

I spread my arms. "My phone is dead."

Peyton nods. I can see he doesn't believe me.

"Really! It stopped working the moment I got here."

"Okay." He flashes me a smile. "Well… like I said, it's good to see you." He looks around, taking in our surroundings—the palm trees, the hammocks, the Caribbean Sea. "Great place for a vacation, huh?"

"This is too much," I say. "I need to walk." I have no idea where I'm going, haven't thought that far ahead, but I'm not about to stand around making small talk with my ex when Paula could look out any minute and see him.

Peyton starts after me as I march through the sand. I can hear him plodding along behind me. I toss a glare over my shoulder and see that he's wearing shiny black shoes that don't belong on this beach, or any beach. Idiot. "You should probably take those off," I tell him, and I keep walking.

He does as I suggest, and then he hurries to catch up. When he's back on my heels, I stop abruptly and face him. "Wow," I say. "I can't believe you followed me here."

"I didn't *follow* you. I came to see you. It's not like I'm some kind of stalker."

I turn back around and head in the direction of the sea grape tree, where this whole mess with me having to extend my visit to paradise began. The thought crosses my mind that I could entice Peyton to take a ride on the swing, and maybe this time, a shark really will be out there… and that will be that. Only with the luck I've been having lately, the shark will be old, with no teeth, and all Peyton will get is a good gumming.

"Where are we going? It's hotter than a blowtorch out here," he calls to me.

"Put a city man on a beach in paradise, and he'll still find something to complain about," I mutter to myself, but loud enough.

"What was that?"

"Nothing. Just follow me," I say, and I continue to lead the way. I stay far enough ahead that he has to struggle to keep up and we walk for what seems like miles—to him, I'm sure—and then I stop at the log where Paula got hurt. Just my luck, it's in the shade, which means Peyton won't die from sunstroke.

I sit. He sits next to me. I scoot away. He scoots closer and plants a hand on my leg. I yank my leg away to make it perfectly clear I am not happy to see him—and that I don't want his hands anywhere near me—*I don't*. I only want Cole's hands near me— and now the full impact of what I've lost makes me gasp as big tears form in my eyes. I wipe them away, but it's impossible to hide how I'm feeling.

"Are you okay?" Peyton asks. He tries to put an arm around me, but I shrug it away.

"I don't want your comfort."

Peyton's hands go up in surrender mode. "Okay. What *do* you want? You don't seem very happy to see me."

I'm confused. "What do *I* want? *You* came here to see *me*!" I laugh a little. "It's a long plane ride to say hi. So, why don't you tell me what's going on here." I poke him in the chest. Hard. I want to hurt him. "Tell me why you're here!"

"Jesus, Taylor, calm down. I just thought we should talk."

"Don't tell me to calm down." I'm practically screaming at him.

Peyton leans away from me. I think he might be scared. He clears his throat, like he needs to prepare himself for what he's about to say. "Okay. I assume you've heard about Gina," he begins.

God. Shit. Are he and I really having this conversation? Here in paradise, for God's sake? It takes all I have in me not to slug him. "I've heard. So what? Did you come here to rub it in, or are you trying to be decent and tell me before I hear it from someone else?"

"Neither. God, Taylor, I realized it would never work with her. It's you I love. I must have picked up the phone a hundred times to call you, but I didn't know what I could possibly say that would make things right between us. I had to see you in person... to ask if it's too late."

My mind is whirring. Peyton wants me *back*? He *loves* me? But what about the last three months? Haven't we both moved on?

I don't even know what to say. I've waited for him to come back to me, but now that he has, I'm not sure I care. Or maybe it's that I've finally become a pineapple, with a hard shell. The thing is, if he had come to me a month ago, I might have considered a reconciliation. But this isn't a month ago. This is now. And I think maybe we're both where we're supposed to be.

I look into his eyes and notice how pale grey they are, like the sky when there's nothing up there but atmosphere. No clouds, no sun, just blah. "What happened?" I ask. I've calmed some. "Did you wake up with the Yorkie's bubblegum in your hair? Did she prefer watching cartoons Saturday mornings, instead of joining you for your morning jog and coffee?"

Peyton looks sheepish, like he knows who I'm referring to when I say Yorkie. Which, I actually feel bad about. I don't enjoy being one of those women who say mean things about another when it's really the man who deserves the anger. It's not the Yorkie's—Gina's—fault. This is all Peyton. He's the one who left me with a scribbled note.

"I'm sorry," I say. "I shouldn't take my anger out on your girlfriend."

"No. *I'm* sorry. And Gina isn't my girlfriend. Not anymore. She was a mistake. *I* made a mistake. But I'm here now, hoping I can repair the damage." He grabs my hand and holds it so tight I can't pull away. "I know I picked a lousy time to walk out on you. You were having trouble at work... the Eversole case... the Crawford case. It was a bad time for both of us."

My thoughts immediately go to Cole and I yank my hand back to safety. "I don't need you to remind me of all the cases I've lost. And my coming here has nothing whatsoever to do with my job. It's you. All you." I jab a finger into his chest again. "It's not even so much about the fact that you hooked up with another woman two minutes after we broke up. It's how you said good-bye. What was I, a one-night stand who didn't deserve anything more than a quick and easy *adios* on a piece of paper? How could you do that to me?"

"I was angry."

"Why?" I ask, incredulous. I'm more confused than ever.

"I felt like we were always in limbo, that our relationship wasn't moving forward. I never knew from one day to the next what would be with us."

"We were *living* together."

"I wanted to marry you," Peyton tells me. His words are coming at me like rogue waves. What he's saying is all news to me.

"Why didn't you ever say anything?"

"I didn't think it was what you wanted."

"I never said that."

"You did. After one of your court cases, you said you couldn't see the value in marriage. That the odds were against couples staying together, that it wasn't fiscally wise for any working woman to get married."

"Yes, but that didn't mean *I* never wanted to get married."

Peyton shrugs. "It's what I thought."

I shake my head. "So you left me for the Yorkie. What was she, my punishment?" I wince, could kick myself for the name-calling. Gina is likely innocent in all this. Or not. And maybe I don't even want to know.

"Don't be silly," Peyton says.

"I'm not being silly. I'm being serious. You left me for her. And now you've left *her*. What gives?" I almost feel sorry for Gina, right now.

"She didn't take life seriously. She had a lot of growing up to do," Peyton says.

I have news for him. Since coming here to St. John, I have a new appreciation for taking life *lightly*. I look over and his soft brown hair is fluttering in the breeze. His lips, the lips I've kissed a thousand times, are now pressed together in sullen silence. In the past, that would bother me, and I'd try to find out what was wrong so I could fix it. But now? I don't think I care to fix anything with him. All I can think about is Cole. When I think of forever, Cole is the only man I see. Peyton never made me tremble the way Cole did. I like trembling.

But Cole doesn't want me anymore.

I practically leap from the log and begin stomping for all it's worth through the sand. "I need to go. You ruined Starbucks for me. I deserved better." I wish I were back in my office, staring out my window at the Space Needle.

"What can I do to make it up to you?" Peyton shouts, coming after me.

"Nothing. Not a damn thing."

"Taylor, please, there must be something."

As I walk, my mind goes to work. He *should* make it up to me. But how? I'm not ready to take him back. Maybe never. So, what? Then I have it, and I spin around and face him. "Can you take me home?"

"Back to Seattle?"

I splay my arms. "Where else would I call home?"

"I can," he says, and he pulls an envelope from his shirt pocket. From the envelope, he takes out what looks to be airline tickets and holds them out to me. "We can leave here in two days."

I'm flabbergasted. "You purchased a plane ticket for me back to Seattle? You were that confident? Wow."

"You're looking at this all wrong. It was hard even getting these tickets. I wasn't sure what your plans were, or would be, so I wanted to be prepared."

"Wow," I say again. "You had it all figured out. You thought you'd come here and say you were sorry, and then all would be forgiven, and then what? Did you think we would fly off together into the sunset and continue where we left off?" I'm fairly fuming, can even feel the top of my head smoldering.

"I won't apologize for wanting you back," Peyton says. "I made a mistake. Now I'm trying to fix it. I won't apologize for that, either."

Chapter Twenty-Five

Peyton and I head back down the beach, and my heart thumps wildly when I see Cole's Jeep parked at the back of The Fish Shack. He's at the wheel and it looks like he's about to leave. I want to shout and stop him, find out if he was here to see me, but I don't. Because Peyton is here.

I kick at the sand in my frustration and my toe hits a piece of storm debris. It's the same toe I hurt previously. I cry out and lift my foot and begin to hop around like I'm on fire.

"Are you all right?" Peyton asks.

"Do I *look* all right?" I reach out and grab the hammock closest to me, and I hold it steady while I slide backward onto it. Once I find my balance, I thrust my toe in the air, straight at Peyton's face. "Is it bleeding?"

Peyton reaches for my foot. "Hold still, let me take a look." He grips my foot like it's a fish that's trying to escape, but I quickly yank it away.

"Don't *touch* it, for God's sake. I asked you to check and see if it was bleeding, not do minor surgery!" I hold my knee and rock from side to side, and then I realize I'm sitting on the same hammock that Cole and I recently shared… before he decided he never wanted to see me again. The gods are against me.

"*I need to get off this island,*" I wail.

Peyton backs off and eyes me from a safe distance. "Jesus, Taylor, if it hurts that bad, maybe you've broken it. Maybe I should take you to the hospital. They do have medical facilities here, don't they?"

I glare at him from the hammock. "Are you trying to be funny? At a time like this? Of course they have medical facilities here." I do some more rocking until the pain starts to subside. And as it does, I begin to feel an all-consuming anger. "This is all your fault. Why couldn't you have waited to talk to me when I got back home?"

"I waited long enough. I needed to see you," Peyton tells me.

"What's going on out here?" a gruff voice calls to us. It's Tug. He's standing several yards away, and he looks like he's in the mood for a fight. He moves closer, taking a few more threatening steps toward Peyton. "This guy do somethin' to hurt you?" he asks me.

Peyton is smart—I'll give him that much—and he wisely moves even farther away from me. He puts his hands up in surrender mode. The look on his face is priceless. Sheer terror. "Easy, pal. My fiancée hurt her toe, that's all." Peyton makes a head gesture in the direction of my foot. "See for yourself."

Fiancée? I immediately forget about the pain in my toe and my eyes meet Tug's. He looks confused like he has no idea what to think. But his jaw is set, and I think Peyton could be in real danger of being pummeled. And who could blame Tug? He's Cole's best friend. They're like brothers. It'd serve Peyton right. The only thing is I'm an officer of the court, and I suppose it's my duty to save Peyton's life. I slip off the hammock and put myself between the two men. "It's okay," I tell Tug. "Peyton is right. I kicked something in the sand. I'll be fine."

The hardness remains in Tug's eyes. He looks as though he might be weighing his options. Should he kill Peyton or just maim him? "I saw you jumpin' around out here…" he says.

"I know. But I'm okay."

195

Tug continues to glare at Peyton. "You sure?"

I lay a hand on his arm. "I promise."

Tug doesn't look convinced. Even so, he grumbles and lumbers away and it's murder averted, I'm sure.

As soon as I'm confident no one else is listening to our conversation, I turn on Peyton. "*Fiancée?*"

"Sorry. Slip of the tongue. I guess I'm getting ahead of myself."

"Yeah. Way ahead. Let's get something straight. You and I may be flying home together, but everything else? Including any kind of reunion between us? Isn't even a consideration at this point. You said good-bye—on a Starbucks napkin, for God's sake. And then you go right out and hook up with a woman who…" I press my lips together to keep from calling Gina a Yorkie again.

"What?"

"Nothing. Never mind. It doesn't matter. Honestly, do you think I can just forget everything that's happened and fall right back into your arms?"

Peyton looks at me, has no answer. So I leave him standing there. And when I get back to The Fish Shack, Paula has emerged from her cave. She's at the end of the bar. Which is just great. I'd really hoped to get Peyton out of here before she saw him.

I take a calming breath. If she sees that I'm angry, she'll know something is up. "You look tired," I say. "Maybe you need to go lie down for a while."

"I've been lying down. Now I'm up."

I press my lips tight, thinking. "We could go do our nails," I suggest. "Why don't you go and get everything set up?"

Paula looks at her nails. They look fine, perfect even. Because we just did them. "What's wrong with you? Have you been out in the sun too long?"

She has no idea.

"Are you trying to get rid of me?" she asks.

I give her a *c'mon* look. "Why would you say that?"

She leans to one side and looks around me, and I know what she's looking at because her eyes have gone all squinty. "What is *he* doing here?" she asks me.

"Hello, Paula," Peyton says. "Or should I say aloha?"

"This isn't Hawaii," Paula says, her voice sounding all kinds of annoyed. She turns to me. "What gives?"

The door to Ella Su's room opens, which saves me from having to explain. Ella Su pokes her head out and gives Peyton a thorough up and down. Then her face turns sour. Obviously, Paula has shared her opinion of my ex, probably with everyone on St. John. "Cole stop by," she announces, looking directly at me.

"Yes, I saw him," I tell her.

"He wanted quickie," she adds, giving me a wink.

Paula spits out a quick laugh. "I'm sure that's not all he wanted."

"Who's Cole?" Peyton asks.

I ignore Peyton. Cole is none of his business. And I see no reason to delay telling Paula what's going on. "Peyton brought me a ticket home. I'll be leaving this Friday. I was just about to tell you."

Paula's face turns to stone. She appears unable to speak and looks like she could chew glass—she's that mad. I don't even have to look at Tug. I'm betting his face is one big scowl. I know mine is.

After a long few seconds, Paula finds her voice and speaks through clenched teeth. "I suppose that means you'll be wanting a going-away party."

I shake my head. "That's not necessary."

Tug grunts and turns his back to us. He pretends to be busy at the bar, but I wouldn't be surprised if he was preparing a special cocktail for Peyton... something blue, with strychnine in it.

"Of course it is," Paula says. "You've made friends here, and they'll want to say good-bye." She shoots Peyton an icy glare. "What do you think, Peyton? Don't you think our girl should have a chance to say good-bye to all her friends?"

"Absolutely. So long as she and I can have at least one evening out together." He glances around the bar. "Somewhere more lively, perhaps?"

Paula's eyes narrow. I think she might be on the verge of telling Peyton exactly where he can go. But then Tug pipes up. "St. Thomas. Beach bar called Duffy's."

"No need to go to Duffy's," Paula says. "We have quite the nightlife here, too. You remember karaoke night, don't you?" she asks me.

"I do, and it was fun. But I've heard about Duffy's and I'd like to check it out." I'm trying to save Peyton. I wouldn't want to bet he'd survive another hour here with Paula, let alone an entire evening.

"How about tonight?" Peyton says.

"Great," I agree. Anything to put some distance between he and my sis. In fact, my back is up from Paula's reaction to Peyton being here. I have no idea why she hates him so, but I'm an adult. This is *my* life. I should be allowed to screw it up however I see fit… the same as me and our mother have had to allow Paula to live her life here on this tiny island. Damn it.

Peyton grins. And then he slips an arm around my waist. "I need to go check in at my hotel, down the beach. Want to come?" He leans close to my ear. "We could spend some time getting caught up."

I jab an elbow into his rib cage as a warning, and he drops his arm from around my waist. "Let's go," I say, and I grab his arm and lead him through the back door. We head out in Paula's Mini Moke, and we're at the Westmark Resort in minutes. We get Peyton situated in his room, and then we immediately set off for St. Thomas before he can get any more ideas about getting caught up. I won't, for one minute, consider doing anything I might regret later, though I can't help but be aware of how much Peyton cares for me. He brought me a plane ticket home, and, yes, I get that it was slightly manipulative on his part, but it will also save me from more anguish. Soon, I'll be far, far away from Cole and all the heartache I caused myself by keeping Lacy's secret. I need to move on and forget that chapter of my life.

If that's possible.

It's a long walk through town when Peyton and I get to St. Thomas and it's bigger than I remember. But when I was here before, with Cole, as excited as I was to look inside all the shops and check out all the vendors, none of that was my main focus. Cole had all my attention.

So much for forgetting.

One of the local shop owners sends us in the right direction, toward Duffy's, telling us to listen for a loud drum beat. But I think it may be a bit early for music, so while we make our way, Peyton and I do some window shopping. And then, when we've had enough of that, we find a bench near the shore where we can sit and watch the sun set. For the first time since what happened with Lacy, I feel like I can relax.

"It's been lonely in Seattle without you," Peyton tells me.

I can't imagine so. "What about Gina. Didn't she keep you company?"

"I told you… she has a lot of growing up to do."

"I don't know what that means."

"It means she had impossible dreams. Dreams I could never fulfill."

I consider his answer, but I'm still not sure what he means. "Like what?"

Peyton hesitates, like he's weighing his answer. Or maybe he just feels uncomfortable talking about her with me. "She wanted me to be more than an artist," he says at last.

I laugh sardonically. "You won the Bill and Melinda Gates project. Wasn't that enough?"

"It seems not. Gina went to Harvard. She wanted a guy who was either highly educated or a guy who… I don't know… wanted to become president of the United States."

I laugh again. "And she wanted to be First Lady?"

"Something like that."

We go on with our conversation that has nothing to do with

politics or life, in general. We discuss work and the weather here on St. John, comparing it to Seattle's weather, and we both conclude that the sun is better than rain any day of the week. Then, as the orange sky turns to magenta, we decide it's time to continue on to Duffy's. Eventually, we hear the drum beat the shop owner told us about. It's faint at first, then grows in volume and intensity until we can see Tiki torches flickering down the beach.

"It's loud," Peyton says as we make our approach.

"I know," I say. "Let's go have fun." I grab his hand and pull him along. I'm excited. I've heard so much about Duffy's, and I can't wait to get inside.

When Peyton and I walk in, I see several of the customers—women—on the bar, hooting and strutting their stuff. And there's a line of patrons who are all connected via a conga line that's grooving to the classic "Love Shack," by the B-52s. They're winding around between all the tables and spilling onto the beach, and all I can think is that I want to join them.

"What do you want to bet they're but a single shot away from taking it all off?" Peyton says. He's talking about the women on the bar.

"They're just having a good time. Don't be so old," I tell him.

Peyton and I are escorted to a table, where we sit and watch the action for a minute. Duffy's is quite possibly the biggest and rowdiest party joint in the Caribbean. I won't tell Paula that, but it's the truth.

Soon our waitress appears and we haven't even had a chance to look over the menu.

"What I be gettin' for ya?" she asks, her face beaming. She has a great tan to go along with her smile and so many beads in her hair that they look like they're growing from her scalp.

"We need another minute, but I definitely need something to drink," I tell her. I look around at the other patrons and nod at the women dancing on the bar. "I'll have whatever they're having."

The waitress laughs, and her yellow hair beads swing gaily about her face. "They all be drinkin' rum. Dat what you want?"

"Rum is perfect," I say. I might as well let myself go wild.

Peyton orders his standard—gin and tonic—which I find boring... but that's just me.

After taking our order, our waitress leaves and the space between me and Peyton grows wider. I'm not sure us coming here was a good idea. I can think of nothing worthwhile to say, and not only that, but I'm still miffed at Peyton. The way he said good-bye, the way he took up with another woman so soon. I'm miffed, period. About everything.

In only a few minutes, our waitress returns, and she sets a coconut shell before me. I'm not sure what it is, but it's filled with a frothy white liquid that looks yummy.

"It be called Lime in Dee Coconut," she tells me. She shows me her thumb and index finger. "It only be havin' teensy amount da alcohol. You be sure to take dee coconut shell with you when you leave here. It be souvenir."

And then she sets Peyton's gin before him. The glass is plain nothingness. "I be back to take your order in a few minutes," she says. And then she leaves.

"That's quite a drink you have there," Peyton says to me.

"Yes, it is," I agree. I rub my fingers over my souvenir coconut shell. And here I thought all I'd be taking home from St. John is a broken heart.

One thing is sure, any feelings I had for Peyton when I arrived here in St. John have all but dissipated. I'll always care about him, but after being with Cole, I know that what I felt for Peyton was simply comfortable, not at all the kind of love it takes to get through the hard times in life. I think maybe I had that with Cole.

And then I blew it all away.

Chapter Twenty-Six

"I've missed you," Peyton tells me.

I have no response, just a smile. This is the first date he and I have been on in over five months. It's only been three months since he left me, but we'd both gotten so busy we hadn't taken any time out for ourselves in some time. And now I'm wondering if that was part of what happened to us, why we ended. Funny thing is, I've wanted the opportunity to ask questions, but now it doesn't seem nearly so important to hear his answers. And, too, where can talking take us? I've been with Cole, heart and soul, practically since I arrived. Have even fallen in love with him. I doubt Peyton wants to hear that.

I take a sip from my coconut souvenir shell, and it's so strong I'm surprised I don't have flames shooting from my mouth. A few of these and I might not remember Cole's name later. Though, somehow, that's not very comforting.

Peyton chuckles at the face I make. He's not used to seeing me drink anything stronger than wine. "Maybe you shouldn't have that," he tells me. "It's probably one of those drinks that sneak up on you."

I clamp my hands around the coconut shell and take a few

more sips, ignoring Peyton's advice. The alcohol goes down easier with each swallow. "Aren't you going to drink yours?" I ask.

"We should order some food," he tells me, and he opens the menu. The lighting isn't great, so he has to squint, and I'm happy to sit back and let him do all the work. I'm enjoying the tingly sensation that has taken hold of my extremities. In fact, I might have another Lime in Dee Coconut before the evening is over.

While Peyton peruses the menu, the music picks up and everyone in beach seating comes out of their chairs. Several people form a new conga line. It's a real party. Fun time. I get an idea that I'm sure Peyton won't like. "Let's join them," I say, but I don't wait for his response. He's not a conga type of guy. Nor am I a conga type of girl. But that doesn't matter. I'm up and on my feet and attached to the back of the conga line before I can talk myself out of it. Peyton quickly catches up, and he grabs the back of my hips and makes himself the caboose. I'm sure he's hating every second of this.

The conga line weaves through the bar, between tables, and then out to the beach. We pass a couple of women who are dancing on a tabletop, and I make a mental note to do the same at least once before I turn fifty, as I'm sure it will take me that long to get up the nerve.

Peyton keeps up, holding on to my hips, which surprises me. I'd have thought he'd have fallen off at the first turn.

We make it through the first playing of "Love Shack," and then halfway through the second playing, the conga line begins to shrink. Some of us are exhausted and some of us have simply found that we can no longer make our limbs function. I fit both categories, but I'm a trooper and I hang on until it's just me, Peyton, an old couple, and a robust woman who is now our leader. She takes us on two more trips around the bar, and then on the last turn, she swings around too fast and lands on her keister. Those of us who can still stand pause briefly to make sure she's okay, and then we move on. When the line reaches my and Peyton's table, I let go of the man in front of me and I land in my chair. Peyton follows. He looks somewhat relieved, but I'm amazed he even joined in.

We laugh. It's been fun, and my head is clearer from the activity. But I'm also aware that I'm enjoying myself too much. I shouldn't be doing this with Peyton. I should be having fun with Cole. I pinch my eyes shut, don't want to cry again in front of my ex. But the tears come, anyway.

Peyton looks at me like he'd prefer I was dancing on the tabletop. He picks up his menu again and then waves to our waitress. "I'll order you some food," he tells me.

"You think I'm drunk?" I ask.

"Aren't you?"

"No."

"Then why are you crying?"

I wipe my eyes. "I'm not. It's all the smoke. My eyes are burning."

Peyton looks around. "There are no walls. The smoke is hardly your problem."

He's right, but it doesn't matter because our waitress has wiggled over to us, and she's standing next to our table.

"What else I be gettin' for da lovebirds?" she asks. "You be here for your honeymoon?"

"No! We're not married. Nor are we lovebirds," I tell her.

"Okay, no need to get riled, sista. So, what you be havin'?" she asks.

"She needs food, no more drinks," Peyton tells her. "Bring her a salad and some bread sticks."

"Salad," I say. "Just salad."

"And I'll have the cowboy steak," Peyton adds.

I glare at him. "You're having the cowboy *steak*?"

"Yes, I'm hungry." Peyton gestures at the waitress to skedaddle, and then he leans over the table and tries whispering to me, but the music is too loud, so he ends up shouting. "What has gotten into you?"

"What do you mean?" I shout back.

"Last time we were out together, you didn't say a word when I ordered filet mignon. Have you gone vegetarian?"

No. I've gone cowboy. I lean way over the table to answer him. "Maybe I'm not in the mood to sit here and watch you eat something that used to have *big brown eyes*."

Peyton pulls back from me. He looks exasperated. "How about I make a donation to the ASPCA. Will that make you happy?"

I know he's being sarcastic, but since he offered. "How much?"

"I don't know, five hundred."

"Not enough. Make it a thousand and I promise not to throw up on your plate."

Appropriately alarmed, Peyton nods. Mostly, I think he wants to shut me up.

Time passes and I listen while Peyton talks about work and life and more work. It's all I can do to keep from holding my eyes open in feigned interest. Which is surprising. I used to enjoy hearing about his latest art project, hoping someday he'd make a big splash in the art world. And now that he has, I don't care so much. Because I'm in love with another man... who may no longer love me back. But at least he didn't say good-bye with a few scribbled words on a piece of paper.

"You're an ass," I say, though I can tell by the look on his face that he can't hear me.

"What?" he says.

"I *said* you're an ass." It feels good to say it, even if I'm saying it to thin air.

"I can't hear you," he tells me.

"Yes, I know."

When our waitress returns with our order, I try to avoid looking at Peyton's *cowboy* steak. I eat my salad in silence... and think about Cole. How he smelled walking next to me on the beach... how his lips felt on mine... how I shivered under his hands while we made love.

"Feel better?" Peyton asks when we've finished our meal.

Not at all. "Much," I tell him, and I even manage a smile.

"I have something for you," Peyton says. He digs around in his pocket and comes up with a small black box, which is alarming, considering what's happened between us the last few months. My mind is whirring. "I know things haven't worked out the way we'd hoped," he tells me. "So I thought I'd try again." He opens the box and shows me a ring, and it's sparkly and brilliant, even under the Tiki-torch lighting, and it makes me gasp. "It's the ring you pointed out to me in the window at Tiffany's the last time we were at Bellevue Square," he says. "It's for your birthday. I told you I'd buy it for you. Remember?"

I do remember. I'm surprised *he* did. "That was six months ago," I say. My feelings are all over the place. "You shouldn't have." And I mean it. "This is too much. You can't expect me to accept this."

He shrugs. "At least try it on."

I reluctantly put it on the only finger it fits—my ring finger—but it doesn't feel right, so I immediately try to remove it. I pull and twist, but it won't come off. "It's stuck," I tell him.

Peyton tries, but gets nowhere. He smiles, showing a hint of satisfaction. "Wear it until we leave here. I can't return it until we get back to Seattle, anyway."

I look at the ring. Maybe a bar of soap would do the trick… but it's so beautiful… maybe it's okay if I wear it for a while. I give him the best I-mean-business look I can muster, considering my condition. "Just so we understand each other, my wearing this ring doesn't mean a thing."

"Understood." He smiles and reaches into his pocket again. "And because I expected that response, I got you something else." He hands me a picture.

I take it and my heart nearly melts. "It's a litter of puppies," I whisper, tracing my finger over the photo, counting each perfect brown and white bundle of fun.

"Yes. They're King Charles spaniels," Peyton tells me. "I know how much you've always wanted a dog."

The puppies are so cute I could squeeze them.

"Taylor? Are you listening?"

"What?" I ask, not sure of anything he's said.

"One of those puppies is yours. All you have to do is go pick him or her out."

"What?" I say again. I can't be hearing right.

"I bought you a puppy," he tells me.

What? "No. Peyton, what were you thinking?" I shout over our table. "I can't take in a dog and expect him to be happy while I'm off at work fifteen hours a day. It wouldn't be fair. Not to mention, he'd get bored and chew everything in sight." I immediately have visions of coming home to chewed shoes, purses, furniture, et cetera.

"You don't have to worry about that. I also found you a dog nanny. Her name is Amy, and she lives just a block away from you. She's agreed to come over every day and take your new pup out for playtime."

I'm stunned, can't even respond. This is too much. I was so not prepared for this, for such acts of kindness from Peyton—the plane ticket home, the puppy. God, a puppy! He doesn't even like dogs, always complains about the mess they make. But I know he's going for gold right now, hoping I'll give him another chance, trying to make things right between us. Not that I'm anywhere near ready to forgive and forget. But I can't ignore this bold gesture. It's so surprising and unexpected. He must really want me back.

I stretch out my hand and look at the ring once more—it's so beautiful. And then I look at the picture of the puppies. My heart fills with warmth. A puppy. For me. From Peyton.

I look at him. His face is hopeful, almost boyish.

"You don't have to decide anything right now," he tells me. He glances at the people on the dance floor. "How about a dance?" He holds a hand out to me.

I look at all the people, wrapped in each other's arms. One dance? Can it hurt? No, I decide.

Peyton leads me out onto the dance floor, where he pulls me close. It feels foreign to have him touch me, but I go along with it, and it's not long before I settle into his arms. It's like old times.

Comfortable. I lay my head on his shoulder and it's like we were never apart. He kisses my forehead, and then, as our dance ends, he kisses me on my lips. It's nothing passionate, jut a simple kiss, but it's unnerving and I push him away. Then, as I turn to go back to our table, I see a couple leaving Duffy's, and through the atmosphere of people, I see that it's Toby and Ariel. I duck my head, hoping that Toby didn't see me, but I know he did. No doubt about it, he saw Peyton kiss me.

Chapter Twenty-Seven

I didn't kiss Peyton. Peyton kissed me.

That was the day before yesterday, and Peyton has since made himself scarce. When we left Duffy's, I was so mad at him I couldn't think straight. I told him I needed time to sort things out... to calm down. Which I have to some degree, but now it's likely I'll see him again tonight, because it's my last day here, and I doubt he'll miss my going-away party. I'm already dreading it.

It's not that I don't like parties, but Paula has threatened to invite the entire island, and I'm in no mood for festivities. But since I haven't been here long, I don't expect a large turnout. Maybe just a handful of locals.

The one person I would like to see before I leave is Cole. Though I can only guess what he must be thinking if Toby told him about seeing me with Peyton... that maybe what we had was just an island fling. It wasn't. But how can he possibly think any different, after all that's happened?

Tomorrow I go back to Seattle, where I'll reclaim my office and reenter my life as Taylor Grant, attorney at law. Cole is not my future. But what do I do with the feelings I've developed for him? We had three tremendous, beautiful times together making love… and memories. And now nothing. It makes my heart ache just contemplating the days ahead.

"You look like you could use one of my special drinks," Tug offers. He's moved down to my end of the bar after catching me perusing the shelves filled with colorful bottles.

I smile a small smile. "Thanks, but I'm not into drinking anything that reminds me of antifreeze. Or anything right now."

"Suit yourself," he says, and he turns away and goes back down to the other end of the bar, where a customer is waiting for service.

Tug doesn't seem to know anything about what's happened between me and Cole. Which I find hard to believe. It's a small island, and news travels fast. He may not have heard that Peyton and I shared a kiss, but he has to know by now what's happened with Lacy. Maybe Paula asked him to go easy on me.

I head outside, where I'm greeted by Bananas. He's at the bottom of the steps, purring and jerking his tail, which I've come to learn is cat speak for wanting attention. I oblige by sitting on a step and pulling him into my lap.

"Why are you so damn happy all the time?" I ask him. His response is to purr louder, like he has no idea I'm about to leave, that he may never see me again. But he's a cat. He doesn't know a thing about real life or that things change… sometimes in the blink of an eye.

I should have been honest with Cole.

I look down at my hand, at the ring on my finger. I try once more to take it off, but my fingers have become permanently pudgy and it doesn't budge. I'm sure it's some kind of punishment.

Bananas purrs louder, reminding me of his presence. I rub the top of his head, and then I push him gently from my lap. I go stand at the tide line, and I count seven shades of blue as I watch the water curl around my feet. It makes me think of the day I first met Cole, when I watched him with his dog, throwing sticks at this very spot. It was the same day Paula made her ridiculous bet about me sleeping with Cole. Little did she know I'd already spent the morning thinking about that very thing.

I move down the beach and I don't stop until I get to the sea grape tree. I look up to the fork, the jumping point, and decide that if I wanted to, I could swing. I might scream, but no one would hear me. No one would know what a wimp I really am.

I look up again, then out to the water. And then I think about Paula swinging back toward the tree. She was caught, couldn't free herself. I wouldn't have that problem. My shorts are hemmed.

I do want to swing.

Once I commit to something, I rarely change my mind. So in only a couple of minutes I'm at the fork, looking out at the sea. It's like before, so clear and blue, though minus the lurking shadows that I thought might be a shark. *I can do this*, I think. I don't know why I was so afraid before. Maybe I was just looking for an excuse not to let myself go. In my job, which is full of constraints that keep me in check, I can never do something wild. Or crazy.

My heart is racing, thumping hard in my chest. I'm still afraid. But I'm excited, too. All I have to do is let go.

Just let go.

I don't think about it—that would only give me time to change my mind. I just push off from the branch and let what's going to happen, happen.

In a flash, the swinging is over and I have bubbles fizzing from my nose. Plus, I have a small amount of sea water in my mouth. But I'm otherwise okay. I'm okay. I've done it. I've swung from the tree. And it's possible I even peed myself.

I spend a moment treading water, looking at all the colors surrounding me—yellow, blue, purple—that I quickly realize is a school of tiny fish. Their scales are glinting and flashing like neon lights as they swish first in one direction and then the next.

Some great white. I feel foolish for ever thinking such thoughts.

As I make my way back to shore, I'm almost giddy at what I've accomplished. I could tell Paula I swung from her tree, but she may not believe me. I could tell Cole, too… but I may never see him again.

The sun is warm on my back as I dress. I'm not ready to go back to The Fish Shack, so I sit on Paula's log to dry for a few minutes. It doesn't take long in this heat. And now my hair is a curly mess, but I don't care. I've conquered that damn tree.

On my way back to The Fish Shack, I hear music even before I get to the hammocks. The fun has already begun. Yippee.

I drag my toes through the warm sand, taking my time and wishing more than ever I hadn't agreed to this going-away thing. This party. It would be so much easier if Cole were here. But he won't be and I'm beginning to think maybe the romance he and I shared was all in my head. That it wasn't real and beautiful.

But it was. And I'll always remember my time here with Cole.

As I walk up the steps to The Fish Shack, I see hundreds of miniature white twinkly lights hanging from the ceiling and everywhere else. The Fish Shack has been transformed. And the place is packed with people. They cheer when they see me and I'm embarrassed, because I can't remember all their names. I smile big though, because I appreciate their coming, and then I perch on a stool at the end of the bar.

I look around at all the lights and the crowd. This is so much more than I expected. Impossible, really. In Seattle, it would take me twenty years to make this many friends. Seattleites are so busy, and in-person relationships don't seem nearly as important as tweeting, leaving comments on Facebook, or texting. Texting is huge.

I don't get the attraction to social media, but I have a feeling it's here to stay. Myself, I'd rather have a face-to-face to learn that a friend had a great spaghetti-and-meatball dinner at a fabulous new restaurant than see a picture of a full plate. And I'd prefer to see the light in a friend's eyes as she tells me she just got a promotion, or see her tears if her jerk of a boyfriend has done her wrong. How else can I wrap my arms around her and let her know how much I care? To those who don't need an occasional arm wrapped around them, great. But got life?

I see Tug move over to the corner of the bar. He's about to hook up the karaoke machine, which will be loads of fun, but I hope he doesn't expect me to perform.

Ten, twenty, thirty minutes pass and even more people show up, but the absence of certain individuals is duly noted. Toby and Ariel, for instance. Though I suppose expecting them to show up after Toby saw me with Peyton is a stretch.

Paula appears and sits next to me at the bar. "Did you and Peyton have a fight?" she asks. "I haven't seen him since the other night, when the two of you went over to Duffy's." Her eyes are sparkling, and she looks like she couldn't be happier with Peyton's absence.

"No, we didn't have a fight," I say.

"Darn." Paula pokes her lips out. "I suppose that means he'll be making an appearance tonight."

"Unless you have him tied up somewhere."

"Gee, I wish I'd thought of that."

I swivel my stool around so that she and I are face to face. "What is it about Peyton that you find so distasteful?"

"Are we being honest?" Paula asks.

"By all means, be honest."

"For starters, he dumped you. On a Post-it."

"It was a napkin. And I doubt that was the catalyst. You stopped liking him five minutes after you met him."

"You're right. I've never liked Peyton."

"But why?"

"Are we *really* being honest?"

Now my curiosity is acutely stirred. "Yes. I'd *really* like to know."

"He kissed me," Paula says.

"What?" I could not have possibly heard right.

"Peyton kissed me. It was that first night, when he and I first met. The three of us—me, you, and him—were at your place and you were cooking dinner. You were in the kitchen, checking on the spaghetti noodles, and he kissed me."

I frown. I don't remember making spaghetti, but I do

remember that night. I wanted Paula to meet Peyton because I thought he was "the one." Turns out, he wasn't, but I didn't know that then. "What do you mean? Like, out of the blue, he just grabbed you and kissed you?"

"Something like that," Paula says,

"Why do I get the feeling there's more?"

"Okay. I cannot tell a lie. Maybe he didn't *grab* me. Maybe I gave him a little encouragement."

"What kind of encouragement?"

Paula's face takes on a pained look. "I wanted to make sure about him. I knew you were serious, but he just seemed a little too smooth, like he knew what to say to a woman."

"And?"

"And I might have suggested he and I could hook up."

I hadn't even realized, but I'm wringing my hands in my lap. "God, Paula."

"What? Don't be mad at me. He's the one who made the move."

"Right." I don't even know what to say at this point. Though what does it matter? Peyton and I are done… even if he thinks we're not. "Why would you wait until now to tell me something like this?" I ask.

"I wasn't going to tell you at all." She looks at my finger. "But you're wearing his ring."

I look at the ring on my pudgy finger. "It's not what you're thinking. I was only trying it on, and now it's stuck. I don't intend to keep it." I make a real effort to get it off to convince her, but she still looks doubtful.

"*Really!*" I tell her, and I hold out my finger to her. "You try to get it off."

"It doesn't matter. You shouldn't have even put it on. Peyton is a creep." She looks over my shoulder. "Speaking of, look what the sand crabs just dragged in."

"Have I missed all the fun?" Peyton asks, coming up behind me.

I swivel on my stool to face him. And then Paula nods in

Tug's direction. "I think I'll mosey on over and see if Tug needs any help with the karaoke machine," she says and she's gone.

Peyton survey's the room. "Looks like you've made quite a few friends here."

I make no comment. I'm confused on so many levels that I can't even think straight. I want to hit him or curse at him or… anything. But what would it change? I've fallen in love with another man, so why even bring up the subject of him kissing Paula?

The only thing I'm sure of at this point is that I love Cole. I love him with all I have in me, and I don't think that will ever change. He and I may not ever find our way back to each other, but that doesn't mean I'm ready to settle. I refuse to be with a man I can't even trust to spend a few minutes alone with my sister.

"You're an ass," I say to Peyton.

He looks confused. "Are you still mad about the other night? Jesus, Taylor, it was just a simple kiss. If I'd known it was that big a deal, I would have kept my lips to myself."

"You should have," I say, and I swivel my stool around.

The time goes by and Peyton and I just sit in silence. He has no idea what's going on with me and I don't care to tell him. And, anyway, I'm more interested in karaoke than talking to him, so I give all of my attention to the room. Several people have gathered at the front of the bar. They're going to sing, or at least try to and I'm ready for the distraction. Something to do to pass the time.

"Are you going to take a turn?" Peyton asks.

"After you," I say. Which gets me off the hook, because he and I both know it'd be a snowy day here on St. John before he'd do karaoke.

I continue watching, while at least a dozen people bravely step forward to entertain the crowd with their singing prowess. But my mind is elsewhere. On Cole. I want so badly to see him, to say good-bye. But when two hours have passed, I have to accept that he's not going to show, and I decide to take a break from the smoke and noise. "I'm going out for some fresh air," I tell Peyton.

"Want some company?"

I shake my head. "If I'm not back in fifteen minutes, maybe you could bring me a drink."

"Anything special?"

"Tug will know," I tell him, and then I leave. As soon as I hit the sand, I see Bananas crouched beneath a bush. I wait to see if he wants some attention, but he stays put, so I sit by myself. Not even ten minutes pass when I hear footsteps coming down the steps. I turn, ready to tell Peyton to come back in another fifteen, but it's not Peyton. It's Cole.

Cole.

I stand, my heart pounding. It feels like it's in my throat. I want so bad to throw my arms around him, but I don't. He steps down next to me. My chest is tight, like the air has been sucked from my lungs. "I was hoping I'd see you tonight," I say.

"I thought I should at least say good-bye," he tells me.

"How have you been?"

"I'm gettin' by." The lines at the corners of his eyes seem deeper, and he looks as though his nights have been as sleepless as mine.

It feels odd, the two of us making small talk, pretending that we're just casual acquaintances. But we're no longer lovers, are we?

"I've been thinking," Cole continues, "about a lot of things. I didn't want you to go away believing that what we had didn't matter to me. It did matter. *You* matter. A whole hell of a lot. That's why it hurt so much when I found out about Lacy."

I open my mouth to respond, but I don't even know what to say. And anyway, Peyton has shown up and he's brought me a drink.

"You were right, Tug knew exactly what you'd want," Peyton says. He comes down the steps and hands me a glass, filled to the brim. "Pardon me for interrupting," he says. He extends a hand to Cole. "Peyton Harris."

"Cole McKenzie," Cole says. He accepts Peyton's handshake.

I smile tightly, feeling hugely awkward. Feeling like a cheater.

But I'm not cheating. Never was. Peyton and I were over. *Are* over. And right now I'd like nothing more than to have him disappear so that Cole and I can continue our conversation.

"Your name sounds familiar," Peyton tells Cole.

Cole glances at me. "I'm a friend of Paula's. Now a friend of Taylor's."

Peyton puts an arm around me. "I'm glad my girl made so many friends while she was here."

My *girl*? I could kick Peyton right now.

Cole smiles thinly. His face changes and he tips his hat. "It was nice seeing you, Taylor. Have a safe trip home." And then he's gone and I feel like the life has been sucked out of me.

I turn on Peyton. "Your *girl*?"

"What?" Peyton says.

I'm so mad I can barely see, let alone talk. I need to stop Cole from leaving. I rush up the steps, but Cole is already at the back door, walking out. By the time I fight my way through the crowd, he's in his Jeep, and all I can see are taillights streaming off into the night.

My knees practically buckle. My heart feels like it's been kicked. It's like I've lost Cole all over again.

217

Chapter Twenty-Eight

It's the dead of night and sleep won't come. Every time I close my eyes, I can see the look on Cole's face when Peyton called me *his girl*.

Dammit.

But damn Cole, too. He could have given me a chance to explain before he stormed out into the night.

Men!

But at least I've managed to remove Peyton's ring from my finger. Too little too late, though. Cole is gone and I may never see him again.

I close my eyes as the ache in my chest grows ever deeper. I don't want to disturb Paula, so I get up to leave the room. I'm practically out the door when she raises her head from her pillow.

"You want my advice?" she asks.

"About what?"

"Cole. Isn't that who we're talking about?"

"I didn't know we were having a conversation," I say.

"Go tell him how you feel," she continues. "He's obviously smitten with you, too. You don't think he showed up here tonight just to shoot the shit with Tug, do you?" She snags the Moke keys from her nightstand and tosses them to me. "Go. Drive safe. I'll see you in the morning."

I catch the keys and clench them in my fist. But it's late and I'm sure Cole is asleep. "I wouldn't want to get him out of bed," I tell Paula.

"So crawl into bed with him," Paula says. "I'm sure he wouldn't mind."

I'd love to be in Cole's bed with him, but it wouldn't change a thing. I did my best to try to get him to listen, but he was too hurt. And now it's up to him to decide what he wants. I gently set the Moke keys back down on Paula's nightstand. She's already turned over and has gone back to sleep.

I make my way out to the beach, where the moon is full and big in the sky, and I sit in the sand at the waterline. The warm tropical breeze, full of floral scents, washes over me as I let my mind drift, recalling all the good times I've had since coming here. Not just with Cole but with everyone. Including Paula. She and I didn't get to do all the things we'd talked about, but the important thing was spending time together. We had plenty of that, and now it'll be a while before I see her again. I'm going to miss her.

My emotions bubble to the surface, bringing the threat of tears, but I manage to hold them off. I'm all cried out. Going back to Seattle will be good for me. I'll be so consumed with work and the rush of city life that I won't have time to feel sorry for myself.

I feel something brush against my back, and I turn and see Bananas sitting in the sand, looking lonely. I scoop him into my lap, and there he and I sit, taking in our last evening together on the beach. It's a comfort, holding him. He makes me forget all my sad feelings. I even smile a little. Maybe Peyton really has done me a favor, getting me a puppy. I'm sure I'll have plenty to smile about watching my new housemate play and grow into his big fluffy ears.

I spend several minutes stroking Bananas and thinking about a name for my new pup. Scout, Jake, Tucker. But I finally decide that I need to see him first, so that I can choose something that truly fits.

When I've had enough alone time, I walk back across the sand to go inside. But as I reach the top step, I'm startled to see the shadow of a person near the end of the bar. I've grown accustomed to sleeping with one wall open to nature, and to whatever or whomever might wander down the beach, but it's late and the bar is closed, and now I'm on guard. My mind immediately goes to Cole, but that's wishful thinking and it's not who this is. The shadow is too small. It's not Paula, either. "Is that you, Ella Su?" I call out.

"It's me, Lacy. Can we talk… about my dad?"

I step toward the shadow, my breath caught in my throat. I have visions of some crazy Jeep accident—a tourist traveling on the wrong side of the road or a collision with a donkey or even some leftover storm debris—and now Cole is lying injured in a room at St. John's medical center. "What's happened? Is your dad hurt?" I ask.

Lacy steps forward. I can see her enough that I can tell she's smiling. "Wow, you and my dad really have it bad, don't you?"

"I don't understand," I say. I usher her out to the front porch, where our conversation won't disturb Paula. My pulse is racing. I can't bear the idea that Cole might be hurt and I'm not with him. "Was there an accident?" I need an answer.

"Don't worry. It's nothing like that. I think it's called lovesickness. He came home tonight, ranting and cursing like he'd gotten himself tossed off the back of one them ornery ol' bulls, and when I asked him what was wrong, he mumbled your name and headed to the sofa with a six-pack of beer."

Relief. I can breathe. Cole hasn't had a head-on with a donkey. "I saw him tonight," I say. "It didn't go well. I'm sure he'll feel better in the morning."

"I don't think so. I've never seen him so bad off. I think you should go talk to him."

I want to, but I can't.

I settle on a step, and Lacy sits next to me. A chorus of night sounds surround us—the clicking and buzzing of insects, hermit crabs scrabbling along in the dirt beneath The Fish Shack, chirping from some unidentifiable creature. I'm used to them now, but it was hard at first. They kept me awake some nights. Now I don't know how I'll sleep without all their noise.

I drop my head and stare down at my bare feet. I'm in dire need of a pedicure, but that can wait. At the moment, Cole is my focus. I lied to him, and now he's miserable and I'm miserable and I don't have any solutions for the mess I've made. But I'm not about to bring Lacy into the drama I've created with her dad. She'll have enough drama of her own as she goes through life.

"Sometimes," I begin, choosing my words carefully, "no matter how much two people care about each other, they still can't make it work. It's not that they don't want to, but for whatever the reason, they just can't get it together." I look at Lacy to see if she understands, and she nods… and then she shakes her head.

"That's lame," she says.

"What?"

"You and my dad. You're both willing to let a good thing go when all you need to do is kiss and make up."

I almost laugh. When she puts it like that, it sounds so easy. Though it's not. "I don't think your dad is interested in kissing me right now."

"I know, and it's because of me. But I think you should go talk to him anyway. You can make him understand. Isn't that what attorneys do… explain and make people understand?"

"In theory. But it doesn't always go the way we want. And, too, I'm leaving in the morning. That doesn't give me and your dad a lot of time to work out our differences."

Lacy shrugs. "Then don't go. Stay here and work on them."

I smile a small smile. "I wish I could."

"I don't get it. You adults are a funny bunch. You act like you care about each other, but then you let it all go away." She laughs a little. "We teens seem so desperate compared to you. We think it's the end of the world if the boy we like even looks at another girl."

221

"But it's not," I say.

"I know that now," Lacy admits. "But what I don't get is why y'all make it so hard on yourselves. Can't you just say 'I love you?' and then kiss each other and let it be over?"

"If only it were that easy," I say.

"It is. Just do it," Lacy tells me.

When morning comes, and after I've had only a few hours sleep, the first thing I think of is the conversation I had with Lacy. She left here still not understanding, and I'll admit it doesn't make much sense to me, either. Two people who love each other should be able to fix things. But that's just it. I'm not sure anymore what Cole feels for me.

It's interesting how far I've come with my thinking about not wanting children. I'm still not convinced I'd be the best mom in the world, but after my experience with Lacy, motherhood doesn't seem nearly as scary. She's given me a good taste of the worst and I'm still standing. I've even come to care a great deal for her. And isn't that how it goes… you finally figure something out, and then it's too late.

Paula and I have a fruit smoothie for breakfast, and then, after giving me a dozen kisses and a warm hug, she sends me off to the airport with Tug. It's the end of our time together. She doesn't want to see Peyton. He's still not her favorite person. Mine, either, but it is what is. He bought me a ticket, and now I'll be sitting next to him all the way home. From there, I don't know what will happen.

Peyton is all smiles when he sees me, but I'm dragging from lack of sleep. He'll have to find some way other than my company to amuse himself on the flight home.

The line to get through security isn't long, and Peyton and I reach the checkpoint in enough time that we'll be able to relax for a while before we board our plane. A man and a woman in front of us go through without any problems, but when Peyton steps up, a woman who's built like a lady wrestler gives him a suspicious look. Her name tag says Ms. Morse.

"Step back, sir," Ms. Morse says. She pulls Peyton's bag over to one side, and then gestures for me to come through the checkpoint. I do as told, but she doesn't appear to be any fonder of me. "Ma'am, you step over there while I finish with the gentleman."

At least she's polite. I take my place at one side, to be searched or questioned or whatever it is they intend to do, and the stream of people behind us continues on their way.

"I just goin' check in here real quick," Ms. Morse tells Peyton. She zips open his bag and begins removing things—a couple of shirts, a pair of slacks, an extra pair of sunglasses, and a plastic bag filled with travel-size items that look like skin-care products. She looks at Peyton, giving him a good once-over. "These be yours, sir?" she asks.

Peyton's face turns a rosy pink. "Of course they're mine! They're in my bag!"

Ms. Morse ignores Peyton's ire. She continues going through his things, pushing aside a book, a couple pairs of socks, and what looks to be a map of the islands. After finishing with the main compartment, she focuses on the side pocket, which has Peyton looking nervous.

"This is ridiculous," he speaks up. "Look at us. Do we look dangerous?"

"Danger be comin' in all forms, sir," Ms. Morse responds. She shoves a gloved hand inside the pocket and pulls out a piece of black, shimmery material that's been folded neatly into a small square. I stifle a laugh. I know what it is—Peyton's favorite pair of silk boxers. He likes to sleep in them, says they keep him cool at night.

Ms. Morse picks up the square and shakes it, causing Peyton's secret undies to unfold, which reveals them to anyone who might be looking. I don't think I've ever seen Peyton look so discombobulated. I lean and whisper in his ear, "Gee, I sure hope your undies don't get confiscated."

223

"Give those to me," Peyton tells Ms. Morse. He grabs the boxers, and she lets him, but then a big black man wearing a security uniform steps forward, ready to assist should the need arise.

I take Peyton's arm and pull him close. I can see this situation easily going from bad to worse. "Let them do their job," I whisper fiercely. "The sooner they finish, the sooner we'll be able to board our plane." Though I have to admit, it does seem strange that Peyton and I are getting such scrutiny.

Peyton listens to me, and he and I settle and wait while Ms. Morse finishes making a mess of his belongings.

This is the kind of thing I'd expect to happen in Seattle. People think we're so mellow and civilized there, but in recent years, we've become like so many other big cities. Angry people, everyone in a hurry, needless frustration. I'm not sure I want to live like that anymore. After living on a beach for a while, where the pace is much slower, it'll be torture going back to city life.

When Ms. Morse and her cohort are satisfied that Peyton's bag is clear of dangerous items, she turns to me. "We be goin' where we can have some privacy," she tells me. She nods at a door marked SECURITY and ushers me through. We enter a small room and she motions for me to sit. "It be but a minute," she says. And then she leaves me by myself where I'm surrounded by stark, grey walls.

Something must be terribly wrong. I have a bad feeling about this. I can think of no reason for this kind of treatment other than they suspect me and Peyton of wrongdoing. I rack my brain, trying to think of anything I might have packed that would be cause for concern. Nothing comes to mind. This has to be a mistake.

I'm tense as I sit and wait. Peyton is on the other side of the door protesting in my defense. But it doesn't make me feel one bit better.

My mind goes to Cole. Thinking about him eases my stress. I remember every bumpy road we drove here on St. John. I think about when we were lying together on the hammock and how we got busted by Lacy. I remember sharing conch and crab cakes and how he made me realize I could love again. We sat on the beach and listened to the sound of waves lapping the shore, and I watched him help Sophie give birth to her baby. We shared so much, including a few deep, dark secrets… and then I made a great big mess of things.

I sigh as all my good memories with Cole fade. I'd give anything to have him kiss me one last time. But, clearly, our love trip is over.

My back is rigid against the hard chair. I become aware that I can no longer hear Peyton. I get up and listen at the door, but I hear nothing. I hope that doesn't mean bad has gone to worse.

I sit back down, but then the door opens, and when I turn, it's like the sun has filled the room. Cole is there, standing in the doorway.

"What are you doing here?" I ask. I can barely speak. It's like that first day he and I met at Cruz Bay Beach, when my tongue felt all tangled in my throat.

"I heard you were havin' a problem with security," he says. "I'm here to see if I can help."

I rush to him, getting as close as I dare. I'm confused and happy at the same time. I don't know how, but Cole always manages to show up right when I need him. "I'm an idiot," I say. "I should have told you about Lacy. I don't know if you can ever forgive me, but I need you to believe I never meant to hurt you."

Cole puts his hands in my hair. "I know, and I apologize to you, too, for not listening when you tried to explain."

"You were hurt," I continue, wanting to say more because I really need for him to understand. But he stops me from talking by putting a finger to my lips.

"What's done is done. It's time we move on."

"We?" My heart is thumping wildly. I'm afraid to hope for anything more than a good-bye kiss.

"Yes, we," Cole says gently, and he takes my face in his hands. "I'm in love with you, Taylor Grant, attorney at law. I think I have been since the moment we met. I'm not sure I can let you leave and I never see you again. If I have to, I'll come to the mainland with you. I need to be wherever you are."

My head is swimming with emotion, but I refuse to cry. I am so done with the tears. "I will!" I say. "I do!"

Cole laughs. "I haven't got to that part yet. Could be I'm just trying to get you to spend the night with me."

"In your swinging bed?" I laugh in my joy. "Yes! I will… and I do!"

Cole steps back. "Guess we better make it official, then." He shoves a hand into a pocket, and brings out something brilliantly shiny that's as bright as a crisp new star. It's a ring! The most beautiful ring I have ever seen. "Will you marry me?" he asks.

I'm so happy, I'm practically speechless. Even so, I need to consider the idea of making him leave the home I know he loves. No doubt, Lacy would be happy, but if Cole isn't, then I couldn't be either. "What about your life here?" I ask.

"Damn, girl, you've got me this far. Don't leave me hangin' now. We can work out the details later."

It's not a perfect answer, but he's right. We can work out the details later. "Yes," I say. "A thousand times, yes!"

Cole kisses me and it's that big screen kiss that feels like forever. I'm smiling so big my cheeks hurt. This is how it feels to really be in love, and this is how it feels to really *be* loved. Lacy was right. All Cole and I needed to do was kiss and make up. But for me, it goes much deeper than that. As far as I'm concerned, it's in the holding. As long as Cole holds me in his arms, nothing else matters. And if his home is here in St. John, then this is where I want to be.

I think I am already home.

THE END

A NOTE TO READERS

Thank you for reading *Love Trip*. If you have been entertained, please consider posting a review to help others when they are selecting a new book to read.

To see where you may purchase my books, go to www.alexadarin.com/books. If you would like to hear about upcoming releases, etc., you may subscribe to my mailing list at www.alexadarin.com. Or if you'd simply like to send me a quick note, go to www.alexadarin.com/contact. I always enjoy hearing from you.

Many thanks for your support!

ABOUT THE AUTHOR

Alexa Darin makes her home in Washington State, where she is surrounded by nature and spends most of her leisure time hiking in the Alpine Wilderness. She is an animal lover, a big-time dreamer, and a woman who believes that every romance writer should have a survival kit that contains dark chocolate, red wine, and tissue. Readers can learn more about Alexa and her upcoming books at:

www.alexadarin.com

62159899R00144

Made in the USA
Middletown, DE
24 January 2018